A MIND OF HER OWN

A MIND OF
HER OWN

Rosie Harris

severn
House

This first world edition published 2018
in Great Britain and 2019 in the USA by
SEVERN HOUSE PUBLISHERS LTD of
Eardley House, 4 Uxbridge Street, London W8 7SY.
Trade paperback edition first published
in Great Britain and the USA 2019 by
SEVERN HOUSE PUBLISHERS LTD.

British Library Cataloguing in Publication Data
A CIP catalogue record for this title is available from the British Library.

ISBN-13: 978-0-7278-8847-1 (cased)
ISBN-13: 978-1-84751-971-9 (trade paper)
ISBN-13: 978-1-4483-0186-7 (e-book)

All Severn House titles are printed on acid-free paper.

Severn House Publishers support the Forest Stewardship Council™ [FSC™],
the leading international forest certification organisation. All our titles that
are printed on FSC certified paper carry the FSC logo.

Typeset by Palimpsest Book Production Ltd.,
Falkirk, Stirlingshire, Scotland.
Printed and bound in Great Britain by
TJ International, Padstow, Cornwall.

A final thank you to all my family, friends and
fans who enjoy reading my books.

This is my final book because my eyesight is now so diminished that
I am unable to read the screen on my computer or
the manuscripts afterwards.

This book would not have been possible if it had not been for
the help of Carmel Bevan who has read through every page and
checked for typos and punctuation.

I am also grateful to my grandson, Robert,
for his persistent encouragement.

Thanks, too, to Caroline Sheldon of the
Caroline Sheldon Literary Agency and also to all at
Severn House for their support.

One

'Of course, I miss him! I'm surprised you even ask. I thought you of all people would understand,' Betty Wilson said, sharply.

She was a trim woman of medium height with neat grey hair and brown eyes. She was wearing a dark-brown dress with discreet make-up.

'I'm bound to; we were married for fifty years, so of course I miss him!' She sighed. 'The first thing I was aware of when I woke up in the morning was his head next to mine on the pillow. In later years when he retired, I not only saw him at breakfast time, I saw him throughout the day when he was doing odd jobs around the place. I saw him at lunchtime, and asleep in his armchair in the afternoon, as well as for the rest of the day.

'Of course, I miss him, so why must people keep asking me do I miss him? Of course, I do. You miss Jeff, don't you?'

The woman she was speaking to, her friend Sally Bishop, nodded slowly. She was a few years younger than Betty but she looked older with her rather severe white blouse fastened high to the neck, and a plain grey cardigan.

'Oh yes, I do,' she agreed solemnly, 'even though it's almost two years since he died.'

'Well, so do I,' Betty told her, 'and in my case it's only four months, remember. I'm not going to stop doing everything I did in the past, and I'm doing his jobs out here in the garden as well his jobs indoors. That's the least I can do,' she said determinedly, her head proudly raised. 'I'm fit and well so why shouldn't I do the jobs that he did over the past few years, even though he was getting more and more shaky.

'Not that he would ever admit it. He liked to think that he was as fit as he ever was but, of course, he wasn't. The list of things he couldn't do were endless and the older he got the shakier he became and everything was an effort.

'Nevertheless, I'm not going to dwell on that. I'll pick up where he left off and run the place just the same as we always did. I have no intention of moving to one of these sheltered flats for the elderly, no matter what the family say.

'This is my home. It's been my home for almost the past fifty years. I remember the day we moved in. It was raining all morning and as I waited for the furniture van to arrive, I thought everything we owned, and that wasn't a lot, was going to be ruined by the rain.

'Of course, it wasn't, because the moment the lorry drew up the rain stopped, the sun came out, and it was a beautiful May day. I couldn't have asked for anything more perfect.

'We didn't have a lot of furniture but what we had was precious since it had been given to us by various members of our family. To other people it must have looked like a hodgepodge of mismatched chairs, tables, cupboards, crockery and ornaments.

'Even so, it was ours and this was our first home. We'd been married for almost three years and had been living with Jeff's mother and father. They were very kind to us but I could see they were fed up of having us there, and I can well understand that.'

'Yes,' Sally agreed, 'I know what you mean. We lived with my mum and dad for two years and, though we got on well enough, we badly wanted a place of our own because they were settled in their ways and they didn't want a young couple coming along and disturbing their routine.'

'I thought it was all my prayers come true when we found this place. It was my dream cottage,' Betty sighed. 'It was the sort of place I always wanted. Friends raised their eyebrows when I said we were moving into Clover Crescent. "Why buy an old place like that when you could have one of the new modern houses they're putting up in the village?" they asked. "Because being tucked away in a quiet little lane off the main road is what I want," I told them. "I like the cottage far better than one of those boxes they're putting up." I know it's small and I must admit it was a bit of a squash when the children were growing up, but nevertheless it was ours. It has so many memories that now I couldn't bear to live anywhere else.'

'And I wouldn't want you to move,' Sally Bishop told her. 'We've been friends now for so long that I just couldn't stand it.' Her pale blue eyes filled with tears and her mouth trembled.

'I don't like the way everything is changing all around me these days,' she went on. 'Everything seems different. Even this place is no longer a village, but a small town. The traffic is faster, the shops have all become supermarkets, and even most of the people are strangers and so busy with their own affairs they haven't got time for each other.

'As for the children, well you wouldn't know they were children these days. The little girls don't play with dolls and prams; they wear trousers, or jeans as they call them, to be the same as the boys, and all they want to do is fiddle with these little machine things they carry around with them. They all go to school in cars and none of them ever play ball games in the road, or seem to do things on their own. If they go to the park their mums or dads go with them to make sure they are safe.'

'Well, we haven't changed,' Betty assured her. 'We might be getting a bit slower but we've still got plenty of time to do things, and I intend to carry on and keep my home going the same as it always has been. I've made that quite clear to Tim and to Mary,' she added.

'And what did they say?' Sally asked, pursing her lips questioningly.

'They say it's my life and I must do as I wish, but they'll help if I need them to. Tim's wife, Brenda, is the problem. She always has had too much to say for herself has that one. She thinks herself a cut above the rest of us, but when all is said and done she is only a receptionist. Sits out there preening herself, patting at that bush of fiery red hair and smiling at people when they come up to her desk for information.

'She'd like me to go in a home so that they can wash their hands of me, but she's got another thing coming. I may take half a day to do jobs around the house that only used to take half an hour, but I can still do them and intend to go on doing them,' Betty said clamping her lips together grimly.

She didn't tell Sally that Brenda was not only constantly saying that she would be better in a home, but was forever pointing out things she hadn't done in the house; finding dust on ledges, or raising her eyebrows if she saw a few crumbs on the kitchen floor.

She never had seen eye to eye with Brenda but she always managed to stay reasonably friendly for Graham's sake.

Graham, their son, Betty's grandson, was now in his twenties and, like her, he didn't relish squabbles. Ever since he was a child he had done everything in his power to avoid them.

For the most part he stayed neutral but she knew she had only to ask him and he would help her in any way she needed.

Mary's husband, Toby Parker, was rather like that, too. He said little or nothing. He wasn't overly friendly but neither was he unfriendly, and she knew that he would always be there to offer a helping hand if she ever needed one.

The other person, who was such a long-standing friend that he was almost part of the family and always eager to help her, was Peter Brown. She'd known him practically all her life and he'd been a close friend of Jeff's. In his younger days he'd been in the Navy and travelled the world. He was still a bachelor but he had his own house and did all his own cooking, and his garden was a picture.

He and Jeff had always been friends and helped out in each other's gardens when there was a big job to do. They exchanged cuttings and ideas all the time. They had regularly gone out together for a drink on Friday nights and Peter had come to them most weekends for Sunday lunch.

He still came on a Sunday, and he made no secret of the fact that he would like to see her more often. He kept telling her that he would happily take over the garden and keep it as immaculate as Jeff had always done.

Her reply was always the same. She would tell him that for the present she didn't need to call on his help, or anyone else's.

'Why not let him do it? You feed him once a week and he's always round here on some pretext or the other, so why not let him take care of the garden for you?' Sally asked.

'That would be the thin edge of the wedge,' Betty said tartly. 'Next thing he'd be doing the shopping for me.'

'Well, he takes you to the shops in his car each week as it is,' Sally pointed out.

'I know that, but I still do my own shopping,' Betty insisted. 'No one tells me what to buy, or picks out the fruit and vegetables, or tells me what joint of meat I should buy.'

'No, maybe not, but he carries them home for you and when he comes on Sunday for lunch he always has a bottle of wine under his arm,' Sally rallied back. 'You want to think yourself lucky,' she went on. 'Not many of us in our seventies have a friend like that, and he's several years younger than you. The way you turn down his help it's a wonder he hasn't cleared off and found someone younger who would appreciate him. He's still got a good head of hair and he dresses well and takes good care of himself.'

'I know what you're saying and I do appreciate his help,' Betty admitted, 'but he keeps telling me that he wants to look after me, and all that nonsense, and I want none of it. What with that and my family talking behind my back about me going into a home, I don't know where I am.

'It's my life and I'm going to ignore the lot of them and live it my way to the best of my ability.

'Tomorrow,' she went on, 'I intend to give this big hedge a good trim. Cut it right back.'

'Do you think you can do that?' Sally said doubtfully. 'I think you ought to let Peter tackle that job or else hire someone to come in and cut it for you. Get it cut down really low so that you don't have to stand on those high steps. Your Jeff never looked safe when he was up on them.'

Betty laughed. 'I know they're a bit wobbly but Jeff always said they'd last a lifetime and see him out.'

'Well, they've done that all right,' Sally agreed, dryly. 'I still think you should get someone in to cut it and cut that great hedge for you, even if it's Peter or your son.'

'No,' Betty shook her head determinedly. 'First thing tomorrow morning I'll give it a go. You can bring me out a cuppa about ten o'clock, now don't forget,' she added with a smile.

Two

Betty Wilson was as good as her word.

Dressed in Jeff's old boiler suit, and a scarf tied round her hair, she was ready for action and ready to accept the challenge she had made the night before.

She went straight to the garden shed for the very ladder which Jeff had always used to cut the high hedge. She struggled valiantly to get it out of the shed, across the lawn and fix it into position at the beginning of the hedge. It was tricky; the ground was uneven and the ladder extremely heavy. It took her almost ten minutes to fix it to her own satisfaction. She returned to the shed to rummage for the hedge cutter, plugged it in to the long lead attached to a socket and extension, so that she could run it across the lawn and have the extension close by the foot of the ladder.

Having satisfied herself once again that the ladder was now quite safe, she picked up the power trimmer and began slowly and carefully to climb the ladder steps. She was about halfway up when the ladder began to tilt for a moment as she clung on, petrified that she was going to fall. Then, carefully adjusting her position on the ladder, she steadied it, waited a couple of minutes and then, convinced that it was safe to start up once again, slowly proceeded to climb upwards so that she could reach the top of the high hedge.

Sally Bishop was watching from her kitchen window. She had already switched the kettle on ready to make tea for Betty and herself, but her heart was in her mouth as she saw the ladder swaying. She wanted to rush out and see if she could steady it, but she was afraid that might only startle Betty and she might make a movement that would send the latter tippling over onto its side.

As she watched, Sally saw Peter Brown moving quietly down to the bottom of his own garden, which was adjacent to Betty's, and edging his way through a gap in the fence into Betty's garden. She suspected that there was a sufficient gap in his fence to allow him to come and go as he pleased.

Like her, he was scared of frightening Betty, making her jump and upsetting the position of the ladder, so he remained just inside his own garden, watching and waiting.

Sally decided to take Peter some tea, as well as Betty and herself, so she put another mug on the tray, took the milk out of the fridge, and began filling the mugs from the big teapot. Then she added a tin of biscuits and opened the back door, ready to carry the loaded tray out into the garden.

Cautiously she stepped out into the garden.

Sally paused and looked to where Betty was perched high on the ladder, she seemed to be in full control of the situation. Sally could hear the noise of the hedge trimmer. Sally waved a hand in greeting to Peter and waited as he finally edged in to the garden.

'Would you mind carrying this tray down to Betty?' she asked with a smile. 'Put it down on the garden table. She will see it is there and come down for her drink,' Sally smiled. 'She told me to make her one at about this time.'

'I imagine it will be very welcome,' Peter acknowledged, as he took the tray.

'I've made you one as well,' she told him, 'so drink it before it goes cold, and help yourself to a biscuit.'

As she spoke the noise of the trimmer stopped. Suddenly there was a bright flash, followed by a startled scream from Betty. She seemed to be surrounded by acrid smoke.

'My God!' Peter yelled as he dumped the tray and ran towards the hedge, 'she's cut through the cord.'

Shaking like a leaf, Betty was clinging to the ladder, which was swaying precariously. Almost at the same moment as Peter managed to reach her side, the ladder toppled sideways. Peter grabbed out desperately, trying to break her fall, but he was too late and both Betty and the ladder fell in a heap at his feet.

'Whatever happened?' Sally gasped as she arrived at the scene.

'At a guess, I would say that she cut through the cable and then let go of the trimmer because at that same moment she felt the ladder slipping. It was lucky she did let the trimmer drop or she would have been electrocuted!'

'I saw it swaying just a few moments earlier, I should have told her to get down,' Sally cried.

'She had a very heavy fall and she's unconscious,' Peter pronounced as he took control of the situation. 'Go and call an ambulance. I'll stay here with her in case she comes round. Also, can you bring out a blanket or something to cover her over so that she doesn't get cold, and perhaps a pillow to put underneath her head to make her comfortable,' Peter asked.

'Yes, of course I will,' Sally called back to him, as she hurried off.

Ten minutes later they heard the approaching vehicle, and Sally rushed to let them in through her house and into Betty's garden.

The two paramedics came armed with bags of equipment, and they listened carefully as between them Peter and Sally explained what had happened, or at least what they thought had happened.

They examined Betty carefully, then one looked at the other and nodded, then went off back to the ambulance to collect a stretcher.

'We're taking her in,' they told Peter and Sally. 'If one of you wish to come with us you can.'

Peter and Sally exchanged looks. 'I'll go,' Peter said.

'No, I think I should,' Sally told him. 'It might upset her if she woke up and found you sitting at her bedside.'

There was a moment's silence, after which Peter nodded his head in agreement. 'Yes, you're probably right,' he said resignedly. 'Let me know how she is as soon as you can though.'

'Don't worry, I'll do that,' Sally promised.

She followed the two paramedics out to the ambulance, and took the seat they indicated.

Betty was still on the stretcher, and her face was completely devoid of colour. Even her lips were so pale that they looked translucent.

When they reached the hospital Sally followed the two paramedics carrying the stretcher into the A & E and stood there waiting, wondering whether she should go into the small single ward where they had taken Betty or whether she should stay in the general reception area. Not knowing what to do for the best, she followed the stretcher-bearers and waited as they transferred Betty from the stretcher onto the narrow bed and told the nurse who had directed them what details they knew about the accident.

Sally remained there, uncertain about what to do next. She almost jumped out of her skin when a dark young man with a stethoscope around his neck entered the room. He nodded in Sally's direction but went straight to the bedside and began checking Betty over. A nurse entered and their voices lowered as they exchanged comments about Betty's condition, so that Sally was unable to clearly hear what was being said.

'Is she going to be all right?' Sally asked in a frightened voice.

The nurse looked at her quickly. 'Are you a relative?'

'No,' Sally admitted, 'I'm her neighbour, but I was there when she fell off the ladder.'

The dark-haired doctor looked across at her as if seeing her for the first time. 'You witnessed the accident?'

'Well, yes,' Sally admitted. 'She was trying to cut a high hedge. She was standing on a sort of ladder and it became rickety as she was holding an electric trimmer in her hand trying to cut the hedge. I'm not sure quite what happened, whether she cut the cord of the trimmer first, or whether the trimmer cut itself off as it fell when she fell.'

The doctor frowned as if not quite understanding what the situation had been, then he looked at the nurse with raised eyebrows.

'You mean she could have electrocuted herself?' the nurse asked.

'Well, yes I suppose she could have done, but I think she fell first and it was then that she let go of the hedge trimmer so that she could hang onto the ladder. Anyway, it ended up on the ground beside her.'

'The trimmer was switched off at the time?' The nurse pressed her.

'Well, it certainly wasn't running when we went across to pick Betty up,' Sally admitted.

The doctor and nurse went out of the cubicle and stood together outside, talking in low voices once again. They moved away after a few moments and about ten minutes later a porter came in and wheeled Betty away in the bed she was lying in.

'What's happening, now?' Sally asked the porter.

'We're taking her for an X-ray and after that she will be transferred to a ward. Sister will tell you which one and take you there when she is settled in.'

'So, do I wait here?' Sally pressed.

The porter nodded and quickly manoeuvred the bed out of the small ward and towards the double doors that lead to a corridor, and then disappeared from sight.

Sally felt helpless. She stayed sitting on the chair for several minutes. When the nurse came into the room she jumped up guiltily. 'I suppose I shouldn't be here now my friend has been taken away,' she said nervously.

'No, she won't be coming back here so I would sit outside in the waiting area. When they know which ward she has been taken to someone will let you know.'

The waiting seemed endless. People arrived on stretchers bought in by paramedics, relatives came in, patients were taken away on stretchers or if, like Betty, they were too ill to be moved they were wheeled away by porters in the very bed in which they lay. It was all so busy that Sally was quite sure they had forgotten all about her.

It was then that a nurse came in telling her which ward to go to.

'How do I get there?' Sally asked, bewildered by the complicated instructions.

'Give me a moment and I'll take you there,' the nurse told her in a clipped voice.

Five minutes later the nurse came bustling back and hurried Sally through the double doors where she had seen Betty disappearing earlier. They walked for what seemed like miles down corridors, and round corners until eventually the nurse stopped outside some glass-topped doors. She pushed them open and indicated for Sally to follow as she led the way down another corridor, past individual rooms. Sally found herself being directed into the very last one.

Betty's eyelids fluttered open as they entered the room. She stared in bewilderment; first at the nurse and then at Sally.

'Where am I? What happened?' she asked in a faint voice.

'You had a bit of an accident, my dear,' Sally told her. 'You're in hospital.'

'Well, I know I'm not at home in my own bed,' Betty told her tetchily. 'What's more I'm aching all over . . .' She paused and stared down at her arm that was plastered from wrist to elbow and was lying on top of the bed cover. 'Have I broken my arm?' she asked, as she tried to lift it and failed to do so.

'It looks like it,' Sally admitted. 'I wondered why you were away so long being treated, obviously they were putting your arm in plaster.'

Betty didn't answer, she simply stared round the room in bewilderment. 'I can't stay here, I don't like the place,' she said, almost aggressively. 'I've got to finish cutting that hedge.'

'You won't be doing any more hedge cutting,' Sally said emphatically. 'Do you want me to let your Tim know what's happened? I'll just say that you fell off the ladder, you can tell him the rest when he comes in to see you. I won't tell him that we're not sure if you cut through the cable of the hedge trimmer or whether that happened when you dropped it as you fell. I don't know if you realize it but you could have electrocuted yourself. In fact,' she added, severely, 'you should consider yourself very lucky! Not only that you didn't electrocute yourself, but that you're awake now too.'

'Sorry about that but accidents will happen,' Betty muttered in a grim voice.

'We know that, and you were very lucky that you got away with it. That ladder should have been condemned years ago, it's lucky Jeff didn't have a fall when he was using it. As for the hedge trimmer, all the cable on that was so old and cracked that again you've been lucky that neither of you were electrocuted.'

'You sound like an authority on the subject,' Betty said, accusingly.

'No, I know nothing about it except what Peter told me.'

'And what makes you think you can believe him?'

'Oh, he knows what he's talking about, and believe me if he hadn't been there to tell me what to do you'd be in a much worse state than you are!'

Betty closed her eyes and was silent for several minutes. 'Can you call a nurse,' she said opening her eyes and staring fixedly at Sally.

'Of course, is something wrong? Are you in pain?'

'Call the nurse,' Betty repeated slowly and weakly.

Sally did as she asked.

'Yes, what's the matter?' the nurse asked briskly as she came to the bedside. Automatically she picked up Betty's wrist and checked her pulse.

'I want to know when I can go home,' Betty stated.

'Not for a while, I'm afraid. You will have to stay here until your temperature and pulse are back to normal. In the meantime, you must rest and I think it is time your friend left. You shouldn't be worrying about anything.'

'We were only chatting,' Sally said defensively. 'I haven't said anything to upset her, she simply wanted to know what happened and I was telling her about the accident.'

'Yes, well that will do for the moment. I think Mrs Wilson needs to rest,' the nurse repeated, emphasizing the word rest.

'Very well, I'll leave. Can I come back later?'

'Not today. Mrs Wilson needs all the rest she can get. I am going to give her a sedative and it would be better if you left visiting until tomorrow.'

'Make sure it's you that comes back and not that Peter Brown,' Betty said, weakly.

'Do you want me to let your family know what has happened?' Sally asked.

'We will have already notified the next of kin,' the nurse said quickly.

Betty groaned, 'Oh dear, that means they'll be here like a bunch of vultures all saying I ought to go into a home,' she murmured, as she closed her eyes wearily.

Three

Betty was in hospital for just over a week. Sally went to see her once, but the room was so full of relatives that she decided it would be better if she stayed away. Anyway, she had plenty to do.

Peter Brown had taken it upon himself to complete the cutting of the hedge. It was now trimmed down to a very manageable five feet. He had also tended the garden; weeding the borders, digging out dead plants, trimming back bushes, and generally making the whole appearance neat and orderly.

Sally had carried out much the same task inside Betty's house. She had washed up all the dirty dishes, and cleared away a lot of the old newspapers, wrappers and boxes so that the kitchen was now sparklingly clean and looked as if it hadn't ever been used. She also tackled the rest of the house, cleaning the bathroom, changing Betty's bed, and laundering the sheets and duvet cover.

The whole house was now in pristine condition and ready for Betty's return.

Her son, Tim, came round with groceries to fill the fridge and smiled appreciatively at Sally when he saw what she'd done. 'You've done an excellent job here,' he said softly. 'Let's hope she can now keep it neat and tidy.'

'Well, she did have the garden, as well as the house, to look after,' Sally explained.

Tim walked over to the window and looked out into the garden, and then turned around to face Sally.

'You didn't do that as well, did you?' he gasped.

'No, no, Peter Brown did the garden. Made a nice job of that, hasn't he!'

'Yes. It certainly is neat and tidy and he's saved me a job,' Tim said happily.

'He'll be round here in a few minutes for his morning cuppa, so I suggest you tell him that,' Sally chimed. 'It was a lot of hard work, I can tell you, and he's an old man, you know.'

'Well, he didn't have to do it! I would have tidied up the garden, but she refused to let anyone help her.'

'Yes, I know that, but sometimes it's the way you put it,' Sally pointed out.

'And what is that supposed to mean?' Tim asked, hotly.

'Well, Betty doesn't like to think that she is putting pressure on people. She doesn't want to be any trouble. I could have helped out in the house but she made it clear that wouldn't do at all.'

Their eyes met.

'Yes I know, and I am grateful to you, and to Peter, and believe me I will tell him so when I see him.'

When Betty came home she stared around in wonderment.

'I didn't know there were still fairies working here. Invisible ones that come when you're in the hospital to clean and tidy,' she murmured looking straight at Sally.

'Just a bit of a clear up, that was all. I thought you'd like it done for when you came back, sort of start afresh,' Sally said with a smile.

'I would've got around to doing it once I got home,' Betty told her. She raised her eyebrows and smiled. 'And what about the garden? Has Peter been out there fiddling around?'

'He's certainly been out there and worked very hard,' Sally told her.

Betty went to the window to take a look outside, and stared in surprise at the low hedge, beautifully tended borders, trimmed bushes and the new plants that had been put in appropriate places.

'My, my he has worked his socks off,' she commented dryly.

'He worked very hard, I can tell you,' Sally said. 'In fact, there were times when I thought he was doing too much.'

'He's certainly done that,' Betty's said sharply. 'Given a few days home and I would have tackled it myself.'

'Would you? Could you with your arm?'

Betty looked down at her arm, still encased in plaster. 'Well perhaps you have a point,' she conceded.

'Then make sure you thank Peter when he comes to see you, he'll be here any minute for morning coffee.'

Betty pulled a face. 'Lazy old devil, too idle or too mean to make his own,' Betty said witheringly.

'No, nothing like that, he was working so hard in the garden but I felt he needed a drink. I didn't want him passing out from dehydration,' Sally stated.

Before Betty could answer, Peter arrived.

'Anyone in?' he called as he pushed open the back door.

'Come on in, Peter,' Sally called. 'My word,' she said in surprise, 'you do look smart this morning. Is that a new pullover?'

'Yes, it caught my eye and I thought it was about time I bought myself something new to wear,' he told them, rather sheepishly.

'Betty's here and delighted by what you've done in her garden.'

'I wouldn't go as far as to say that,' Betty muttered softly, but there was a smile on her face as she greeted Peter.

'My word, it's good to see you back home and looking so well,' Peter greeted her warmly. 'You certainly had us all worried. Do you remember what happened?'

Betty winced as she raised her broken arm very slightly. 'How can I forget when it weighs so much,' she said dryly.

'How long does the plaster have to stay on?' Peter frowned. 'It must make doing things very difficult,' he added, with feeling.

'I'll find out when I go back to the hospital in a couple of weeks' time for a check up,' Betty told him.

'She's very pleased with the garden,' Sally persisted.

Peter's eyes lit up. 'I know how much it means to you, Betty, that everything is tidy. I'll be keeping it in order until you are better, so don't worry about it.'

'It looks all right at the moment and by the time it needs attention I'll be able to do it myself,' Betty said quickly.

'There's no rush. I'll carry on doing it for as long as it needs it. In fact,' he said hesitantly, 'I'm hoping that you will let me go on doing it for good. You certainly must never attempt to cut that hedge again. For one thing, that old ladder isn't safe and I think it should be thrown away. As for the trimmer, well the cord on that was so cracked that it's a wonder old Jeff didn't do himself some harm when he was using it.'

'Well, he didn't,' Betty snapped, 'and as soon as I can get out and about I'll buy a new hedge trimmer.'

'Don't trouble yourself, I'll use mine,' Peter told her.

Sally could see that Betty was about to refuse so she quickly changed the subject. 'Come on,' she insisted, 'let's drink our coffee before it goes cold. And now don't you worry about anything, Betty. Concentrate on getting better.'

'I expect you'll have to go for exercises to get that hand and arm working,' Peter said thoughtfully.

'I need to get the plaster off first.'

'Yes, of course. I understand that,' Peter mumbled. 'I was just trying to say don't do anything until your hand and arm are working properly again. If there is anything in the house that needs attention just let me know and I'll come and do it for you. I'd even move in if you wanted me to look after you properly; I'd wait on you hand and foot if only you would let me.'

There was an uneasy atmosphere in the room. Sally looked across at Betty and raised her eyebrows questioningly. 'That mightn't be such a bad idea,' she mused. 'Peter would be on hand to bring you a cup of tea when you wanted one or help you with anything else.'

'Like putting me to bed,' Betty said caustically.

'I know that you wouldn't want me to go that far,' Peter said quickly, his face going red with embarrassment. He looked across at Sally. 'Although I'd even do that it if she wanted me to help her. I'd do anything to help you, Betty, as you well know,' he added sincerely.

'I know what you are all saying and I don't want your help,' she told him, sharply.

Peter looked crestfallen. 'I only meant that I'd help and do anything you couldn't manage to do,' he told her.

'So, you've told me countless times,' Betty said crossly. 'Leave me alone in peace. If I want your help I'll ask for it, and the chances are I'd sooner manage without!'

'What about shopping? I'm sure you won't be able to get to the shops for a while, and it would save Sally here having to do it for you.'

'Drink your coffee and go home,' Betty told him, 'and stop calling on Sally to make you coffee every day, you can make your own.'

Sally waited until Peter had said goodbye and left before saying firmly to Betty, 'I think you should be grateful to Peter and treat him better.'

'I'm fed up with him constantly pestering me and wanting to help,' Betty retorted. 'It seems to me that there is always someone who knows better than I do about what I should and shouldn't do. I had it from my family all the time I was in hospital. Even my own daughter, Mary, was lecturing me about going into a home because it wasn't safe for me to be on my own, especially at night. How would you feel if your family treated you like that?'

'I'm sure it is because they are worried about you, especially being on your own at night, in case you have a fall.'

'I know that, and Tim says he is going to get me one of those button things to hang round my neck that I can press if I fall and call for help. He says the call will go through to a help centre and to him at the same time. I don't want that! He takes no notice and you can bet your boots he'll be turning up with one in a few days' time. I don't intend wearing it.'

'Be rather foolish not to do so,' Sally murmured. 'Anyway,' she went on with a twinkle in her eyes, 'if you don't want to do that, then accept Peter's suggestion and let him move in with you.'

Betty laughed. 'You should have seen the look on Mary's face when I told her he had offered to do so. "He's after your money", she warned me. "Whatever happens you mustn't do that".'

'Rubbish!' Sally stated.

'That's what I said. I told her he had his own house, and a good pension, so what did he want my money for.'

'Your daughter is only trying to protect you, I suppose,' Sally said warily, 'but surely after all these years of living almost next door to him since she was a child, Mary must know that Peter isn't like that?'

'I know but how would you feel if you were in my shoes?'

'Probably tell her to mind her own business.'

'That really would cause a family row. They would probably say I had gone out of my mind and get a couple of doctors to verify the fact, and have no trouble putting me into a home. I'd have no say at all.'

'Then go ahead and accept Peter's help and be grateful for it,' Sally told her. 'He means well.'

'He's too pushy. I can't stand it and all this business about trying to please me.'

'He means well,' Sally repeated.

'I suppose he does but I don't want him looking after me doing things for me, or preventing me from doing the things I want to do in my home, or in my garden.'

'No, but it is better than your family insisting that you go into a home!'

Four

Betty had been home six weeks when she received a telephone called from her bank to say that a large sum of money had been drawn from her account and they needed to verify that it was not fraudulent.

For one moment the caller's voice was driven out by the horrifying thought that filled Betty's mind: had her daughter Mary been right? Had she made a foolish mistake in letting Peter handle her affairs? She felt shocked, how could things have gone so wrong when everything had seemed to be running so smoothly.

Although she didn't want Peter moving in with her, she had conceded that he was her rock and had to come to depend upon his help more and more. He did her shopping, he kept the garden under control and he took her out whenever she needed to go somewhere. More and more he was taking over, even doing the shopping for her. She had given him her credit card and told him what her pin number was so that he could pay for groceries, and she had handed him her debit card so that he could even draw out cash for her so that she had no need to go to the bank.

'Sorry, I was distracted, could you repeat what you said?'

'Yes, of course,' the cultured voice told her. 'A large sum of money has been withdrawn from your account and we need to check that you were aware of this.'

'Oh, my goodness,' Betty exclaimed in alarm. 'Are you sure?'

'Well, if you tell us your account number and pin number we can confirm this.'

'You told me never to disclose those to anyone,' Betty said worriedly.

'Quite right, madam,' he paused as if trying to think of a solution. 'I tell you what we will do. We'll send a courier round to pick them up. Put them in a sealed envelope and hand them over to the man who will be in uniform and who will show you his identity card.'

'I'm not sure,' Betty prevaricated. 'I don't know who I'm talking to.'

'I understand your reluctance, and it's very sensible of you, so I tell you what I'll do. I'll hang up and you ring your bank and ask the manager there to confirm what I have told you. Right?'

'Very well,' Betty said hesitantly.

'Have you the number handy?'

Before she could answer he reeled it off to her and she recognized the number and was convinced that it was the bank she used. With a feeling of relief, she did as he told her. She put down her phone and then picked it up again and dialled the number. A different voice answered her and Betty explained what had happened.

'I'm sorry you've been troubled like this, Mrs Wilson, but if you could do as my colleague has instructed we will verify how much has been taken and tell you what we are prepared to do about it.'

'What do you mean by that?' she asked in a bewildered voice.

'If the fault is ours, then we will recompense you, but if someone who is known to you has taken the money then there is not a lot that we can do. Has anyone except yourself got access to your bank cards?'

Betty hesitated. 'Well yes,' she admitted. 'A friend has. You see, I find it difficult to get out these days and so when I need some shopping done this friend does it for me and I have to let them have my credit card number so that they can pay for the goods.'

'I quite understand. Although it is rather irregular, I can see that you may find it necessary. Now don't worry, we will look into the matter immediately. The courier is already on his way so put the phone down, find your cards, put them into a sealed envelope, and hand them over to him.'

'Is that safe?' Betty asked anxiously.

'Quite safe. He will be wearing an identification badge so you can check that you are handing it to the right person.'

As Betty hunted for an envelope she found herself again remembering what Mary had said. Although she was sure Peter wouldn't do anything like that, she couldn't help wondering.

When she'd put both her debit and credit cards into the

envelope she made doubly sure they were safe by using a strip of Sellotape to seal them, as well as the gum on the envelope. Then she went down the path to wait by her gate for the courier.

Peter was working in the garden. He looked up and greeted her as she came down the path.

'Going to the post office?' he said, nodding towards the envelope in her hand.

Betty shook her head. Then on the spur of the moment, and because she felt she had to warn him about what was happening, she told him about the call she'd had from the bank.

Peter frowned and let out a low whistle. 'I don't like the sound of that,' he said.

'Neither do I. You haven't told anyone else my pin number, have you?'

'Of course not!' His eyes narrowed. 'It sounds fishy to me. I tell you what, find another envelope and put something about the same thickness as your cards inside it for the guy to collect and the moment he's taken them from you I'll drive you to the high street and you can go into the bank and make sure about what is going on.'

'I've already phoned them and spoke to the manager,' Betty told him.

'I know, but a double-check isn't a bad thing. If you should have handed over your cards than you can tell him what you've done and give the real ones to the bank to deal with.'

Betty looked confused. 'All right, if you think I should,' she agreed.

The moment the motorcyclist had collected the second envelope from Betty, Peter fetched his car and they drove to the bank.

Betty explained to the teller what had happened and he reported it to the manager immediately. They were shown into a private room and the manager listened intently as Betty related the phone calls and the courier who had called to take away her cards.

'Oh, my goodness, Mrs Wilson, I wish you hadn't done that,' he told her. 'I'm afraid you handed them over to the very people who have been tampering with your account. I don't know how they got hold of your number, but obviously they have, and as a matter of fact money has already been transferred from your savings account into your current account ready to be withdrawn.

Previously it looks like a small amount was taken, maybe as a test. Now you have given them carte blanche to withdraw everything you have in it.'

'What do you mean?' Betty said looking at him in amazement. 'I phoned you after I'd had their call to verify that I was to hand over the cards. In fact, they told me to confirm it with you.'

The manager shook his head. 'No, when you picked up your phone again the line was still open to them and the man's accomplice spoke to you.'

'How do you know that?'

'Because it's a scam, Mrs Wilson.'

'A scam! You mean they're imposters?'

'I'm afraid it's exactly that, a scam. I will immediately call our security people and explain what has happened and see if they can stop any more money being taken from your account, but they may have already used the cards you handed over to them to clear your account.'

Betty smiled. 'No, they can't do that. The envelope I gave to the courier just had bits of an old card from some estate agency that was lying around. I didn't put my credit card or my debit card in there. I've got them here.' She held out the two cards to the bank manager.

He stared at them in astonishment as he took them from her. 'Mrs Wilson, how very clever of you!'

'I hope so,' she said, her smile broadening. 'Actually, it wasn't my idea it was Mr Brown's.'

The bank manager looked at Peter. 'You are the one who uses her cards and knows her pin number, are you?' he commented.

'Yes,' Peter admitted. 'I knew them on both her cards. You see, I go shopping for her and she gives me the cards instead of money. We thought it was safer that way.'

The bank manager looked grave. 'Yes,' he said, 'you would think so but tell me have you ever actually handed the cards to anyone and let them take them away.'

Peter looked thoughtful. 'There's only one place that I can think of and that was the new chancellery shop that's just opened in the next village.'

'So why did you do that?'

'It was just the credit card,' he said. 'I hadn't been in there before and the assistant said that he needed to check that it was genuine.'

'He would have known whether it was or not when you put it in the machine. If it wasn't genuine the bank would reject it and refuse to pay.'

Peter nodded. 'I did think that, but I didn't know enough about it to be certain so I didn't argue with the man.'

'So, he took the card and went out into the back of the shop with it?'

'That's right.'

'And what happened next?'

'Well, when he came back he said it was OK. I put it in the machine and paid the bill.'

'When you passed it over to him, did you tell him the pin number?'

Peter looked rather sheepish. 'I'm afraid I did,' he said. 'The man said that he needed that to check with the bank.'

'I bet he did,' the manager said cynically. 'Well, since you haven't handed your cards over to the courier today I don't think you have very much to worry about, Mrs Wilson. The bank will make good the money they have taken from your account. I would suggest, though, that you change your PIN just to be on the safe side. In future be very careful,' he said, addressing Peter. 'Never let anybody take your cards away from you on any pretext whatsoever.'

As they came out of the bank Peter and Betty exchanged glances and then both of them started laughing.

'That was a lucky escape,' Betty commented. 'Don't you forget, Peter Brown, don't you go handing my cards to anyone or telling them my pin number!'

'Don't you worry, I've learnt my lesson,' Peter said. 'Come on, let me take you for a drink to celebrate how well everything has turned out for us.'

'At this time of day!'

'Why not? We've had a very lucky escape. You could have lost all your money, but instead it's safe and sound, and we've fooled the scammers. I'd like to see their faces when they open your envelope and find a load of rubbish inside.'

'Thanks to your cleverness,' Betty said admiringly.

'Your trouble is you are too trusting. You think everyone is as sweet and honest as you are. You never think badly about anybody.'

It was on the tip of Betty's tongue to tell him what Mary had said and admit that for a brief moment she really had doubted him and wondered if he'd had anything to do with the money being withdrawn. Then common sense prevailed.

'Alright,' she said with a beaming smile, 'we'll have that drink to celebrate, but only a small one, mind. Why not,' she added. 'We've certainly got something to celebrate. We may be old, we may be doddery, but we are not stupid!'

Five

Betty Wilson couldn't sleep. She tossed and turned, changed her pillows round, took a drink of water, settled down again, but it was all to no avail. The events of the day were churning wildly in her head.

So much had happened since Jeff had died. The constant nagging by her family that she wasn't capable of looking after herself, and all of them in turn pointing out things she should have done but for some reason hadn't, irritated her.

She understood that they now felt responsible for her and that if they could persuade her to go into a home then they would feel they had nothing more to worry about, but she wasn't having any of it. She considered the idea utterly ridiculous. She was fit and well apart from a few aches and pains but those were what you expected when you were in your late seventies.

First, it had been the state of her home, then the work that needed doing in the garden, and now both Tim and Mary were trying to persuade her to sell the car.

'I don't want to sell it,' she told them firmly.

'Why not?' Tim demanded. 'You don't drive it.'

'I might do one day,' Betty argued.

'You've never driven it. Dad always drove wherever you went.'

'He liked driving, and he didn't like being a passenger,' Betty told him.

'You've never driven it,' Mary argued, backing up her brother.

'No, not that car, but all the other cars we've had.'

'Rubbish,' Tim persisted. 'I don't remember you ever driving.'

'How about the school runs?' Betty argued back. 'I used to take you to school and pick you up.'

That comment had shut him up, but what with one thing and another all the arguing was making her life unbearable.

She went through in her mind again the business of the ladder slipping and making her cut through the cable of the hedge strimmer. Had it been in that order, or had she cut through the cable and had a small electric shock and then lost her balance and fallen?

She would never know for certain, either way she supposed she had been lucky, but it had certainly undermined her confidence.

'Lucky, when I broke my arm,' she muttered out loud.

She turned over and tried to sleep but it was no good. Although she had put the accident out of her mind she was now thinking about the way she had nearly fallen for the scam which might have ended up with her losing every penny she possessed. That would have given the family something to berate her about.

Then again, she had been exceedingly lucky and she had Peter to thank for that. She would never have thought of putting false cards into the envelope. That had saved the day and her money, there was no doubt at all about that. Two heads could certainly be better than one when it came to sorting out a problem.

That was the difference between her family and Peter. They nagged; he did something useful. Either he took over and did the job himself, or cleverly guided her on what she ought to do.

She really should be grateful to him, she thought guiltily. The trouble was that she was afraid to thank him or praise him because he might then take it as a sign that she was weakening, and she didn't want to be taken over completely by him.

Why was he so keen to move in with her, she wondered. He had no problems looking after himself. He was a reasonably good cook, took housework in his stride, and when it came to odd jobs and doing things in the garden, or in the house, he tackled them all efficiently.

Was he lonely? She wondered. Was that the reason he was so keen to move in with her? True, the evenings were long during the winter months, and half the stuff on the television was not worth watching. Sometimes she switched that off and turned to the radio. Some of their plays were good, but it wasn't much fun listening on your own because you had no one to talk about the programme with afterwards.

Still unable to sleep she got out of bed, put on her dressing gown and made her way to the kitchen and switched the kettle on. A cup of tea might help to calm her down, she decided. Even if it didn't help her to sleep, it might help her to clarify what she was going to do in the future. If she got her mind in order it would make things easier when it came to arguing with the family.

She sat at the kitchen table, drank her tea and planned ahead.

By the time she returned to bed she felt quite sleepy and within minutes of her head touching the pillow she was away, her mind occupied by a wonderful dream in which she was driving their Mercedes down the motorway.

When she woke next morning, the memory of her dream was still clear in her mind and, as soon as she had her breakfast, she decided to put it to the test. She opened up the garage doors and surveyed the Mercedes. It was a big car and she was sure she could handle it, but would it start? That was the question. Tim was quite right, it had been standing there for quite a long time.

Never mind, she could give it a try, she decided, as she put in the ignition key and pressed the pedal. The second time she turned the key the engine fired.

Triumphantly she backed out of the garage and down the drive onto the main road and headed for the M4 which was less than two minutes away. Once on the motorway, she felt her confidence soaring. She stayed in the slow lane, surprised by the number of heavy goods vehicles there were at that time of day. She kept her speed low until finally she found herself almost crawling behind a heavily loaded lorry, so she pulled out into the middle lane put her foot down and felt the car react immediately. Betty was gloriously happy to be doing what she wanted; this would show them she told herself. The road ahead was so clear that she increased her speed. She looked at the dials and saw she was doing nearly ninety miles an hour. 'I'd better slow-down,' she muttered aloud.

Before she had time to do so, she heard a strange noise coming from the car. As she looked into her rear mirror, she saw something lying in the road and clouds of smoke coming from the back of the car. Then the steering started to lurch and she hastily pulled into the slow lane.

She returned to her snail's pace as she waited for her heart to stop hammering and her breathing to slow down. That was some fright, I wonder what happened, she mused. Should she get out and walk back, and see what it was that had dropped off her car, or would that be too dangerous on a motorway?

Before she could decide she heard a police siren coming up behind her.

'Oh dear,' she said aloud, 'do I pull over or hope that it goes by?'

Nervously, she decided to continue on. She stayed in the slow lane and then wondered if she'd done the right thing because the police car followed her, flashing its lights at her. In her driving mirror she could see there were two policemen in it, and that the one sitting next to the driver was signalling to her to stop.

She did as she thought she was being asked to do and put her brakes on and moved into the hard shoulder.

The police car stopped right behind her and the elder policeman, the one who was a passenger, jumped out and came up to her car indicating to her to lower her window. He looked grave.

'May I see your driving licence,' he said quietly.

'Driving licence,' Betty frowned. 'I don't carry that with me,' she said. 'In fact I am not even sure I know where it is.'

'You do have a current driving licence?'

'I think so,' Betty said vaguely. 'I did, but it's ages since I looked and I'm not even sure where it is.'

'You mean it could have run out.'

'Run out?'

'Expired,' the policeman said.

'Well, it could have done as I haven't seen it lately.'

'Surely, you realize that it has to be renewed periodically,' the policeman said in an exasperated voice.

'Well, my husband saw to all those things.'

'And where is your husband?'

'He died about six months ago.'

'Did you drive when he was alive?'

Betty gave a sigh. 'No, it's years since I drove regularly, but I must say I'm enjoying it today.'

'Maybe you are, madam, but not only are you exceeding the speed limit, but you have lost part of your exhaust pipe, and you have a flat tyre.'

'Really! So that's why the steering is odd. I thought you could go as fast as you wished on these motorways.'

'No, madam, there is a speed limit and if you exceed it there is a heavy penalty.'

'Oh dear! I'm sorry about that,' Betty said contritely. 'I'll try and remember in future. Can I go now?'

'I'm afraid it's not quite as simple as that, madam. The fact that you can't produce your driving licence is a problem, you will have to bring it down to the station. The other thing, as I have pointed out, is that you have been caught speeding. Furthermore, we need proof that this is your car and that it is insured in your name.'

'The car is probably still in my husband's name,' Betty said. 'I just told you my husband has died.'

'Quite so, madam, in which case has the insurance been transferred to you?'

'Dear, oh dear, you are worse than my children always worrying about these trivial matters. I really don't know about the insurance. He always dealt with the insurance and little things like that.'

'I see. Please wait here, madam.'

The policeman returned to the car and talked to the driver who got out and walked across to Betty's car. Part of the interrogation was repeated virtually word for word. Betty was becoming both alarmed and irritated.

'I don't think you should be driving at all, madam,' the elder of the two policemen stated. 'In fact,' he said, taking a notebook from his pocket and noting down her name an address in it, 'you are being charged with dangerous driving and for exceeding the speed limit, as well as not being unable to produce your driving licence, or prove that this car is yours and that it carries the relevant insurance cover. Do you understand?' he said, as he handed her a piece of paper.

'I've got to pay this amount,' Betty said in dismay as she stared at the figure he'd written there.

'They are all things you are not allowed to do without permission. It's outside the law to drive without a current driving licence, without current insurance, and there is no proof the car belongs to you or you have permission to drive it. Do you understand?'

'Not really,' Betty said looking at the list again. 'Now can I go?'

The two policemen exchanged glances. 'Your car is not drive-able in its present state,' one of them told her. 'You must arrange for it to be collected. Are you a member of the AA?'

Again, Betty looked vague and shook her head.

'Right. Then I'll arrange for it to be picked up by one of the local garages and they will let you know what repairs are necessary and their charges. Is there someone in your family who can handle this for you?'

'I'm quite capable of dealing with it myself,' Betty told him.

'Very well. Can you tell me the garage you normally use?'

Betty shook her head. She felt tears pricking behind her lids and knew that any minute now she was going to break down in tears.

'Are there any personal items you need to collect from your car?' asked the elder policeman. 'Then we will drive you home.'

Betty looked startled. Then she felt relieved. She knew she had broken the law, so she gave in gracefully and didn't argue because she didn't want to make matters worse.

As she was driven home she started rehearsing in her own mind how she was going to explain all this to the family. Or, should she simply pay the fine and say nothing, and the whole matter would be over and she could forget all about it.

That was impossible, she told herself, because sooner or later Tim would start asking about the car and when he looked into the garage and the car wasn't there she'd have to explain everything. Anyway, she would need his advice about what to tell the garage about repairing the car. Was it even worth it, or should they ask the garage to make them an offer for it?

Six

Betty saw curtains twitch and faces appear at several windows as the police car pulled up beside her cottage in Clover Crescent.

It was only to be expected, she thought wryly. After all, it was not often they had a visit from the police in their quiet little backwater.

Peter and Sally were at her door almost before she had her key in the lock.

One of the policemen walked with her to her door and then with a brief nod went back to the car, which drove off immediately.

'What happened?' Sally exclaimed, worriedly.

Peter stood by Betty's gate and said nothing, but he looked equally worried and listened intently as Betty explained she had gone out in the Mercedes and it had broken down on the motorway.

'Heavens above! It hasn't been out on the road for months. It's probably a year since Jeff last drove it,' Peter exclaimed. 'Why ever didn't you let me go over it and make sure that it was road-worthy before you took it for a run?'

'It started up with no trouble at all, it fired up on the second turn of the key,' Betty told him.

'What were you doing on the motorway? Where were you going?'

'I was just going for a drive,' she said lamely. 'Well, if you must know, Tim wanted to sell the car and I was against it. He said that I've never driven it and I wanted to prove to him that I could drive it.'

'You seem to have done that all right,' Peter said. 'What you going to tell him?'

'I was contemplating not telling him anything. I don't see that there's any need to do so.'

'He'll find out, don't you worry. Anyway, where is the car now?'

'Well, that's the problem. You see, the exhaust came off and one of the tyres went flat so the car is still by the side of the motorway. The police are asking a garage to come and collect it.'

Peter shook his head in dismay. 'That's going to be expensive!'

'Yes, yes I know about that,' she sighed. 'I've also got a heavy fine to pay because I couldn't produce my driving licence, and I wasn't sure who the car was insured with or where the documents were.'

'It probably isn't insured at all,' Peter commented, a worried look in his dark blue eyes. 'After all, it's six months since Jeff died and he hadn't driven it for at least three months before then.'

'If that's so, I've got a hefty fine to pay,' Betty repeated.

'More reason than ever to tell Tim,' Peter said solemnly. 'You can't hide it all from him,' he went on. 'For a start, if he is set on selling the car then won't he wonder where it is when he comes to collect it?'

'I don't want him to sell it, I want a car to drive.'

'You know I will always drive you anywhere you want to go,' Peter told her.

'Yes, I do know that but I want to be independent; to be able to jump into the car and go off at a moment's notice, without having to ask or explain to anyone where I am going or why!' Betty proclaimed stubbornly.

'Tell Tim that. Let him sell that big old brute and get you a smaller car, one that is only a couple of years old, not an old banger out of the Dark Ages,' Peter told her.

'One like yours, you mean. Small, neat, and modern but run of the mill,' she added sarcastically.

'See what Tim thinks,' Peter said, ignoring her jibe.

'He'll be so furious about what has happened that I daren't mention having another car at all,' Betty sighed. 'Still, let's get this matter settled and then I can rethink the whole thing and perhaps talk him round.'

Tim was aghast when Betty told him what had happened. His brown eyes darkened, his mouth tightened and his chin jutted out aggressively as he stared at his mother.

'Don't be cross!' he exploded. 'What do you expect me to be?

In the first place, why didn't you say that you were going out in the car and then I could have advised against it, or suggest you had the garage give it the once over before you took it out.' His voice rose, 'It's been standing in the garage for almost a year! The types were bound to be flat and it's a wonder the engine didn't seize up! I simply can't believe you could have been so st—'

He stopped himself from saying 'stupid' but he was so angry that, for the first time in her life, his mother felt frightened of him.

'Even so,' she spoke sharply. 'That's how matters stand, Tim, so I'm asking you to help me to sort them out. You can do whatever you wish about getting rid of the car. Contact the police and ask them to give you the name of the garage, find out what repairs are necessary and get them done, and then sell the car. I don't want to hear any more about it; do you understand!'

Tim stared at her in silence for a minute, then at last he turned on his heel and walked away.

Betty stood where she was for several minutes trying to collect her thoughts and regulate her breathing. Her heart was thumping, and she felt that if she moved she would probably fall over. It felt as if every ounce of energy had been drained from her.

She hated rows but then so did Tim, so he claimed, which no doubt was why he had said nothing.

Once the car was disposed of then, and only then, would she suggest buying a smaller one to replace it. Something like Peter was driving. She was sure that she could manage that quite comfortably. She had to admit that driving the Mercedes had been nerve-wracking. It was such a big car, which was one of the reasons why she had taken it on the motorway as she had thought there would be no pedestrians and therefore fewer hazards.

'Well . . .' She shrugged her shoulders and slowly walked back indoors. What was done was done and there was no turning back; she'd learned her lesson, she thought.

Peter looked very relieved when she told him she'd decided to sell the car.

'Glad to hear it,' he told her. 'It was far too big for you to drive. Great cumbersome thing! I never did like it. I thought Jeff was crazy to buy it in the first place, but then he always did like

something ostentatious when it came to motors I remember . . .'
His voice trailed off. 'Ah well, you don't want to hear all that
again, do you,' he said briskly. 'Put your coat on and I'll take you
out for a coffee.'

'Oh dear, is that a good idea?' Betty said worriedly. 'By now
everyone there in the village will know about the accident, because
they will have seen the police car bring me home, and be talking
about it.'

'Yes, I expect you're right so the sooner you face up to them
the better. Put a brave face on it, there's nothing to worry about.
Most of them will be worried in case you've been injured. When
they see you out and about drinking coffee they'll know that
everything is all right. Go on, get your coat.'

Betty looked at him with raised eyebrows. 'When did you
become so bossy?' she asked with a smile.

'Oh, I can take command if I have to. Remember I was a
captain in the navy.'

'That was a 100 years ago,' she said, with a teasing smile.

'Not quite, but we won't argue. Get your coat, let's be off.'

She pulled herself together.

'Did you tell Tim about your decision about the cars?' Peter
asked as they sat in the café drinking their cappuccinos.

Betty nodded her head. 'Well, I told him to go ahead and sort
out the repairs on the Mercedes and then sell it. I told him to
pay my fines out of the money he gets for the car. I didn't
mention replacing it with a small car though. I thought it best
to let the matter die down and be forgotten before mentioning
that. It's bound to cause an argument and I don't want to stir up
any more anger than I have to.'

'Aren't you going to appeal the fines they've imposed on you?'
he asked.

'What's the point? I committed the offences so I'd sooner pay
up and forget about it.'

'I suppose that's one way of looking at it. Accept that the
punishment fits the crime.'

They sat in contemplative silence until Peter said, 'So you think
that the money you get for the car should cover the cost of your
fines.'

'Of course!! I expect to get more than that,' Betty stated.

'I doubt it,' Peter warned. 'Old bangers don't fetch much these days, especially ones that have been involved in an accident because it's not easy to get hold of the spare parts. Tim will want to get rid of it as quickly as possible so he may even suggest to the garage that they handle the sale after they've repaired it, or else buy it from him for scrap.'

'Oh, let's forget it for the moment and see what happens,' Betty said firmly.

Peter was right. A few days later Tim turned up at her door holding out an envelope. When she opened it, she found a few notes and coins inside.

'What's this?' she asked, puzzled.

'That, my dear mother, is the change from selling your car and paying your fine.'

'Is this all?' she said in a dismayed voice.

'What did you expect? You're lucky there was enough from the car to cover the fines! I hope you take it to heart and that you'll be a bit more careful in the future. Thank heavens you won't be driving again.'

It was on the tip of Betty's tongue to argue with him on that point, then she felt it would be more prudent to say nothing; to simply take the money and look contrite.

Tim wouldn't stay for a coffee, he didn't want to discuss the matter any further. He had done a deal as she had asked and, as far as he was concerned, that was the end of it. Betty had no chance to ask him anything about another car. Anyway, she didn't think it was the right moment to do so. She would let his anger subside, and the incident be forgotten, before she brought the subject up but she was more determined than ever to have a little car of her own.

Having your own car was a mark of independence, she thought. It meant you could go where you wanted, when you wanted, and not have to ask a friend or relative to take you. She knew she was lucky, and that Peter would take her wherever she wanted to go, but that wasn't the point. Sometimes she just wanted to go somewhere on the spur of the moment, like into Burnham Beeches; park the car, sit in it, and watch people go by or to go for a stroll on her own. Peter couldn't understand why she wanted her own company, nor would anyone in her family, and to take a taxi just to go for a walk seemed to her to be something you just didn't do. In her young days taxis were only used in an emergency, certainly not for frivolous things like going for a walk because you felt like it.

No, she resolved, she'd be patient. She'd got over this one and should be grateful that she had come out of it smiling. She wasn't out of pocket, even though the fines had been enormous. She had already renewed her driving licence to make sure that it was current because the police had been quite right, the old one had expired, although only by a few weeks fortunately, so she'd had no trouble in renewing it.

That taken care of, she would now bide her time, and when she thought it was prudent to do so she would talk to Tim about buying a small second-hand car. Tim was good at doing deals of that sort so he'd find her the right car at the right price. She'd be happy and peace would be restored.

Seven

Betty Wilson hoped that by having everything to do with her accident dealt with by her son, Tim, it would mean that her mishap would be handled discreetly and that friends and family would be none the wiser about what had happened.

Needless to say, news of her accident did leak out and became general knowledge in Ashmore. Some people were aghast that she had been driving without a current licence and up-to-date insurance; others were very sympathetic.

Her daughter, Mary, was incensed and she had an angry scowl on her plump face when she came to visit her. 'What on earth did you think you were doing, Mother! To take that car out when it hasn't been on the road for years,' she scolded.

'I know, it was one of the reasons I was taking it out. I wanted to find out if I should keep it or not.'

'Keep it!' Mary's scowl deepened. 'Dump it, that's the only thing to do with that old wreck.'

'Yes you're quite right. It was an old wreck and the cost of the repairs didn't make it worth having them done.'

'So you are going to get rid of it,' Mary said with relief.

'Tim has dealt with the matter. I suggested that he should ask the garage if they will buy the car from us.'

'You mean by it from him?'

'Of course. They agreed but at scrap value.'

'Well, it's such an old wreck what can you expect.'

'Yes, I suppose it was,' Betty sighed. 'It seemed to be the best thing to do with it.'

Mary sniffed disapprovingly. 'I suppose you've let him keep all the money.'

'No! After he'd paid for having it towed in from the motorway and then paid my fines, he brought me the change. You can have half of it if you'd like,' her mother told her.

Betty went over to her bureau, opened the drawer and took out an envelope and extracted a note and a few coins from it.

Mary face fell like a balloon being deflated as she looked at the money that her mother had put in her hand.

'What's this?'

'Your share of what Tim got for the car.'

'Are you joking! He surely didn't let it go for twenty pounds!'

'Oh no, they paid a fair price, even though it has gone for scrap, but as I've already told you he had to pay my fines out of the money.'

'Your fines?'

'That's right. My driving licence was out of date, and I wasn't able to produce the insurance for the car . . . I didn't even know which company it was insured with.'

'And, of course, they negotiated as low a price as they possibly could by telling you that it was an old heap and that it should have been done away with years ago because it was so old that it was dangerous to drive and shouldn't have been on the road,' Mary said, tight-lipped.

'They probably did,' Betty agreed, 'but you'll have to ask Tim about that because I wasn't there.'

'Dad should have bought a new car that was much smaller, more economical to run, and easier to handle,' Mary stated.

'Yes, yes we know all that and it's too late now,' her mother agreed again. 'Anyway, that's your share so look after it,' she added with a faint smile.

Mary didn't smile. She stared again at the money in her hand, her round face registering disbelief. 'I would have thought Tim would have managed a better deal,' she said cryptically, 'since he's regarded as such an expert salesman.'

'Selling property is totally different to selling a car,' her mother pointed out.

Mary raised her eyebrows and said nothing.

'He did have to pay all my fines, don't forget,' Betty stressed. 'In fact I think he did quite well, we have got rid of the car so no longer have a problem, and the whole thing is over and done with and best forgotten.'

'Except that now you will have no car,' Mary pointed out.

'No!' her mother agreed. 'That is very true, but who knows what will happen in the future. For now let's put the whole matter out of our minds. I don't want to hear another word about it. Do you understand?'

Mary nodded and slipped the money into her pocket. She wasn't happy about the deal but there was nothing she could do about it. After all, it had been her mother's decision to sell the car and she herself had described it as an old banger so, as her mother suggested, the only thing to do was to forget the whole incident.

Betty found that forgetting about selling the car was the last thing she could do. The news spread like a forest fire through the family. Mary, she reflected, must have spent the rest of the day on the phone telling everyone about what had happened. Her twenty-eight-year-old granddaughter, Clare, was the first phone call she had telling her that she had been foolish to sell it as scrap since it was probably quite valuable as an antique. This was followed by a call from Mary's husband, Toby, to say that he fully agreed with what their daughter had said and that Betty should have consulted him before disposing of the old Merc.

Tim's son, Graham, also phoned to express his dismay that the car had been sold but, unlike the others, he actually congratulated her on her decision. 'What you need to buy, Gran, is a nice little runabout. You let me choose one for you when you're ready to replace it,' he told her with all the authority of a twenty-six-year-old.

Betty sighed. They'd all be talking about what she'd done for the next couple of weeks, she presumed. Telling all their friends and either praising her for getting rid of the old banger, or deriding her for selling a valuable antique for scrap.

It possibly was a veteran, and had some antique value, she mused, but she didn't really care. She had done what she wanted to do. Her mind was free, and in due course she would get Tim to look for a new car for her, she decided, as she made her way up to bed.

Worn out by the events of the day, Betty decided to have an early night. She was about to get undressed when she remembered she had left her mobile phone downstairs; she liked to keep the it by the side of her bed.

It had been Tim's suggestion that she did this in case she was feeling ill or needed help in the night. He had keyed in his own number so that all she had to do was to press the letter 'A' and she would immediately be through to him.

Switching on the landing light she made her way back downstairs.

To her surprise, there seemed to be a shadow of light coming from her living room.

'Heavens,' she muttered, the family were right, she really was getting past it. She must have forgotten to switch off the lights. She pushed open the door. It wasn't that the light was left on at all, it was a beam of light coming from a torch that was being shone into the room and it was coming from the direction of the window.

Mystified, she stood transfixed as she looked across at the room and saw that the sash window was wide open and someone was trying to climb in through it. They already had one leg on the sill.

Silently, but quickly, she walked across the room and slammed down the sash window trapping the leg that was on her side.

She drew in her breath sharply as she heard an ominous crunch as the bone shattered. It was followed by a blood-curdling scream from the owner of the leg.

Raising her voice, Betty said, 'I don't know whether you are coming in or just leaving, but get out!'

'Get this bloody window off my leg,' the young man howled.

His voice was muffled by groans, so much so that Betty had a job to hear what he was saying.

Swiftly, she picked up her mobile which was on the table where she had left it. 'I think you need an ambulance,' she said as she pressed the 'A' to alert Tim that she needed him, and then immediately dialled 999.

When the police answered, she explained the situation. 'Yes. That's right, an intruder and he's astride the windowsill. The window is a sash window and his leg is trapped and he is unable to move. I think his leg is probably broken and he needs an ambulance!' she said in one breath.

'We understand and we'll be right along to help you deal with the matter,' the voice on the other end told her.

Within minutes she heard the siren of the approaching police car.

The intruder also heard it. 'Look, Mrs, if you just lift this bloody window I could free my leg,' he cried. 'The pain is killing me.'

'If I lift the window, to let you free your leg, you'll fall over into my flower border and I don't want all my flowers crushed,' she told him sternly. 'Another minute and the ambulance will be here and there will be someone to help you.'

At that moment the police car drew up and two burly policemen jumped out and rushed across the garden to where the young man was suspended.

'My word, this is a fine sight,' one of them said, a wide grin spreading across his face. 'Now if we can lift the window we may be able to free you. Were you going inside or leaving?'

With Betty's help from the inside, the two policemen pushed up from outside. The boy fell out straight into their arms with a blood-curdling scream of pain.

They were about to hustle him out to their car when the sound of the ambulance could be heard.

'There you are,' Betty said to the boy, 'I told you I had sent for an ambulance. Now they'll take you to hospital and find out just how badly you've hurt your leg.'

'We'll sort him out all right, don't you worry,' one of the policeman said grimly, as he snapped handcuffs onto the lad's wrist and onto his own. 'A very clever way of trapping a burglar,' he added with a smile.

'I don't really know what he was after. I've nothing much worth stealing,' Betty said.

'Even so, you want to make sure your windows are shut when you go to bed at night and when you go out during the day,' the policeman told her.

'I will be back tomorrow for a statement,' the other one said, 'but now we're going to accompany this gentleman to the hospital and get his leg attended to. We will be keeping him under arrest until we know his full story.'

As the policemen accompanied their prisoner into the ambulance, another car drew up.

Betty saw that it was Tim and breathed a sigh of relief. Now that the excitement was over she felt breathless and exhausted.

'What the devil is wrong now, Mother,' he exploded as he got out, slamming his car door shut, and hurrying towards her.

'It's all right, sir, nothing to worry about. Your mother caught a burglar breaking in and she very cleverly trapped him by bringing the sash window down on his leg. She is quite a heroine, I can tell you.'

'Someone will be back to see you tomorrow for a statement,' he said again, turning to address Betty. 'You get to bed now and don't worry.'

'You'd better let me in first and tell me what has actually been happening,' Tim told her.

Over a cup of coffee, which Tim made because Betty was shaking like a leaf, she told her son exactly what had happened, and how she had come down to collect her mobile and found the young man astride the window sill.

'So you don't know whether he was coming in or leaving?'

'No.'

'Have you even checked to see if anything is missing?' Tim said.

'No! It never entered my head to do so.'

'Well, go on. Make sure. If anything has been taken then you can tell the police when they come around to see you tomorrow.'

Betty crossed to the bureau and opened it. All her papers were in order, and neatly arranged as always. She burrowed underneath them and brought out a purse, opened it and counted the contents.

'Everything is here,' she said with relief.

'How much have you in that purse?' Tim frowned.

'Three hundred pounds,' Betty said, closing the purse and putting it back underneath the papers.

'Why on earth have you that much in there?' Tim asked.

'In case of an emergency. I might need money and not feel well enough to go to the bank,' she said.

'Madness keeping all that money in the house,' Tim said crossly.

'No, it's not. I've just explained I might need it.'

'If you weren't well enough to go to the bank then all you have to do is phone me and I'll bring you what you need,' Tim said crossly.

'I know that, but I do like to be independent and make sure I have some,' Betty repeated.

'I understand, but you don't need to keep quite such a large amount,' Tim insisted.

They looked at each other and Betty was the first to break the silence. 'What do you suggest?' she asked.

'One hundred pounds for emergencies would be ample,' Tim told her firmly. 'After all, you have only to press a button and I'm right here – you proved that today.'

Eight

The first thing the next morning, Peter Brown was at Betty's door, closely followed by Sally Bishop.

'Are you all right?' Peter asked anxiously.

'Of course she is,' Sally laughed. 'You didn't think that the ambulance was for her, did you?'

'I didn't know what to expect,' Peter said, shaking his head. 'I heard someone screaming but it sounded like a man's voice not a woman's. Then the police arrived and the ambulance just minutes later, and I didn't know whether to come help or not.'

'I was the same,' Sally confessed. 'When I saw Tim drive up I thought it was best to mind my own business. He knows where I live and, if there was anything I could do, I knew he'd come and tell me.'

'So what was all the fuss about?' Peter asked. 'Why were the police and an ambulance here?'

Peter roared with laughter when Betty told him about what had happened.

'That was a damn clever move on your part,' he said with a broad smile when she told them how she had trapped the intruder and held him captive, with his leg stuck in the sash window.

'I had to leave him sitting there on the window sill until the police came and helped to lift the sash window back up again. Judging by his screams and groans, he was in terrible pain. I feel awful now!'

'Serves him right for trying to break in,' Sally stated.

'He won't forget that in a hurry,' Peter said.

'No, I'm afraid he won't because the window came down much quicker than I expected it to and it not only trapped his leg but broke it.'

'Broke it!'

'Yes, it was horrible when I heard the bone crunching,' Betty said shaking her head sadly, 'and he screamed and called me terrible names when I refused to lift up the window and free him.'

'You mean he had to sit there on the sill with a broken leg until the police came and helped you to lift up the window?' Peter questioned.

'Yes,' Betty replied with a nod, 'I'm afraid he did. Those sash windows are so terribly heavy that I couldn't do it on my own.'

'No, and you probably didn't want to even try,' Sally Bishop said, the smile spreading across her face as she spoke.

'Did he manage to take anything?' Peter asked.

'I think he was probably just on his way in,' Betty admitted. 'You see, nothing has been touched and nothing taken.'

'You've been very lucky,' Peter concluded.

'Yes, that's what Tim said. He also warned me about not keeping so much money in the house.'

'Keeping money in the house is damn silly, I agree with him,' Peter said firmly.

'Oh don't you start, I've had enough from Tim to last me a lifetime.'

'I should jolly well hope so. Why have more money in the house than what you're going to spend over the next few days?'

'For emergencies, of course,' Betty explained.

'Emergencies! What emergencies?'

'If I was taken ill and I couldn't get out to buy any milk or food, and I had to ask one of you to go and get it for me you would want the money, wouldn't you?'

'Not at that moment I wouldn't,' Peter said. 'I'm quite sure that neither Sally nor I are so hard up that we couldn't manage to buy you a pint of milk and a loaf of bread if we have to do so.'

'That's not the point,' Betty said firmly. 'I like to be independent; I like to pay my way.'

'We all know that,' Peter told her, 'but surely to goodness, if you needed some money one of us would let you have it if you couldn't get to the bank.'

'Yes well, that's what Tim says so I will not keep as much in future.'

'Don't keep any at all,' Peter said, 'then you won't attract burglars. Now that's all over and you've had a good telling off, what you need now is something to cheer you up,' he told Betty firmly.

'Oh yes and what's that mean?'

'You and Sally get your coats on. I'll take you to Windsor, leave you over there, and come back for you in a couple of hours' time.'

'What do we want to go to Windsor for?' Betty asked frowning.

'Have a couple of hours out enjoying yourselves. Spend some of the money you've been hoarding for emergencies!'

Betty and Sally exchanged looks.

'Oh, very well if that's what you think we should do then we will do it,' Sally said, winking at Betty as she spoke.

'Right, I'll give you half an hour to get yourselves ready; put on your best hats and I'll drop you right in the centre of Peascod Street, and you can shop to your hearts' content.'

'You mean you'll drop us outside Daniels?'

'Yes, if that's what you want.'

'I don't think you can drive down Peascod Street,' Betty said.

'Well, I'll drop you somewhere near there, even if it is the top of Peascod Street, then you can make your own way down and when I come back I'll wait for you outside the castle.'

Half an hour later Peter was outside Betty's front door. Betty slid in beside him and Sally took a seat in the back of the car.

'My word, you are both looking smart,' Peter commented, his blue eyes twinkling, as he surveyed his two passengers.

Betty was wearing a dark-red fitted coat with a stylish matching red hat, black gloves and carrying a black handbag. Sally was in a dark-green coat which had a wide shawl collar, but she was not wearing a hat, only a flowing black and green scarf at the neck of her coat.

'Are you belted up?' he asked.

'Yes, we are ready to go so stop fussing,' Betty told him.

She always enjoyed the drive to Windsor, once they were on the relief road and could see Windsor Castle in the distance. She always looked to see if it was the Union flag flying from the turret, or the Queen's Standard which meant that she was in residence. Today, she was elsewhere.

They reached the town centre around eleven and Peter told them he'd be back for them at three o'clock that afternoon.

'Whatever are we going to do for four hours?' Betty grumbled.

'Shop, of course,' Peter told her. 'In Peascod Street you have Daniels, Marks and Spencer, Hotter shoes and a dozen other shops too. Then you can have something to eat, and after that shop again in King Edward Shopping Mall where there's another thirty or more shops like Next, Zara, H&M, Clarks and countless others. Or, you can go for a walk,' he told them.

'I'm sure you'll find something to do. A leisurely lunch will take up at least an hour.'

'Anyway, I'll be outside the castle at three p.m. to bring you home.'

'Thank you, Peter,' Sally said with a smile. 'We'll enjoy ourselves, never fear.'

They found the time passed extremely swiftly. There were so many shops to browse in, so much to see. It was almost two o'clock when Sally pointed out that they hadn't even eaten yet.

'We've left it rather late for a full blown restaurant meal,' Betty said. 'What about a snack of some kind? Perhaps from one of the food stalls here in the arcade? There are any number of them in the place where the platform for the trains used to be.'

There were so many of them, and such a wide choice of food, that it took them some time make up their minds what they would have. Sally wanted to go for a burger, but Betty was more adventurous.

'Did you see that stand Soup and Sushi?' she asked.

'I did, but it's not something I fancy,' Sally protested. 'I wouldn't mind the soup, but you do know sushi is raw fish?!'

'Have you ever tried it?'

'No, and I don't want to,' Sally said with a shudder.

'Well, I do. Let's make this trip memorable and try something new!'

Sally shook her head. 'Not for me,' she protested again. 'You try it if you want to.'

'What about the soup?' Betty pressed.

'Yes, well I'd have a bowl of soup, but not the fish.'

'I'm going to try the sushi,' Betty told her, 'come on, let's give it a go.'

The chicken soup smelled good and looked appetizing. Sally

ordered a bowl, but Betty insisted on the sushi. Sally could tell from the look on Betty's face that she wasn't enjoying it.

'You don't have to eat it,' she laughed. 'Why not have a bowl of soup; it really is delicious.'

Her suggestion only served to increase Betty's determination to finish her sushi.

'I think we had better start making our way back to the castle,' Sally said when they left the arcade. 'Peter might have trouble parking, but if we are there waiting for him then I am sure he can find a space to pull in and let us get into the car.'

As they climbed the hill, from King Edward's Court to the castle, Betty was so quiet that Sally looked at her sideways several times to see if she was all right, and was worried by how colourless her face was.

'Are you all right,' she asked but she got no answer. 'Shall we slow down?' she asked again, concerned she was out of breath. Betty seemed to be concentrating all her effort into getting up the hill.

They had just reached the appointed meeting place when Peter drew up. As Sally had predicted, he had difficulty in stopping long enough for them to get into the car as there was so much traffic in the area.

'Well ladies, have you had a good time?' Peter asked as they headed for home.

'Splendid,' Sally told him. 'Enjoyed every minute of it. Haven't we, Betty?'

Betty nodded, but didn't answer.

Sally then told him about the Soup and Sushi bar where they'd had lunch, and Peter roared with laughter when Sally told him that Betty had insisted on having sushi.

'Did you enjoy it?' he asked, his eyes twinkling as he gave her a quick sideways glance.

Before she could reply, she gave a deep gurgling sound and looked wildly round, then dragged her hat off her head in time to bury her face in it as she vomited.

'Oh heavens!' Peter exclaimed, as he looked frantically for a lay-by so that he could pull in.

Before he stopped the car, Betty had wretched again and this time much of it went down the front of her coat.

As soon as the car stopped, she pushed open the door and stumbled out, drinking in the fresh air.

Peter whipped out his handkerchief, handed it to her, then reached into the side pocket of his car and brought out a roll of kitchen towel.

'Here, I keep this handy to clean the windscreen,' he said, as he tore off a length and handed it to Betty. 'Clean up your coat as well as you can,' he continued, taking her hat from her, before walking over to the ditch, tipping out the contents, and then wiping it out with a length of towel.

'Do you carry any water?' Sally called out to him.

'Yes, in that pocket behind the passenger seat. There isn't a cup, though, she'll have to drink it from the bottle.'

Betty gratefully accepted the water, took a mouthful, swilled it round her teeth and then spit it out. Shakily, she returned to the car and climbed back into the passenger seat. Then, she wiped her forehead with Peter's handkerchief and lay back in her seat, with her head against the headrest and with her eyes closed.

'Are you all right now?' Peter asked anxiously.

'I don't think I'm going to vomit anymore if that's what you mean, but I feel far from all right!'

'I think the best thing is to get us home as quickly as you can and let Betty have a lie down,' Sally advised.

'If you're sure the motion of the car won't make you sick again,' Peter said hesitantly.

'I'll use my hat again if I need to,' Betty said with a wan smile.

'It's caused by the sushi, I expect,' Peter said thoughtfully. 'Do you think I should take you straight to the hospital in case it's food poisoning?'

'No, certainly not,' Betty stated weakly. 'I don't want them using a stomach pump on me. Get me home and let me rest. I'll be better in an hour or so.'

Nine

It was almost a week before Betty felt completely well again. She refused to let them call the doctor, and both Sally and Peter were very worried about her.

Peter suggested that she looked so washed out that he would stay in her cottage overnight in case she needed help, but Betty stoutly refused to let him do this.

'What on earth would people think if they ever got to hear that I had let you stay all night,' she exclaimed.

'I planned to sleep downstairs in an armchair or on the settee,' he told her.

'Who would believe that! It would be a choice bit of scandal that would have everyone gossiping about us.'

Two days later, when Betty's face was still very puffy and her eyes sore and watery, Sally told Peter that she was going to let Tim know.

'I think you should,' he agreed. 'I've been expecting him to pop in and see if she had recovered from the ordeal of the intruder, but he hasn't been near,' Peter grumbled.

'Don't say a word to Betty,' Sally warned him, 'I'll pop into his estate agency as I pass and tell him what has happened.'

Tim was aghast when Sally told him about the sushi incident. 'For heaven's sake, why didn't you take her straight to the hospital?'

'Your mother refused to go,' Sally told him, tight-lipped.

She felt annoyed by his tone of voice. Here she was doing what she thought was the right thing and he was berating her as if it was her fault. Then, as she looked at the worried expression on his face, she forgave him immediately. Poor lad, he's worried stiff and really, he is blaming himself, she thought.

'She's more or less her old self again now,' Sally said reassuringly.

'That's as maybe, but anything could have happened to her in the meantime, all alone there at night.'

'No, she wasn't alone. Peter Brown was here with her.'

'What all night?'

'He slept down here on the settee or in the armchair, but he was there if she needed anything,' Sally confirmed.

Tim shrugged and said no more. Sally wondered just what was going on in his head. Did it help relieve his worry to know that or not, she wondered.

'Thank you both for looking after her so well, but next time anything like this happens send for me,' he said.

'As I understand it there's a button on her mobile for her to contact you,' Sally defended.

'She was probably feeling too ill to do so,' he murmured.

Sally looked at him quizzically, but said nothing. They both knew that she had deliberately not done so because she didn't want to see a doctor or go into hospital.

As soon as Betty was feeling well enough, Peter took her and Sally on little jaunts out into neighbouring villages where they would enjoy a cup of coffee or pot of tea at the village café.

Every time this happened Betty wished she was able to make little trips of this kind on her own, whenever the mood took her to do so. Her own wheels were the answer, but after the sushi incident she didn't think it would be wise to ask Tim to indulge her in what he would term a 'mere whim'.

Yet, the more she tried to forget it the more she yearned for her own car. A small manageable one like Peter's, she thought longingly.

She didn't say a word to either Peter or Sally because she was afraid they might mention it to Tim, but she spent more and more time thinking about it and wondering that if she could prove to all of them how efficiently she could drive Peter's car, then maybe Tim would give in.

She thought several times about asking Peter to let her trial his car, but a second sense warned her that he wouldn't agree.

A couple of weeks later, when she asked him to take her to Maidenhead the next day, he said he would as soon as he came back from the barbers. He had booked a haircut and he didn't want to lose his place.

She nodded in agreement, but the moment he told her, a plan

had started to take shape in her head. Would he mind if she took his car, she wondered. She wouldn't go to Maidenhead because the roads would be busy, but just a little tootle around the village and up one or two of the quiet roads would be enough to prove her prowess and wipe out the memory of what had happened on the motorway.

Everything depended on whether or not he took his car keys when he went for his haircut, she thought.

Next morning, as soon as she saw him leave, she went into his house and held her breath in anticipation as she entered the hall and looked on the rack where he put all his keys. There was a car key hanging there. Whether it was the spare or not she wasn't sure. Anyway, it didn't matter.

Taking the key, she went to the driveway, her heart thumping with a mixture of hope and nervousness.

It was the right key. Gingerly, she started the engine and then cautiously backed the car out of the drive and headed north, away from the village. It was a glorious early autumn morning and she decided to drive to Burnham Beeches. That was no more than three miles but, by the time she reached there and came home again, she would have proved her point that she could handle a small car efficiently.

The run up to the Beeches was uneventful and she parked in one of the open spaces and spent a few minutes simply sitting there, admiring the lovely view of the beech trees changing colour, and catching her breath back.

She felt immense pleasure at her achievement, but decided she had better get back and return Peter's car before he came home.

She decided to go back the same way as she had come. About a mile out of Ashmore, a fox ran across her path. It was quite a young fox, with a lovely shining coat and bushy tail. It was such a lovely creature that, even though she knew many people considered them to be vermin, she swerved wildly to avoid hitting it.

She was so intent on avoiding the animal, and making sure that he reached the other side of the road safely, that she didn't see the approaching lorry until the loud blast of a horn signalled that it was almost on top of her.

The lorry stopped, but Betty was unable to do so in time. There was a clash of metal, a mad jarring and shuddering of the car, and she found herself thrown forward so hard that her forehead impacted with the windscreen.

As she looked up all she could see was a huge lorry looming over her. She felt paralyzed by fright as she realized that she was on the wrong side of the road and that the metalwork of Peter's car was inextricably entwined with the lower part of the lorry.

After what seemed an eternity, the lorry driver jumped down from his cab and came to speak to her.

He was a burly, sandy-haired man in his early forties, and he looked extremely angry.

'What the hell were you playing at? You drove straight over to my side of the road and slammed into me! If I hadn't got good brakes you'd be dead!'

'I'm sorry,' Betty said, her mouth so dry that she could hardly enunciate the words.

'Sorry?! I should damn well think so! What the hell did you think you were doing?'

Betty swallowed hard. 'I was trying to avoid hitting a young fox,' she told him.

His bellow of sarcastic laughter scared her far more than any verbal abuse would have done.

'Tell that to the court when my firm prosecute you for dangerous driving,' he guffawed. 'Vermin!'

The sound of a police siren sent a fresh wave of despair through Betty.

She didn't recognize the young police officer who came to interrogate them, but he recognized her immediately.

'You again!' he exclaimed, as he took his notebook out of his breast pocket.

'I do have a current driving licence but it's in my handbag, and I haven't brought that with me,' Betty said quickly.

He ignored her and looked at the lorry driver. 'What happened?'

'This woman cut right across the road to my side. I braked and stopped instantly and sounded my horn. She ignored it, and seemed to be unable to brake, and crashed right into the front of my lorry. She's done a fair bit of damage to it, as well as to her own car.'

The policeman turned to Betty and raised his eyebrows questioningly. 'Is that right, madam?' he asked with studied politeness.

'Well, yes, but you see I was trying to avoid an animal that ran out across my path,' Betty said lamely.

'An animal?' he questioned.

'A young fox,'

'I see,' he murmured, making an entry into his notebook.

'I told her they're only vermin,' the lorry driver said. 'One of the blighters killed off a half dozen of my hens only a matter of weeks ago. I'd like to see the whole damn lot of them exterminated. Now if it had been a dog then I could understand her swerving to avoid it, but a fox . . . well, I ask you.'

The policeman said nothing. Then, when he had finished writing in his notebook, he said, 'Insurance details?'

The lorry driver gave him all the information he required, together with one of his firm's business cards which the policeman put away safely in the back of his notebook.

'And yours, madam?' he said looking at Betty.

'I'm sorry I have no idea,' she said lamely. 'I can get them for you though.'

'I seem to have heard that excuse from you before,' he said, his mouth tightening grimly. 'You don't even know the name of the company; would it be the same as last time?'

'No, no, not at all. This isn't my car, you see, but I am sure that the owner will have all the details you require back home as he is very conscientious about those sort of things.'

'Not so concerned though about who drives his car.'

'Well, actually he doesn't know I'm driving it.'

'You mean you took it without his consent,' the policeman said with a frown. 'You do know that is a serious offence?'

'It's not really because, you see, he's a very close friend,' Betty said quickly.

'In that case then why didn't you ask his permission?'

'I wasn't sure he would let me have it, because I have never driven it before,' Betty confessed, the colour rushing to her face as she realized how guilty this made her appear. 'Look, officer,' she said giving him a warm smile, 'let me explain. After my mishap on the motorway I got rid of my Mercedes and I have decided to replace it with a smaller car, one I will find easier to handle. A car like this Citroen,' she added, waving a hand towards the damaged car. 'I had never driven one of these but thought I would try it out. I knew my friend wouldn't mind,' she added hastily.

'I rather think he will mind when he finds out what has happened to it,' the policeman told her.

Betty sighed. 'Yes, you are probably right,' she agreed.

'His name and address please,' the officer said curtly.

'Peter Brown, Clover Cottages, Ashmore, Buckinghamshire,' Betty told him.

'Mr Brown's telephone number?'

'You're not going to phone and tell him what's happened, are you?' Betty prevaricated. 'He'll be so upset. Let me tell him when I get home.'

'His telephone number, please,' the officer repeated.

Reluctantly, Betty gave him the details.

The policeman noted it down and then spoke into his radio.

'I see,' he said in response to what was said by the person he was calling. 'Tell him we have located his car, and the person who took it. I'm afraid it has been seriously damaged,' he added as he ended the call.

'Is your vehicle still drivable?' the police officer asked the lorry driver.

'Not sure, I haven't had the chance to try,' the man scowled. 'As far as I know there's some damage to the front, but nothing very serious. But my headlights are smashed and, anyway, I don't fancy risking the ninety-mile drive back to my depot with it in that state as there may well be other damage that isn't visible. One close call is enough for me,' he added with a guffaw.

'We're not ready for you to leave, but I was hoping you could move it off the road. At the moment there is a serious hold up of traffic, so if you can run it up onto the grass verge then it will allow cars to pass.'

'OK, I'll see what I can do once you've assured me that this accident is not my fault.'

'My colleague is marking out the area and we will need a statement from you but, as far as I can tell, the accident was not your fault.'

Ten

As she listened to the long discussion, about how they should attempt to disentangle the car from the lorry, Betty's heart sank when she heard a familiar voice from close behind her say, 'Heavens, that does look a mess. We're going to have to do something drastic about her before she kills herself; this is the second road accident she's had in just a couple of weeks.'

Before she could make up her mind whether to turn around and face Tim, or try to move away before he spotted her, she heard an even more familiar voice say, 'As long as Betty is all right, that is all that matters. After all, a car is only a heap of metal.'

'Well, yours certainly is now,' Tim answered with a dry laugh.

It couldn't be them, she thought guiltily, as the blood rushed to her face. She turned her head and looked over her shoulder in the direction the voices were coming from, and her doubts were confirmed. A crowd of onlookers had gathered and, amongst them, Tim and Peter were standing together only a few yards behind her, and she knew they were talking about her.

She pushed her way towards them. Peter was the first to see her.

'Are you all right, Betty?' he asked, solicitously moving towards her and putting an arm around her protectively.

'Apart from this,' she said pointing to the bump the size of a duck's egg on her forehead, where she had banged it against the windscreen.

Peter bent down and gently kissed the huge bruise, shaking his head in dismay.

'Hasn't anyone suggested that you go to hospital in case you have concussion?' Tim said worriedly.

'I'm all right so don't fuss, Tim,' she said sharply.

He gave a small dismissive shrug, as if resigned to the fact that it was pointless arguing with her.

'The same can hardly be said for Peter's car,' he said snidely.

'No, and I'm sorry about that, Peter,' Betty said contritely.

Peter smiled at her forgivingly. 'You didn't do it on purpose,' he said softly, and once again his lips pressed gently on her brow.

'You must be mad to let her take it out on her own,' Tim said looking at Peter.

Peter and Betty exchanged glances and she waited for him to tell Tim the truth; that she had taken it without his permission. Instead his arm tightened around her shoulders, and he said nothing.

As Tim moved away and went closer to where two mechanics were struggling to wrestle the two vehicles apart, Betty turned and looked directly at Peter. 'What on earth made you bring Tim with you,' she said in an annoyed voice.

'I didn't bring him, he brought me. As your next-of-kin he was informed about the accident. He wondered if it was my car you had been driving, so he phoned and told me what the police had just told him about you being involved in an accident. As my car was missing it wasn't difficult for us to put two and two together. You were missing and so was my car, and you were both involved in a road accident.'

'So you decided to come here together.'

'Yes, because knowing that my car was missing, Tim offered to drive me and it seemed to be a speedier way of getting here than ringing for a taxi.'

'It all sounds so very logical, Peter, when you put it like that,' Betty sighed.

'Does it? Well, perhaps you can explain what you were doing driving my car?'

'I wanted to prove that I could handle a small car. When you went off to have your haircut, I had the bright idea of borrowing yours for half an hour and proving to myself, and the rest of you, that I could do it.'

'That also sounds logical,' Peter agreed, 'but not so much when you see how it has all ended up. When I first caught sight of the two vehicles my heart was in my mouth in case you had been hurt or, worse still, killed,' Peter told her. 'I wouldn't have wanted to go on living if that had happened.'

'Oh Peter!' Betty rested her head on his broad chest, tears prickling her eyes. 'I'm so sorry about your car, but I really couldn't run that fox over, now could I?'

'Fox?' Peter frowned. 'What are you talking about?'

Betty told him about how the crash had come about and then had to repeat her story to Tim, who had given up watching the men struggling to free Peter's car from the lorry and returned to join them.

'You swerved to avoid a fox,' he said in disbelief.

'It was barely more than a cub, and so beautiful and full of life,' Betty murmured.

'I suppose that got away safely,' he added dryly.

'It must have done. I didn't give it another thought after I looked up and found that huge lorry towering over me. Your car seemed awfully small then,' she told Peter with a smile. 'I could only just see the driver's face, he was so high above me. I'm very sorry. I'll pay for the repairs, of course.'

'Repairs!' Tim scoffed. 'Judging by what they are doing to it, it won't be a case of repairs but of Peter needing a new car.'

Betty's hand flew to her mouth but she said nothing.

'This sort of caper has got to stop, Mother,' Tim said in a censorial tone. 'You seem to have lost the ability to think sensibly. Now perhaps you understand why we want you to go into a home.'

'That's rather extreme, isn't it,' Peter intervened, hotly. 'There's nothing at all wrong with your mother's power of thinking; accidents will happen.'

'Accident! Why have an accident over a fox? Common sense should prevail in a case like that.'

'Let's be fair about the matter,' Peter protested. 'Your mother didn't want to harm a wild animal so she swerved. It's a natural reaction. If the lorry had stopped more quickly she wouldn't have crashed into it.'

'From what I can understand, the lorry driver had no alternative and it's lucky for her that his brakes and his reaction were as good as they were. Another few feet and she wouldn't be standing here defending her thoughtless action. She'd be in hospital or in the mortuary. She needs to be somewhere under constant supervision. I'm surprised, Peter, that you can be so lenient when your car is a write-off.'

'As I said before, a car is only a heap of metal and your mother's life is far more important than my car.'

'Surely you are concerned that she took your car without asking you.'

'I'm sorry she had an accident in it, but as for taking it without asking me first, well—' he shrugged – 'she knows that what is mine is hers. She probably didn't even think it was necessary to ask me, and rightly so.'

'I still maintain that she needs to be under constant supervision,' Tim muttered.

'Right, then tell her to marry me and I'll be responsible for her,' Peter said, his jaw set and his eyes as hard as grey flint.

Tim didn't answer. He looked at his watch. 'If you are ready I'll run you both home. That's if the police say that you are free to go,' he added, glaring at his mother.

The officer in charge looked at his notes and frowned when Tim said he thought he should take Betty home. 'Give me a minute, sir. The gentleman whose car she was driving is here and he may wish to prosecute her for taking and driving his car without his permission.'

'No, no, nothing like that,' Peter said quickly. 'No, I don't wish to make any charges, officer.'

'She had taken it without your permission?' the officer persisted.

'Technically, I suppose you could say that, but as I wasn't at home she had no option if she wanted to use it right away.'

The officer pushed his hat back and rubbed his brow. He didn't know what to say. Most people were incensed that someone had taken their car without their permission, but this chap seemed almost resigned to the fact, even though it was so badly smashed up that it almost certainly needed to be written off.

Tim took his silence to mean they could go, and began shepherding his mother through the small crowd, leaving Peter to follow.

Peter stopped to speak to the officer and Betty wondered what he was telling him. After a few minutes, he followed them to Tim's car.

No one spoke on the journey back to Ashmore. As they approached the village Peter said, 'If you drop us off at the top of the high street you can get straight back to your office. I'll see your mother home.'

'Are you sure you don't mind? After what's happened, I mean.'

'Let's forget about it,' Peter said brusquely.

'I don't think we can do that, I wish we could,' Tim said. 'There are going to be all sorts of repercussions, not only with the police, but also with your insurance company as well. If you need any help sorting things out do let me help. I have a very good solicitor.'

'I am quite sure I won't need any help,' Peter told him. 'There were plenty of witnesses. The police seem to have all the details they need.'

'I'm not so sure,' Tim said cautiously. 'That lorry driver looked pretty angry. He may find himself in trouble with his boss when he gets back, even if it is only because he can't deliver his load on time.'

As he stopped at the start of the high street to let them out of the car, Tim once again queried with Peter that he didn't mind seeing Betty home.

'I'll pop in when I close the office and check she is all right,' he promised.

'There's no need for you to do that, Tim. I'll make sure she is safe and sound. I'll fix her a cup of tea, sit with her, and talk over what happened, so don't worry. If I think she ought to have someone with her overnight then I'll phone you or Mary and let you know.'

'Or you'll do nothing and stay there with her,' Tim said quietly.

'Yes, I'll do that if it is what she wants,' Peter assured him.

'Your cottage or mine?' Peter asked as Tim drove off.

'Mine,' Betty said firmly. 'My shoes are killing me, I want to get them off and put my feet up. Look,' she went on, 'you don't have to come in with me. I'm quite capable of making myself a cup of tea.'

'I know that but I want to hear your version of exactly what happened, and why you took my car without saying a word to me. As Tim said, another few yards in to that lorry and you would have been killed outright.'

'I'm sorry if I've given you all a fright, and very sorry about your car, Peter. You see—'

'Not now,' he said, cutting her short, as they reached Clover Crescent. 'Wait until we're indoors and you have taken your shoes off and put your feet up. By then, I will have made the tea and you can relax and tell me everything while we drink it.'

He bent and kissed her, this time on the lips, not on her brow. 'I want to hear every detail, remember,' he said earnestly.

Betty looked at him gratefully. Why did she always put up so much resistance whenever Peter wanted to help her, she wondered. She studied him; he was tall, broad-shouldered and, for a man in his seventies, although his hair was grey, he was still good-looking with a firm jaw line and intelligent brown eyes.

He was kind, understanding and good company. So why didn't she turn to him when she needed a helping hand? She knew the answer immediately. She wanted to keep her independence. She sighed. So far that seemed to have resulted in one thing after another going wrong. Did it mean that she really was getting old, that she really was losing the plot?

Eleven

For the next few months, in the run up to Christmas, Betty decided to be nicer to Peter. He no longer had a car, but he hired one in order to take her into Windsor to do her Christmas shopping.

She wanted to buy him something very special for Christmas but she couldn't see anything that seemed to be suitable. The one thing that she wanted to buy him was a car, but even if she spent her savings she knew it wouldn't be enough money to do so.

She toyed with the idea of asking him to buy a car in their joint names and she would pay off the hire purchase instalments, but she knew in advance what his answer to that would be.

She looked round her cosy sitting room and wondered if there was anything she could sell to raise money. Tim was always saying that the room was overcrowded and that she would find it easier to get around it if there were less things in there. Tim liked the minimalistic look. His wife, Brenda, called bare walls and no ornaments soulless, and claimed it was all right as long as you chose the right items and accessories, which of course she did.

Betty took closer scrutiny of the room. She was sure that Brenda considered it be a hotchpotch of bits and pieces of rubbish and junk. She was attached to most of them because she had grown up with them. There were ornaments that had belonged to her parents, and even her grandparents. She studied them critically, wondering if any of them were of value. She sighed. She had absolutely no idea at all; it needed an expert eye.

She was quite sure that none of the family had any idea, so she looked through the *Yellow Pages* to find out where the nearest antique shop was. The she telephoned and told the man who answered that she was thinking of disposing of some pictures, ornaments and pieces of furniture so was he interested in buying them. He promised to send someone along to have a look and if there was anything there he was interested in he would tell her a price.

A few days later a young man did turn up and said he had come to see what she had for sale.

Betty hesitated. He was well dressed in his late twenties, and he certainly looked as though he was a businessman. He was very charming, but he looked rather young to know anything about antiques.

'You can come in and have a look and give me a price,' she told him.

An hour later her walls were practically bare. All the ornaments had gone from her shelves and from the glass-fronted display cabinet in her sitting room.

Betty looked around the rather empty room and shuddered. She had never really valued any of those things and yet, now that they were gone, it seemed to be a tremendous loss; almost like losing old friends.

She set about rearranging what was left and by the end of the afternoon, tired out but satisfied that she had done a good job, she sat down with a cup of tea in a contented frame of mind.

Ten minutes later there was a knock on the door, so she hauled herself up again and went to open it. She found Tim standing there with an enormous grin spread across his face.

'This is a surprise. You're just in time, I've just made a pot of tea. Would you like one?'

'Great! I've just driven back from London. I've been to an auction there and I've some incredible news for you!'

As he entered the sitting room the excitement faded from his face, and he looked puzzled as he stared around. 'What on earth is going on, what are you doing, Mother? Where have all the pictures and all the ornaments gone?'

'I'm trying to do what you said I should do; I'm being minimalistic and getting rid of all the clutter.'

Tim frowned. 'You haven't thrown them out, have you?'

'No,' Betty told him. 'At long last I've taken your advice and got rid of them. I had a young man over here from the local antiques shop and he's given me a good price for them all.'

'Mother!'

Betty looked puzzled. She didn't like his tone, nor the look on his face. 'They were mine so I sold them,' she stated defiantly.

'No!' he corrected her, 'they weren't yours, they were part of our inheritance. Originally, they belonged to our grandparents and their parents. What on earth were you thinking of?'

Betty bristled. 'Look, I wanted some money to give to Peter as a Christmas present, so that he could replace his car.'

Tim regarded her stonily. 'Does he know you've done this?'

'Of course he doesn't, it's meant to be a surprise. I just told you I was planning on going to give him the money as his Christmas present.'

'So how much did you get for them?'

'I don't think that's any of your business,' his mother retorted.

'I rather think it is,' Tim rejoined. 'I came to tell you that I've just seen a landscape picture that I thought must be a replica of the one hanging here on our wall being sold at auction. I was amazed to see that it had a thumb mark in the bottom right half corner, exactly the same as ours. I couldn't understand that, because I had heard the story handed down in the family about how that came to be there. It was the thumb mark made by your great-great-grandfather, who bought the painting from an artist friend, and was so eager to take it home that he picked it off the artist's easel before it was dry.'

'It's quite true, but fancy you remembering that!' Betty said in surprise.

'And you've sold it?'

'Yes, a few hours ago.'

'How much did he give you for it?' Tim asked again.

'Why do you want to know?' Betty asked clamping her lips tightly together. 'Probably a lot more than it's worth. Your great-great-grandfather only bought the picture because he knew the man who had painted it and he wanted to help him. He only paid a few pounds for it!'

'It doesn't matter how much he paid for it all those years ago, it's what it's worth today that counts, and I'm telling you that it's a very valuable picture so what did you get for it?'

Betty looked uncomfortable.

'Come on,' he demanded impatiently, 'tell me.'

'He paid me more than I expected; I thought that was making me a very generous offer.'

'Mother, you are being very difficult. How much money have

you managed to raise by selling the pictures and the ornaments?' Tim pressed.

Betty hesitated. She suddenly realized that perhaps she should have asked for more, but it wasn't in her nature to haggle.

'Come on, Mother, tell me.'

Tim sounded so authoritative, and indeed he looked hard and businesslike she thought, as she met his dark angry gaze. So much so, that she felt herself shaking.

'Didn't he give you a separate price for the picture?'

Betty avoided Tim's stare and said nothing. Why was she feeling so guilty, she asked herself. She had no need to be scared of him or what he thought. It was her picture and they were her ornaments, they didn't belong to him. They were hers and if she wanted to get rid of them then it was up to her.

'What did he offer you for the picture?' Tim persisted.

When she remained silent, Tim said, 'Five hundred pounds, or somewhere near that figure?'

Betty nodded. That included the ornaments.

'Heavens above!' Tim ran his hand through his thick hair and stared at her in dismay. 'You've given away a fortune; the family's heritage,' he said in disgust.

'I think that Peter will be delighted to receive a check for five hundred pounds,' Betty said defensively.

'I think Peter is going to be pretty mad when he finds out what you've done to get that five hundred pounds!'

'You make it sound as though I've been on the streets,' Betty retorted.

Tim shook his head, his lips curling in distaste at her crude remark. 'I despair of you, Mother, I really do. The older you get, the more rash things you seem to do. Do you know what our picture fetched at auction?'

'Of course I don't, I wasn't there but I'm pretty sure you are going to tell me.'

'Our picture fetched two hundred and forty thousand pounds,' he said quietly.

'How much!'

'Two hundred and forty thousand pounds,' Tim repeated loudly. 'Almost a quarter of a million pounds.'

Betty went white. 'Two hundred and forty thousand pounds,' she repeated slowly, her eyes widening in disbelief.

'What Mary and her family are going to say when they find out I hate to think,' Tim muttered.

'Or your precious Brenda. By the time you finish telling her the story she will probably be hopping mad and then she will come round and lecture me on what I should have done.'

'Yes, Brenda will probably feel the same as I do; that it is a wicked shame to have let such a valuable family picture go in that way. And of course, there are all the ornaments you sold as well.'

'Yes, I did. I was fed up with dusting them!'

'Then why didn't you offer them to the family?'

'None of you seemed to be interested in them before, and I'm pretty sure that you would have got rid of them. Put them in a charity shop or something, when I am dead and gone and you had to clear out the house,' she snapped.

'We won't be able to do anything with them now,' Tim said icily.

'You all said you didn't like them, called them ugly in fact.'

'I may well have done when I was a child and didn't understand their value,' Tim admitted.

'And now, once I've finally got rid of them, you suddenly discover that they're wonderful antiques and worth a fortune.'

'If they don't turn up at specialist auctioneers then I wouldn't mind betting that if you look on eBay you'll find them offered for sale there, and at prices that will astound you,' he said bitterly.

'Maybe!' Betty said her lips tightening once again. 'If you are so fond of them you can always buy them back, can't you,' she snapped. She turned away quickly, hoping that he hadn't seen the tears that were suddenly flooding her eyes.

She had been trying so hard to put things right, and to recompense Peter for his loss, but now she felt utterly deflated. She had meant well. At the back of her mind had been the idea that perhaps she and Peter could possibly buy the car in their joint names, and then she would have her independence and he would have a car to drive once again.

She thought of the sum the picture had obtained at auction and felt physically sick. She had been conned, there was no doubt about that.

It was just another sign that she was getting old, she was far too trusting, and she took people at face value. That smart young man had taken advantage of her. He had taken one look at her grey hair and turned it to his advantage.

She remained silent because she didn't know what to say to Tim. She understood how angry he must feel; she felt it too. She realized she should have talked to him about it, not simply gone ahead with what now seemed like a madcap idea.

It had been such a good plan, but now she could see that it had been foolhardy.

Still, what was done was done and there was nothing she could do to change things, she thought miserably.

Twelve

Betty dreaded meeting the rest of her family over Christmas because by then they would all know about her terrible mistake in letting a valuable picture go for a mere pittance, when it could have brought them a small fortune.

She toyed with the idea of telling her daughter Mary that she was going to Tim's for Christmas and telling him that she was going to Mary's, then she could stay home on her own without either of them being any the wiser.

That idea was quickly scotched when Peter came around to say that Tim had invited him to come over on Christmas Day. That clinches it, she thought ruefully. Peter had no family and if she turned down Tim's invitation then it meant he couldn't go and he would be on his own over Christmas.

She could say that they weren't coming because it meant leaving Sally on her own, but she knew that was impossible because Sally had already told Tim that she was going to her daughter's for a few days both before and after Christmas.

There was nothing for it but to put a brave face on things and to stand up for herself, no matter what criticism or unkind remarks the family aimed at her.

She wondered whether or not to take Peter into her confidence and, in the end, after a great deal of thought, she decided that it would be wiser to do so, otherwise he would hear Tim and Brenda's view of the situation rather than hers. She didn't, however, tell him why she was so anxious to raise the money; that it was in order to partially recompense him for being out of pocket over the damage she had caused to his car.

When she did tell him, he was silent for such a long time that she wondered if he had heard what she had said and all its implications.

When he did comment he was very philosophical. 'What you've never had you're not going to miss,' he commented. 'These people should be reported to the police for taking advantage of elderly people who are out of touch with modern-day inflated prices. Anyway,' Peter went on, 'Tim and Brenda must have forgiven you since they've asked us for Christmas Day. What is the dress code, by the way?'

Betty looked at him blankly.

'How are we expected to dress? Do I wear my best suit, or do I have to go out and hire tails?'

'Tails!' Betty burst out laughing. 'Your suit is perfect,' she told him. 'Or smart trousers and a blazer or jacket.'

'My suit then. So what time do we need to leave?'

'I'm not sure, about midday, I suppose.'

Until that moment, Betty hadn't given a lot of thought to what she should wear, but once Peter had brought the matter up she rummaged through her wardrobes to find what was most suitable. In the end she decided on a dark-red silk dress and a matching collarless jacket.

Christmas Day dawned bright and crisp; the sun shining from a cloudless blue sky. Anticipating that it was going to be cold out of doors, Betty put on her thick winter coat. It wasn't smart but it was wonderfully warm.

Peter knocked on her door just before midday. 'Are you ready, the taxi will be here at any moment.'

'Taxi?' Betty looked taken aback. 'I thought we were going to walk?'

She was about to say she would put on a smarter coat, but before she could do so, the taxi pulled up and she was too busy stowing the bags of presents and wine to have a chance to do so.

Tim and Brenda seemed pleased to see them, but from the first moment Betty felt uncomfortable. Brenda looking very glamorous, with her hair piled up on top of her head, wearing black satin trousers and a white silk shirt. She looked extremely elegant, yet casual. It made Betty feel overdressed in her dress and jacket, especially when, as she removed her heavy coat, she saw Brenda's eyebrows rise as she looked at her. She knew at once that Brenda had recognized it as what she had worn at Graham and Shirley's wedding.

Betty's discomfort increased when Graham, Shirley and little Anna arrived. Graham was in casual trousers and a sweater, Shirley in smart black trousers and a white jumper and Anna was in a pretty party dress and immediately did a twirl to show off the frilly net petticoat underneath it.

'We've invited Mary and her family to join us, Mother,' Tim told her. 'We thought you might like to have all your family under one roof for once.'

The arrival of her daughter Mary and Mary's husband, Toby, and their unmarried daughter, Clare, made Betty feel even more overdressed. They were all wearing jeans and Christmas jumpers.

The meal was a traditional one and Betty enjoyed it knowing that she would not have gone to so much trouble if she had been eating at home on her own.

Afterwards, when they were sitting in the lounge with a glass of port and a coffee, the storm broke. Betty soon found that her family were certainly not as lenient or kind-hearted as Peter.

Brenda's first words set the tone of criticism.

'I couldn't believe it when Tim told us what you'd done,' she said looking at Betty. 'I know you are old and unworldly but really you must refer to Tim before doing anything that involves family possessions. Poor Tim, he was devastated. It would have been a wonderful inheritance not only for us, but for the children and, of course, for Mary and her family.'

Betty said nothing but she felt that there a certain coldness in the air when her grandson Graham and Shirley joined in with their very strong opinions about how she had let herself be taken in by a rogue trader.

Peter remained discreetly silent but, from time to time, he reached out and took Betty's hand, or gave her arm an encouraging squeeze.

Replete with food and wine, the atmosphere improved, although several times Betty felt uncomfortable whenever she became aware of Brenda studying her critically.

The presents she and Peter had brought with them had been placed under the tree, along with the large pile already there. Betty sipped her port out of a crystal-cut wine glass, as the group appointed Peter to act as Father Christmas and to hand round the parcels.

He played his part magnificently by insisting that little Anna should be his assistant and carry the parcels to the appropriate recipient.

It took a lot longer than if he had done it himself, but she was so excited that it was well worth any delay. She especially enjoyed them clapping whenever she handed them a parcel. That over, she had tremendous fun unwrapping her own presents, and then running over to whoever had given the present to her and bestowing a kiss on them.

By this time Anna was so tired that Graham and Shirley said they really must take her home.

Guided by a discreet signal from Betty, Peter said it was time he took Betty home so they would leave at the same time.

'Nonsense,' Tim said. 'You must have a nightcap and then I'll see you both home.'

Betty shook her head, but even as she did so, she realized that grateful though she was to Peter, they could hardly refuse Tim's invitation to stay a little longer.

The moment the door closed behind Anna and her parents, Tim went to the drinks cabinet and Brenda attacked again.

All the pleasure of the day dissipated, as she held forth on how she really thought it was for the best that Betty went into a home where there was someone to take care of her so that she was no longer able to do foolish things like she had done recently.

Betty had expected criticism, but Brenda was so outspoken that she felt tears prickling behind her lids and knew that if she tried to say anything in her own defence she would end up blabbering like an idiot and give Brenda even more reason to promote her idea.

She sat up straighter in her chair, pulled back her shoulders, and faced Brenda squarely.

Before she could say anything in her own defence, Peter took a long swig of the Irish coffee that Tim had handed him, cleared his throat and said, 'I don't think you have any need to worry about Betty or her future—'

'Peter, I know you are very kind and keep an eye on her but, as you have probably heard, she does such foolish things for a woman of her age that I really think that proper care is necessary. Look what happened to your car,' she added quickly.

'Would you kindly let me finish what I was going to tell you both,' Peter said firmly.

'Sorry, Peter,' Tim said cordially. 'Brenda is very worried about my mother and sometimes gets a little carried away.'

'Right . . .' Peter took another drink of his coffee. 'What I was about to tell you was that early next year we are going to move in together. We haven't decided on a precise date yet, but we have been contemplating it for some time. It is one of the reasons why Betty sold that picture and those ornaments. She knew I didn't like them and, since we are planning to move into her house, she was trying to make it as comfortable for me as she could.'

There was a hushed silence when Peter had finished speaking. Betty looked at him in astonishment, but he refused to meet her eyes. She didn't know whether he meant it or whether he was just saying this to placate Brenda and to stop her trying to decide the future for Betty.

All of a sudden, both Tim and Brenda were congratulating them on at last seeing sense, although Brenda did manage to put a damper on things by asking Peter if he was fully aware of the responsibility he was undertaking.

'You're getting older yourself, Peter, don't forget. So, are you sure you want to be burdened by the responsibility of looking after Betty?'

Betty felt so taken aback by what Peter had said that her thoughts were in a whirl, so she clamped her lips together to prevent herself from saying anything. She resented the way Brenda spoke about her as if she was an object rather than a person, or as if she wasn't present.

'Oh, I think we will rub along just fine,' Peter said confidently. 'We've been neighbours now for practically a lifetime so I think we understand each other pretty well.'

'I'm only a phone call away if you ever have any problems, and always ready to help you solve them,' Tim said magnanimously.

Betty waited until the taxi Peter ordered had deposited them outside her cottage. 'Are you coming in for a coffee?' Betty asked.

'I'll come in for a few minutes, but I don't want another coffee. I've eaten and drunk enough in the last few hours to last me the rest of the week.'

Once inside, Betty immediately asked him what he had thought he was doing by telling Tim and Brenda that they were moving in together.

'Getting you out of trouble, of course,' he said blandly.

'Well, you certainly managed to do that! I'm grateful for that but now there will be pressure on us about when we are going to move in together.'

'Don't worry about that. We can prevaricate for as long as you want to but, if you agree with me that it's a good idea, the sooner we do it the better as far as I am concerned.'

Thirteen

It wasn't a very happy New Year for Betty. For the first few days of January she was on edge as she waited for Peter to say something more about the announcement he had made about them moving in together.

Finally, after several sleepless nights, she could stand the strain no longer and so she broached the subject herself.

'Yes, I'd love to move in with you if you are sure that is what you want,' he told her, his eyes lighting up at the thought of doing so.

'I thought it was what you wanted,' she said lamely. 'It is what you said to Tim and Brenda and the others.'

'That was merely to get you out of trouble over selling that picture and those ornaments,' he rejoined with a hearty laugh. 'Saved your bacon there, didn't I? I could see that they were all set to give you a good telling off, and I didn't see why they should reproach you for disposing of what was yours.'

Betty stared at him, speechless.

'I'm all in favour of us doing so though, if you are agreeable,' Peter said in a more serious tone. 'Is it to be your place or mine?'

Betty shook her head uncertainly. 'I don't know,' she murmured.

'You don't know if you want us to move in together or you don't know which house it should be?'

Again, Betty shook her head. 'I need time to think,' she prevaricated.

'Take all the time you need,' Peter told her. 'I've waited long enough for you to decide what you want to do that another couple of weeks won't make much difference.'

'Couple of weeks!' Betty drew in her breath sharply. She would rather it was another couple of years, but she decided she'd think carefully before committing herself.

She was grateful to Peter for using the idea of them moving in together as a means of avoiding a heated argument with her family, but for them to do so would mean a completely different lifestyle for her which had always been her main reason for refusing to contemplate the idea seriously.

To stop Brenda asking awkward questions she decided to start her spring cleaning early and to tell them she was clearing out things she no longer wanted so as to make room for Peter's belongings.

She started with the little walnut bureau that was in her bedroom. It was a lovely item of furniture with intricate carving and moulding, and dating back over a hundred years. It had been a twenty-first birthday present to her mother, and when she had reached twenty-one her mother had given it to her.

She had always cherished it and kept only very special souvenirs in it. There was a lock of Tim's hair, Mary's first shoes, a necklace that had belonged to her mother and, in a slim leather wallet, the most precious items of all, love letters from Jeff when they had been courting.

She sat on the edge of the bed and began reading through them, then carefully folding each one and stacking them in a pile at her side.

They brought memories rushing back, and tears to her eyes. No one else had ever seen them and she didn't want anyone else to read them, certainly not Brenda.

As she finished reading the last one, she looked at the pile on the bed beside her and wondered whether to keep them or dispose of them. They were all so precious that she couldn't put them in the paper box in case someone read them; she didn't feel it was fitting to put them in the refuse bin, so what else could she do with them, she wondered.

If I had an open fire I would burn them, she thought. Cremate them so that no one else could ever read them. She sat for a while pondering. She had matches so why not burn them. She went into the kitchen and placed them in a metal wastepaper bin and, although still unsure, struck a match.

She held it between her finger and thumb, still dithering about whether to burn them or keep them, until the match almost burned out. She gave with a sharp intake of breath as it started to singe the skin on her thumb, and dropped the burning match into the bin.

The letters were so old that the paper was bone dry and flared up in an instant like a giant torch. Betty stepped back as the hot flames rose, fanning her face and in doing so she knocked the bin over. She grabbed a tea cloth to try and beat the flames out, but they had spread rapidly. Suddenly they caught the edge of the tablecloth, spread across the floor and set light to a cushion – and then curtains in the living room.

For a moment she was too numb with fright to do anything. Then she tried to quell the flames with a bowl of water. They hissed and sizzled angrily and it only seemed to increase their fierceness.

Betty picked up the phone and dialled 999.

'I've just set the house on fire,' she told the operator, 'can you send the fire brigade.'

Before she could be transferred, she had dropped the phone and cowered back as fresh tongues of flame reached out towards her. Knowing she hadn't given the operator her address she tried to run into the next room to the extension phone in there, but the flames reached the door ahead of her.

The only other extension was in her bedroom.

Stumbling up the stairs, her heart thudding wildly, she made it into the bedroom and slammed the door behind her in fear that the fire might follow her.

Before she could pick up the phone to dial 999 Betty heard Peter calling her name.

'Don't come in, I'm in my bedroom and quite safe. I've rung for the fire brigade . . .'

Even as she spoke she could hear the shriek of the siren as an engine approached at high speed. She felt dazed, how had they known where she lived. Could they have tracked it from her phone line, she wondered. They must have done, she thought with surprise.

Greatly relieved, she went to open the bedroom door and go back downstairs. The moment she touched the handle she leapt back yelping in agony. The brass knob was red hot and had seared the skin on her palms and blisters were already appearing.

Peter heard her cry and called out anxiously for her to stay where she was as the firemen were coming in.

The pain in her hands was so intense that she had difficulty in staying conscious. The room was filling with acrid smoke. The clamour of the men as they trained their hose on the fire and put a ladder up to the bedroom window seemed unbearably loud.

From somewhere far off she heard the reassuring voice of a man as he broke into the room through the window. Before she knew what was happening, he had a picked her up and passed her through the window opening to another man standing on a ladder outside.

The fresh air stung her face and hands, but she tried not to cry out as she was carried down the ladder before being put on a waiting stretcher and then finally into the ambulance.

Peter was at her side as it drove off in the direction of the hospital. A paramedic gently gave first aid to her hands and questioned her about how the fire had started.

She couldn't remember. All she wanted was a drink of water; a long cold drink to ease the dryness in her throat and help to clear her head.

At the hospital they attended to her damaged hands and to the scorched skin on her face and neck. The area was so tender that they had to cut away the front of her dress so that they treat the blisters that had formed on her reddened skin.

If was a painful procedure and afterwards she would have given anything to have been given a sedative and allowed to sleep, but there were no beds available. Instead, they told her that she could go home, as long as she had somewhere to stay and someone to look after her.

'I will be looking after her,' Peter told them.

'Then we will explain how you should treat the wounds and how to apply fresh dressings,' the nurse told him. 'If you have any problems or any concerns as they heal then contact your local surgery for help.'

By the time they were ready to leave for home, Betty's hands were swathed in bandages over the special dressings, and the skin on her face was also covered by dressings and a bandage that ran under her chin and over the top of her head, hiding her singed hair.

Her dress was fastened together with safety pins to save her modesty, but this only made her feel even more dishevelled and sorry for herself.

They travelled home in a hospital car. When they rounded the bend and drove up to her front door, Betty knew she would never forget the heart-stopping moment when she saw her beloved cottage, blackened and gutted.

She tried to reach out for Peter's hand, but the bandages and the pain stopped her. She could only stare at him, her eyes filled with pain and tears.

In an attempt to comfort her he put his arm around her shoulder and pulled her close. He wanted to kiss her, but her face was so hidden under the bandages that it was impossible for him to do so.

There was still a crowd outside Clover Crescent and the moment the car drew up cameras snapped as two reporters rushed towards them, each of the men trying to be the first one to get an exclusive interview.

Betty refused to talk to either of them. Peter made excuses for her but that didn't satisfy them.

'Was it arson, Mrs Wilson, did someone else do this or did you do it yourself?' one of them shouted.

'Did you do it yourself for the insurance money?' the other asked callously.

Betty shook her head at both of them. She tried to speak, but the moment she did so, the pain in her face was so intense that all she could do was stand there shaking her head, her eyes brimming with tears and turn helplessly towards Peter for protection.

With an arm round her waist he guided her away from her own blackened cottage towards his.

'Come on,' he said softly. 'Don't try to talk, let's get you inside and away from those vultures. Time enough to answer questions when you are feeling stronger.'

Shaking, partly with pain and partly from shock, Betty did as he told her. She even managed a deep breath that helped to steady her nerves.

'A cup of tea and you'll feel like a different person,' he told her confidently.

Betty smiled wanly. She already was a different person, she thought wryly. From this moment on everything in her was going to be different; there was no turning back, she no longer had a home of her own. The decision about moving in with Peter had been decided for her.

Before they could enter Peter's house a car screeched to a halt by the gate.

'So there you both are. Heaven's above! What has happened this time,' came Tim's accusing voice.

'Let's go inside and then we can tell you all about what's happened over a cup of tea,' Peter said quietly.

Tim gave him a scornful glance. 'I imagine there is plenty to tell,' he observed angrily.

He didn't follow them in, instead he pushed Brenda towards Peter's door. 'You go on in, I'm going to inspect the ruins first,' he said grimly.

Fourteen

Peter helped Betty indoors and made sure she was comfortable in one of his armchairs before he went to switch the kettle on.

When he returned to his sitting room he saw that Brenda was staring at Betty with a look of disdain on her immaculately made-up face and for the first time he noticed how dishevelled and weary Betty looked.

Without a word, he fetched a brush and comb so that she could at least tidy her hair.

'Would you like to do Betty's hair, Brenda?' he asked, offering the tools to her.

She shuddered and shook her head. Peter shrugged and went over to attend to Betty.

Gently he brushed her grey hair and neatly combed it so that it framed her face.

Neither of them spoke, but she gave him a grateful smile and he wished he could do more to improve her appearance and bring a little more colour to her pallid face. He let his fingers stroke her cheek before he hurried away to make a pot of tea.

A tray with teapot, milk jug, mugs and a plate of assorted biscuits was on the table by the time Tim returned from looking over Betty's home.

'It's an utter shambles,' he declared lugubriously. 'You certainly won't be able to live there, Mother. I don't know what's going to happen to you.' He glanced towards Brenda, but his wife shook her head emphatically to let him know that his mother certainly wouldn't be welcome in their home.

'I really think that the best solution is for your mother to go into a home, at least for a few weeks' respite,' Brenda said crisply. 'She will get professional care and if she likes it there then possibly we can arrange for her to stay there permanently,' she added hopefully.

'She's living here,' Peter said quietly. 'I've prepared the spare room in readiness. The only thing she won't have will be her clothes, but I'm sure Brenda and Mary will soon put that right,' he said looking pointedly at Brenda.

'Count me out,' Brenda said quickly. 'That is a job for Mary.'

Peter concentrated on pouring out the tea and handed it round.

Frowning, Brenda hesitated when he offered her a mug of tea. 'Peter, I really can't drink from a mug, do you have a china cup and saucer?'

Peter bit his lip but went over to the display cabinet and took down an exquisitely fragile cup and saucer and began to pour tea into it.

'I like the milk in first,' Brenda protested.

Peter tipped out the tea he'd already poured and started again. Tim seemed oblivious to what was going on and Peter wondered if Brenda always caused a scene like this. Or perhaps none of their friends ever used mugs, he told himself, smiling inwardly.

Neither Tim nor Brenda attempted to help Betty hold her cup and, after she had made one or two ineffectual attempts to pick it up between her heavily bandaged hands, Peter went over and lifted it up to her lips so that she could drink. Once again she smiled gratefully.

As soon as he had finished his tea Tim stood up. 'We must be going,' he announced, looking at his watch. 'I have clients due in twenty minutes.'

He looked sternly at his mother. 'Now remember, don't attempt to go into your cottage as the structure is unsafe,' he warned.

Although Betty nodded to indicate she understood, Tim was not satisfied. He repeated the instruction to Peter.

'I heard what you said to your mother,' Peter told him. 'You don't honestly think your mother is in any fit state to go grubbing through the charred remains looking for bits and pieces, do you?'

'No, but she might well ask you to do so,' Tim said sharply. 'The entire building is unsafe and will no doubt have to be razed to the ground. I am pleased to see that the police have cordoned it off.'

Peter didn't reply. He could see Tim's words had upset Betty and he thought the sooner Tim and Brenda left the better it would be.

Tim had not quite finished giving orders.

'The same thing applies to the insurance and anything else to do with the property,' he went on. 'Leave everything to me. I will notify the insurance company and I will deal with them. If they come here or try to speak to you say nothing. Is that clear?'

Peter nodded. He was relieved that Tim was going to deal with the insurance and everything else to do with the property. Tim had the staff and the expertise and it would save Betty a great deal of worry.

Two days later, when Mary came to visit her mother she was far more cooperative about buying new clothes for Betty than Brenda had been. Mary listened carefully to what Betty said she needed and made a great effort to carry out her wishes to the letter.

Betty was more than pleased with everything Mary bought for her. The new clothes acted like a tonic and helped to lift her spirits.

Now all he had to do, Peter thought, was nurse her back to full health and hope that her hands and facial area healed without any complications.

Next morning, refreshed by sleeping in a comfortable bed, she looked so much more like the Betty he had always known that Peter felt reassured enough to ask her if she would be all right if he left her on her own for an hour or so while he went shopping.

'Of course I'll be all right,' she said indignantly.

'I'll be as quick as I can be,' he promised. 'If it wasn't that the larder is running short on basics I wouldn't bother for a few days, not until you are feeling stronger and able to come with me.'

'I'd far rather sit quietly on my own that push my way around a supermarket,' she told him.

It was about an hour later when Betty heard someone knocking at the door. Thinking that it must be Peter and that he had forgotten his keys, Betty made her way down the hallway to answer it.

It wasn't Peter but a man who looked to be in his early forties. He was wearing a short dark overcoat over a grey suit, and his thick dark hair was brushed back from his high forehead. He was clean-shaven and his blue eyes were clear and bright.

'So sorry to trouble you, Mrs Wilson,' he said as she opened the door, 'but I hear you have recently had an accident.'

He had a pleasant voice and an engaging smile and Betty wondered if she knew him. Before she could ask him, he went on, 'I was so sorry to hear about your misfortune that I came straight away to see if I could be of help, if not now then sometime in the future. I thought you might like to consider a personal insurance policy.'

Betty stared at him bemused. 'You mean for the house,' she said. 'You mean you owe me some money.'

'No, no.' He shook his head. 'This would be a policy on your life, nothing to do with what happened to your house.'

He drew some papers from his briefcase. 'May I come inside and read these through to you, it's rather a cold day for you to be standing on the doorstep.'

'Yes, it is and I'm not at all well,' Betty agreed.

'I can see that, Mrs Wilson,' he said nodding at her bandaged hands.

Inside the sitting room he sat down in Peter's armchair and looked round the room as if assessing its value before once more waving the papers at her.

'Shall I read the policy details out to you?' he asked.

'What policy details are you talking about?' Betty asked.

'The policy you have said you want to take out in case of any future accidents,' he said blandly.

'I haven't agreed to take out any policy,' Betty protested.

Suddenly she felt threatened and wished she hadn't agreed that he could come inside. The man ignored what she said and produced a gold-topped pen from an inside pocket and pointed to where he wanted her to sign.

'I can't do this without talking it over with my son,' Betty protested.

'Of course you can,' he said with a light laugh. 'It's a personal policy, just to ensure that if you have an accident we will pay for your medical attention and provide you with a nice little income for as long as six months so that you can remain independent.'

The word 'independent' registered with Betty and immediately she felt herself wavering.

The man was quick to notice and immediately applied more pressure. 'Think of the benefits,' he said. 'Money of your own to do what you like with. Spend time at your favourite resort for a few weeks, or a few months in Spain where it would be warm and relaxing. Or what about a cruise?'

A cruise! Betty's blue eyes grew dreamy. A cruise had been something she and Jeff had planned to take as soon as he retired, but it had never happened. Could she go on a cruise on her own? Or would Sally Bishop be interested in coming with her, she wondered.

The sound of the man's voice urging her to make a decision brought her out of her reverie.

'What's it all going to cost me?' she asked.

'You give me five hundred pounds and then you pay a regular instalment of just twenty-five pounds a month.'

'Five hundred pounds. I haven't that much to give you,' she gasped.

'I can take a cheque made out to cash,' he repeated with a bland smile.

'I don't know, that's an awful lot of money and anyway, at the moment I am unable to write a cheque for you or anyone else because of these . . .' As she spoke she raised her bandaged hands.

'Give me your cheque book and I'll write the cheque and all you have to do is sign it. I'm sure you can manage to do that,' he added with a smile.

'No she can't and even if she was able to then I wouldn't let her do it,' a voice suddenly said in an aggressive tone of voice.

'Peter, I didn't hear you come in,' Betty gasped.

'No, and neither did this young thieving bastard,' Peter said.

'Now,' he said turning to the man, 'collect up your papers and get out and think yourself lucky that I don't call the police to deal with you.'

'You've no call to be so aggressive, Mr Wilson—'

'I'm not Mr Wilson, but nevertheless I'm telling you to scram. One more word and I'll call the police.'

As he picked up the phone the intruder stuffed all his papers into his briefcase and left without another word.

'Oh dear, I shouldn't have let him in, should I?' Betty said contritely. 'You won't tell Tim, will you?'

'No, your secret is safe with me,' Peter told her, 'but you really do have to learn that doorstep salesmen are not to be trusted, Betty, and never have anything to do with anyone who turns up

on the doorstep unless you have made an appointment for them
to come.'

It was three weeks before Betty was able to dispense the enve-
loping bandages on her hands and, although she became used to
her own clumsy movement, she found it still took her an inter-
minable time to get dressed and impossible to do more than dab
at her face with a damp flannel. She longed to soak in a bath or
to stand under a shower, but had been warned that this should
be avoided until the skin had healed.

As well as the dressings beneath the bandages, she was also
taking regular doses of paracetamol to reduce the pain and
inflammation.

Peter struggled to provide her with meals that were easy for her
to eat, and often despaired because of the difficulty she had in
eating them. She simply had no appetite and, because the weather
was cold with occasional bouts of sleet and snow, there was no
question of her going out into the fresh air.

When they returned to the hospital in February the skin on
her face and neck, although badly wrinkled, was completely
healed. The palm of her right hand was still painful, but there
were no blisters or infection and it was decided to leave off the
dressing and let the air help to harden the skin.

Betty found that the palms of her hands were still very tender,
and that whenever she went out she had to wear gloves to protect
them from the cold.

Peter was very protective and wouldn't allow her to carry
anything in case she chafed the newly form skin. When she
insisted on helping with the washing up after their meal, or
helping with the dusting, he made sure that she was wearing
protective gloves.

Tim and Mary's calls became fewer and fewer when they saw
how settled she was, and the care that Peter was taking to make
her life as smooth and comfortable as possible.

Each time he did call in, Tim always reminded Peter that if
there were any problems then he was to phone him, he was
always there to help if he was needed.

When Betty questioned Tim about what was happening about

her home he always came out with the same stock answer that all was in hand, and that there was nothing for her to worry about. He was waiting for the insurance company to deal with his claim and once that was settled and the money in the bank he would start making a move to have it rebuilt.

It all sounded very organized and cosy but Betty silently brooded about the charred wreck only a couple of doors away. It was so unsightly; the blackened remains of what had once been her home was a constant reproach of her foolish action.

Fifteen

The only person who seemed to understand her concern, and how much it distressed her to see the charred ruin every time she walked past it, was Sally Bishop.

'If only we could pull down a curtain and shut it away out of sight,' she said with a smile. 'It must be worse for you than it is for me and I hate walking past it.'

'I wouldn't mind so much if I was able to go inside and see if there is anything I could save,' Betty said wistfully.

'I shouldn't think there is by now,' said Sally in a practical voice. 'After all, it's had months of sun, rain, snow and frost on it; in fact, every element there is has attacked it, including gale force winds. What's more, you know the fire brigade must have done quite a lot of damage when they sprayed their hoses in it in order to out put the fire.'

'Yes, indeed,' Betty agreed. 'You wouldn't think that one small match could do so much damage, would you.'

'You never did say what you were burning,' Sally said, giving Betty a quizzical look.

'Nothing of any importance,' Betty said in a non-committal tone.

'I thought it must be something you didn't want that Brenda to read,' Sally said sagely.

Betty flushed. 'Well, yes it was,' she admitted.

Sally waited for her to explain, but for once Betty wasn't prepared to take Sally into her confidence.

Although they went on to talk of other things the thought of going into the charred ruins of her old home, and making quite certain there was nothing else she didn't want made public, persisted in Betty's mind. She couldn't sleep at night for thinking about it and, in the end, she resolved that given a suitable opportunity she would take a look and find out.

She'd be very careful, she told herself. If she thought it was too dangerous then she'd stop immediately, but somehow the very fact that the house had remained upright and in one piece all through the winter weather made her wonder if it was as great a wreck as Tim and the others insisted that it was.

Her opportunity came a couple of weeks later. Peter had been complaining about toothache and they had decided that one of the fillings in his back molars had either worn away or fallen out.

'It looks as though I shall have to see the dentist,' he said reluctantly. 'I can't stand this pain any longer.'

On the morning of his appointment he made Betty promise him she wouldn't go out shopping on her own.

'Of course I won't,' she told him. 'Why would I when there is nothing we need from the shops!'

'Good,' Peter told her. 'Why don't you ask Sally to come along and have a coffee with you while I'm at the dentist?'

'That's a good idea, and I've got some cupboards I want to sort out and rearrange so I can get on and do that while you are out,' she told him.

It was a lovely spring morning and as she went along to ask Sally to join her for coffee she couldn't help wondering if the snowdrops and crocuses had managed to survive in the garden of her old home. Both she and Jeff had always looked forward to them coming into flower because they both felt that it signalled that winter was over and spring had arrived.

The closer she got to the charred ruins, the greater was the temptation to take a peek through to the back garden. From the gate she was sure that she could see a glimmer of white at the far end of the path that led to the garden and was sure that it must be snowdrops.

Hesitantly she pushed open the gate. She might as well pick them, no one else would appreciate them and she would feel that she had salvaged something from the ruins, she thought with an inward smile.

She'd been right. There was a wonderful clump, fighting to raise their heads above the tangled grass and weeds. She bent down and picked a bunch. Jeff had planted them the first year they had been married and they had meant so much to both of them; harbingers of spring and the year ahead.

Carrying the snowdrops carefully, she went further down the path to see if any crocuses were out in the lawn at the back of the house. The state of the garden horrified her. Tiles had blown off the roof and lay scattered and broken; broken panes of glass and great lumps of blackened plaster that must have blown down from the bedroom completely covered the grass.

She stared upwards at the scorched walls; the broken windows like sightless eyes stared back at her accusingly. The memory would haunt her for the rest of her days she thought as she went back to the path and made for the gate.

For now, she'd go and find Sally. She needed company; someone to talk to who could disperse her gloomy, self-recriminating thoughts.

As she walked past the front door she couldn't resist the urge to just peep inside. She put her hand against the woodwork and a long thin piece broke away and stuck to her hand before dropping to the ground like a discarded scab, sending a shiver racing through her body.

Even so, she couldn't help wondering if the place was really as unsafe as Tim insisted that it was.

Daringly she put first one foot, then the other, over the threshold until she was standing in the dilapidated remains of the hall. All around her everything was blackened and burnt, but when she touched the walls they seemed quite strong, and the floor leading from the hall into the living room seemed as sound and sturdy as she remembered. She was sure Tim had been exaggerating.

Having managed to get this far without mishap she decided to see if there was anything in the living room that she could salvage. One step led to two, and then she suddenly found herself standing in the middle of what had been her sitting room. Betty was astounded to see that the display shelves at the side of the fireplace, which Jeff had built, were not only still intact but that some of her most precious ornaments were still on them. They were covered in grime but she was sure that they were not otherwise damaged.

Carefully she moved closer and stood staring at them in disbelief. Overjoyed that they had survived the onslaught of the fire and the winter elements she reached up to take one down so that she could examine it.

As she lifted it from the shelf it was like the game dominoes

A Mind of Her Own

that Tim and Mary had played when they were small; each one
fell and crashed against the next one. They continued until each
one had tumbled against the next and the entire stretch of them
had smashed. The movement as one ornament hit against the
next upset the actual shelves and they too started to move and
came crashing down around her.

The sharp edge of one of them struck her on the temple. The
pain seared through her head, leaving her so shaken and dizzy
that she was engulfed in an impenetrable blackness. She fell
forward, now striking the front of her head against the edge of
the fireplace with such force that it rendered her unconscious
and she slumped onto the floor.

Although Betty had promised to invite Sally Bishop round for
coffee, Peter made doubly sure that Sally went along to his place
at mid-morning by calling in to tell her to do so before he went
to the dentist.

Sally waited until almost eleven o'clock for Betty to call and
confirm the invitation. When she didn't, she decided that since
Betty must know that Peter had called to tell her so she'd better
go along anyway.

It was a lovely spring morning, but there was a nip in the air
so Sally put on a heavy cardigan. It felt rather too warm but she
could always take it off again when she was at Peter's place, she
told herself. She locked her front door and was singing to herself
as she made the short walk. It was one of those days when it felt
good to be alive.

She was surprised when she reached Peter's place to find the
door ajar but there was no sign of Betty. She walked round to
the back of the house to see if she was in the garden, but there
was no sign of her out there either.

Calling out her name, Sally pushed open the door and ventured
into the house. In the kitchen a tray was laid ready with two
china mugs and a plate of biscuits and the coffee percolator was
bubbling away, but there was no one in there. All was silent.

Puzzled, Sally went through the house, room by room in case
Betty had fallen somewhere and was lying unconscious or so
badly hurt she couldn't call out. The entire house was deserted.

She returned to the kitchen and wondered where on earth

Betty could be. Then, whilst gazing out the window, she caught
site of the blackened ruins. With growing apprehension, she
wondered if Betty had defied all their warnings and gone in to
look inside her old home.

Heart in mouth, Sally made her way back to the blazed remains
of Betty's home. She stood just inside the gate, trying to see if
there was any movement either in the dilapidated garden or the
charred building, but everywhere there was an eerie silence.

Convinced that Betty must be there somewhere, Sally made
her way to the front door and peered into the darkness. As she
lifted one foot to step inside a man's voice shouted a warning at
her, ordering her to stop. Sally froze, then as she turned her head
she saw Peter was pushing open the gate.

Her heart thudded. She would have to tell him why she was
there and what she was doing, but from the angry look on his
face as he came nearer she was scared what his reaction was going
to be.

'What do you think you are doing?' he said in an angry voice.

Sally drew in a deep breath. 'Looking for Betty; I've just
come from your place and she isn't there.'

'Are you quite sure?' Peter's frown deepened.

'I've been all over your house and garden. She isn't there. The
coffee is bubbling away so—'

Peter didn't wait for her to finish. He didn't need her to tell
him where she thought Betty might be.

'Stay here, don't move,' he ordered, as he pushed past her
and went into the house.

From the doorway she heard his exclamation of horror and,
without a moment's hesitation, went to see what had happened.

Sixteen

Sally found Peter in Betty's sitting room staring down and a pile of debris scattered all around him. He was white-faced and tense and instinctively she knew that something dreadful had happened.

She went to his side and gasped when she saw that Betty was lying on the floor by his feet beneath the rubble.

As she moved forward to try and reach her, Peter laid a restraining hand on her arm.

'Be careful, one movement and you may bring more rubble down on her,' he cautioned.

'We can't just leave her there, she's been knocked unconscious and she may be injured.'

'I know that, but if I move that shelf that is pinning her to the ground it may bring the other shelves crashing down. They are all linked together in some way. I remember how proud Jeff was of the ingenious way he had managed to do it.'

'We can't leave her lying underneath that shelf,' Sally reiterated. 'Have you checked her pulse to see if . . . if . . .'

Sally's voice petered out as if she was afraid to complete the question.

'No, not yet,' Peter said.

'I think we should,' Sally told him.

Gingerly he moved a step or two closer and crouched down and then took Betty's hand, his fingers on her wrist. The silence was ominous, but when he looked up Sally could see the relief on his face.

'There is a pulse but it's very faint. Can you go and call for an ambulance? Tell them what has happened so that they can send someone to help lift the shelf.'

Sally found her hand shaking as she dialled 999 from the phone in her own living room. She took a deep breath to calm herself down; she didn't want to appear hysterical when they answered.

As lucidly as possible she told the operator what had happened.

'She is still alive?'

'Yes, she has a pulse but it's very weak,' Sally confirmed.

'Stay with her, don't attempt to move her or the shelf and someone will be with you within a few minutes,' the operator promised.

When she got back to Betty's sitting room, Sally reported this word for word to Peter.

Whilst she had been phoning, he had tried to clear away some of the debris to make it easier to reach Betty and for her to breathe, but he realized that the shelf was far too heavy for him to move single-handed and to try to do so might only end in Betty suffering even worse injuries.

A few minutes later they heard the sound of an approaching ambulance.

There seemed to be two sirens ringing and Peter looked puzzled.

'They've probably sent a fire engine as well,' Sally observed as she headed for the open doorway to look out for them.

She was quite right. As well as the ambulance a fire engine was also pulling up by the gate.

The middle-aged ambulance driver pursed his lips as he observed the situation and then stood back so that the firemen could try and free Betty. There were three burly firemen and they immediately assessed the situation and acted accordingly. Two of them held the other shelving while the third, a muscular younger man, lifted up the shelf that was resting on Betty's chest.

As the heavy wooden shelf was lifted off Betty, one of the paramedics knelt down and assessed her condition. While he was doing this the other paramedic went out to the ambulance and brought in a stretcher.

With great care they lifted Betty and laid her on the stretcher. She was still unconscious but the paramedics waited until they had taken her into the ambulance before they administered an injection and placed a gas and air mask over her face to help with her breathing. Peter and Sally thanked the firemen as they withdrew and Sally followed the paramedics as they carried the stretcher with Betty on it out to the ambulance.

'Are you coming with us?' one of them asked, looking from Peter to Sally and back again.

'I'm coming with you,' Peter told them.

He stopped as he reached the ambulance steps and turned back to Sally. 'Whatever you do, don't try to go in there. All this movement has shaken the rest of the house and it's extremely dangerous.'

'Very well,' Sally agreed with a nod. 'Would you like me to telephone Tim and tell him what's happened?'

Peter hesitated. 'Thanks. I suppose you'd better do that,' he said shaking his head from side to side as if aware of the recriminations that this would bring down on him.

The minute he had sat down the ambulance men closed up the back of the ambulance and they were away. One paramedic stayed at Betty's side, monitoring her breathing, checking her pulse and doing what he could to make her comfortable.

Peter felt at a loss as the ambulance drew up outside the A & E department of the hospital and the stretcher with Betty on it was unloaded and taken inside. He ran a hand over his chin as he followed it and saw her being wheeled into a small cubicle room. There were no doors at the front, only curtains, and as soon as Betty had been transferred from the stretcher to the narrow bed the curtains were swished across by the nurse who had been assigned to look after her.

Peter stood outside uncertain what to do next.

'Excuse me,' he found himself moved aside as a white-coated doctor wearing a stethoscope moved past him into the cubicle.

He was still standing there when the doctor emerged, so Peter plucked up his courage and pulled aside one of the curtains.

'Can I come in?'

The nurse who was inserting a canella into the back of Betty's hand looked up frowning. 'Are you with this lady?' she asked.

'Yes. She lives with me.'

'So, what happened?'

Before Peter could answer the curtain was pulled briskly to one side and Peter looked round to see Tim standing there.

The nurse looked up ready to order him out, but Peter explained quickly, 'This is Mrs Wilson's son.'

'If you are going to talk between yourselves then will you go out into the waiting room or go for a coffee. My patient needs to be able to rest,' the nurse told them in a clipped tone.

'Is she conscious?' Tim demanded, looking sceptically at the prone, white-faced figure of his mother.

'She soon will be if she isn't left in peace and quiet,' the nurse retorted briskly.

'Come on, I want details,' Tim said grabbing Peter's arm and propelling him into the waiting room.

Peter shook off Tim's grasp. 'Let's go for a coffee and I can tell you all about what happened.'

'It's no good trying to avoid the issue,' Tim snapped. 'I want to know now.'

'And I want a coffee,' Peter stated.

They walked down the corridor to the restaurant in silence. Peter ordered the coffees but Tim pushed him aside and paid for them. They carried their drinks to a far corner of the room where they would be left alone.

'So, what happened?'

Peter took a long drink of his coffee before putting the mug down on the table and getting himself comfortable. Then he recounted everything that had happened that morning; from the time he'd left home to go to the dentist until he had come back home again.

'So Sally Bishop was with her when it happened,' Tim mused.

'I don't think so. I think I reached home just as Sally was about to step inside your mother's house to look for her. She had already been to my place apparently and searched everywhere and couldn't find her.'

The coffee seemed to have calmed both men down and, once he had heard how his mother came to be on her own, Tim was more concerned than angry.

'Mother must have taken it into her head to go and look round her house, knowing that you were safely out of the way,' Tim said thoughtfully.

'She must have been in the garden for a while because when I found her she was clutching a bunch of snowdrops,' Peter told him. 'If Sally had been a few moments earlier going around to my place for coffee then none of this might have happened.'

'If only, if only,' Tim muttered to himself. He looked bewildered, as if he needed a motive for her being in there. 'What was she trying to do in the living room when everything in there is blackened and charred,' he asked out loud.

Peter remained silent for a moment. 'She had snowdrops in

one hand but in the other there was a shard of vivid red glass. It was so bright that at first I thought it was blood.'

'Her precious vase that my father bought her for one of their anniversaries,' Tim said with a smile. 'I suppose it was still on the shelf and she saw it and made a grab for it and that was what brought the shelf down.'

'Something like that, I imagine,' Peter agreed.

Tim pushed his coffee cup away from him and stood up. 'We'd better be getting back. By now they might know just how badly hurt she is.'

Peter followed him without a word.

There was a doctor just leaving the cubicle where Betty was when they returned, so Tim stopped him and asked for news of his mother's injuries.

'She has regained consciousness but she has no recollection at all about what happened. I think it will be best if you don't question her. Leave her to tell you if and when her memory of what happened returns. The blow on the head left her unconscious and the heavy wooden object, which you believe to be a shelf, managed to break two of her ribs. Apart from that there is surprisingly little damage. She will be feeling stiff and sore for a few days and it will take several weeks for her ribs to heal. Apart from prescribing painkillers, there is not a lot we can do about the ribs; it's up to her to rest and take things easy.'

'So can we take her home?' Peter asked hopefully.

'Perhaps later today. We need to do a brain scan first to make sure there is no underlying damage from the blow she's received on the head.'

'What happens now?' Tim asked the nurse as the doctor left.

'As you heard, Mrs Wilson is to go for a head scan and if that reveals no damage has occurred, then we will release her either today or tomorrow. She will have to come back again in a couple of days' time for a further check-up,' she added.

'Can we talk to her?' Peter asked, moving towards the bed where Betty lay with her eyes closed. He picked up her hand and spoke to her in a very quiet voice.

She opened her eyes and stared at him and, for one terrifying moment, he thought she didn't recognize him. Then she gave a tiny smile and squeezed his hand.

He moved aside so that Tim could speak to her. The reaction was much the same. It was as if she was too tired to talk.

'I'll wait here until they say she can go home if you want get back to your office,' Peter told Tim.

'Are you sure?' Tim looked relieved. 'Phone me if you have any doubts or problems of any kind,' he added. 'Take care of her.'

'Don't worry, I will.'

At the door Tim paused and looked back at his mother and then at Peter. 'Did you come by car?' he asked.

Peter shook his head. 'No, I came in the ambulance.'

'Do you want me to wait and take you home?'

'No, no. It may be hours yet. I'll get a taxi.'

Tim opened his wallet and drew out a couple of notes. 'This should cover it,' he said holding them out.

Peter was about to refuse then he remembered that he hadn't even stopped to pick up his wallet and he didn't think he had enough small change on him to cover the taxi fare, so he accepted the money gratefully.

'Telephone me as soon as you get her back home,' Tim said as he left.

Seventeen

Betty wasn't discharged from hospital that day, or for several days afterwards, and when she was finally allowed to go to Peter's home she was utterly bemused by her surroundings.

'This isn't my home,' she would state in a puzzled voice. 'It's very similar and there are some of my things here but it's not the home I remember.'

Time and time again Peter explained that she had agreed to share his house and that she had moved in with him, but she seemed to be unable to take it in.

'Why would I want to do that?' she asked in a bewildered tone of voice.

'We both thought it would be a good idea,' Peter said, lamely knowing he couldn't tell her the truth, at least not until she was stronger both physically and mentally.

He could tell that even in her present state she didn't believe him. She wandered round and round, touching things that were his and shaking her head; then picking up things that she remembered from her old home and hugging them to her with a smile of contentment.

She had lost weight while she had been ill and she looked so frail that Peter hadn't the heart to explain to her about the fire that had devastated her home. He talked to Tim about it, but Tim only shrugged and said he didn't know whether it would upset her or not.

'You could try it,' he murmured. 'She knows something is different and it might set her mind straight if she knew the truth.'

Peter waited for an opportune moment. Then one day, when Betty had been particularly fractious, he took her out though his front gate and walked with her down the road to where the charred remains of her old house still stood.

Betty gazed at it in stunned silence, tears streaming down her cheeks. 'Who did that? Who destroyed my beautiful home?' she asked in a pitiful whisper.

Peter mumbled something about an accident but Betty shook her head. 'It was my fault, wasn't it,' she said quietly. 'I caused the fire that damaged my lovely home and that is why I am living with you in your house.'

Peter nodded, placing an arm round her shoulders and hugging her close for a few minutes. There was no need for words. He held her until she stopped trembling, then kissed the top of her head before gently releasing her.

They walked back to his house in silence, holding hands but not speaking. Peter cast sideways glances at her but she seemed stunned and he thought it best to let her absorb the news before he tried to talk to her about the accident.

Afterwards Betty seemed different.

They all noticed it, particularly her friend Sally Bishop. She would spend hours simply sitting and staring vacantly into space. If anyone spoke to her it took a while to bring her back to understanding what they were saying, and even who they were.

When Peter questioned her, and asked if she felt all right, she smiled and said she was thinking about the past, reliving old memories. Betty never shared these memories aloud, not even with Peter, and he wondered if it was her memories of the fire or something else from the past that was worrying her.

When he questioned her on this point she stared at him, as if she didn't understand what he was saying or shook her head and denied it. When he questioned Tim, her son, he merely frowned and made no comment.

Gradually, as her health returned, she lost her pallor and began to put on a little weight. Eventually, Betty's moods passed and slowly she began to take an interest in what was going on around her and even join in the chatter.

She did, however, sleep a great deal. She nodded off after her midday meal and again in mid-afternoon. Peter tried his best to keep her occupied at these times but it was no good. Sleep seemed to be what she wanted, what she needed, and her catnaps, as she called them, only lasted for twenty minutes or so and made no difference to her sleeping at night.

As spring turned into summer, Betty spent more and more time sitting in a comfortable cane chair in the garden. She also enjoyed pottering amongst the flowers that Peter was so proud of and which he grew in profusion. Betty picked some of them most days to take indoors. Peter didn't stop her, even if they were the flowers that he cherished the most and would never dream of cutting himself. After a few days indoors they lost their bloom; he would declare, 'They like to stay out in the fresh air.'

Although Betty accepted this and agreed with him, she continued to pick them and bring them indoors. Whenever her daughter, Mary, came to see her, or Sally Bishop called, they always left with a bunch of Peter's precious flowers.

Peter tried another tactic. She seemed so much stronger now that he felt sure she was capable of going to a short walk each day. At first it was merely a stroll along the roads near their home. Then slightly longer ones along a path through the nearby woodlands and lanes where the hedgerows were still bright with flowers. He encouraged Betty to pick these wild flowers, rather than the ones from his garden.

By autumn, Betty's recovery seemed to be as good as it would ever be. She still became breathless if she walked too far and sometimes complained that her legs were aching and they had to stop for her to have a rest. Her interest in what was going on around her was back to normal, although she did sometimes have lapses of memory when she couldn't remember where she had put things, or the name of something or someone.

'At her age that is only to be expected, and after what she has been through in the last twelve months it's thoroughly understandable. In fact, for her age, she is in very good condition,' the hospital doctor stated when Betty went for her final check-up.

Peter felt very relieved by the news and told Tim that he thought it was about time something was done about Betty's old house.

'It still worries her seeing it in that state, just as it worries me,' he said to Tim the next time he called in to see how his mother was getting on. 'You promised months and months ago to sort it out. You know all the details and you have the contacts to get it put right, so why not get on and do it?'

'I've held back because I thought it might make my mother anxious to get back in there again because you said she often walks down the road, leans on the gate and stares at the house.'

Peter shook his head. 'I don't think so. She seems quite content with things as they are, as I am. I think she does that because she is unhappy about the state the house is in and knows she was the cause of the fire.'

'I see. I'll start putting things in motion then,' Tim promised.

He was as good as his word, and within less than a week there was a smartly dressed man there taking measurements and making notes. At first, Betty was very concerned but when Tim explained to her that the man was an architect and that they were going to restore the house she looked interested.

'You mean I will be able to go back there to live?'

'If you want to do so,' he said slowly. 'I thought you were happy living here and sharing a house with Peter? He does a lot for you and if you go back to living on your own you'll have to care for the garden and do all the cooking and cleaning and so on.'

Betty nodded thoughtfully. 'Yes, you're right. I'll have to think about that.'

She said nothing to Peter but she confided in Sally Bishop.

'You'd be mad to go back there. Peter waits on you hand and foot, you don't know when you're well off.'

Betty smiled. 'I was hoping you'd say that. I'm very comfortable here and, as you say, Peter does quite a lot for me.'

'Quite a lot!' Sally Bishop's eyebrows rose. 'I'll say he does. You've no worries at all and, with winter coming on, having someone to go for the bread and milk and papers when it's raining cats and dogs, or it's snowing, or there's ice on the pavement, is a real blessing I can tell you.'

Betty smiled. 'Jealous, are you?' she teased.

'I'll say I am!' Sally agreed. 'You let them rebuild your old house and get your Tim to rent it out or sell it for you. As an estate agent he will know which is the best thing to do, and then you can enjoy the proceeds.'

From then on, the progress the builders were making became Betty's prime interest. As soon as she'd had her breakfast she would put on her coat and walk along the road to her old house to make sure that the builders were hard at work. If for some reason they weren't there then she asked Peter to make a phone call to Tim and ask him to chivvy them up.

'Why the hurry if you're not going back there to live?' Peter asked nervously.

'Tim has set things in motion and now I want to see it completed,' she told him. 'A sort of tidying up of the past.'

By the time their work was complete in mid-December the builders knew Betty well and were on friendly terms with her. As they began to move the last of their equipment out of the garage, where they had stored it while working on the place, she asked to look and see if there was a bicycle still in there. One of them went to look and came back pushing a very old upright ladies bicycle.

'Do you mean this?' he asked, a big grin on his face.

'That's it!' she exclaimed, a delighted smile on her face.

'It should be in a museum,' he chuckled. 'I don't think I have ever seen one as old as this before. Didn't they used to call them "sit up and beg" bicycles?'

'Don't you be so cheeky, young man. That is my bicycle and I'm going to start riding it again.'

He stared at her, in disbelief, trying not to laugh. Then solemnly he wheeled it towards her and handed it over to her.

'Mind you don't break the speed limit,' he told her.

'And remember you can't use it on the motorways,' someone warned and their remarks were followed by hoots of laughter.

'Don't you need a licence to drive that thing, or a man with a red flag running down the road in front of you,' someone yelled and again there were loud laughs.

No, Betty thought complacently, she may have lost her licence to drive a car but you didn't need a licence to ride a bicycle.

Other voices called after her. She knew they were making jibes about the bike at her expense, but she took no notice.

Delighted to have it back in her possession, she wheeled it away down the road, in the opposite direction to Peter's house. It was so long since she had ridden it that she wasn't sure that she was going to be able to keep her balance, and so she wanted to try it out in private without anyone seeing her do so.

Eighteen

Peter Brown was so absorbed in what he was doing that he lost all count of time. Dressed in his oldest gardening clothes, he was clearing out his shed. He was piling up all the items which were useless and which had accumulated over the years. He was making a bonfire of anything that would burn and collecting up the rest of the discarded items ready to take to the public rubbish tip.

It was a job he had intended to do before Betty moved in with him but instead more and more unwanted items had been rehoused in the shed, until it had reached the point where he could barely get in there and his workbench was buried under the clutter.

Today, after they had finished their midday meal and cleared things up, Betty had retired to her room to have a sleep but he had felt too restless to have a snooze too, so he had decided to tackle the muddle in his shed.

He suddenly felt tired, and since there was no chance of lighting the bonfire because the sky had clouded over, threatening the possibility of rain, he decided to go indoors and make a cup of tea for himself and Betty.

He called out her name as he went into the kitchen and switched on the kettle. It was after four o'clock and if she was still asleep then it was time she was up, or else she wouldn't be able to sleep when it came to bedtime, he thought.

The kettle boiled, he made the tea, but there was still no answering call from Betty. Surprised, he went upstairs to wake her. Her bedroom door was wide open and there was no sign of her. He went all round the house, looking everywhere, but she wasn't there.

He knew she wasn't out in the garden, so where on earth was she, he wondered.

He poured himself a cup of tea and sat down on one of the wooden kitchen chairs. It was not very comfortable but, because of the state he was in, covered with dust and grime, he knew he dare not sit in his favourite armchair.

He stirred his tea, wondering where Betty was. Although she

was now almost back to full health, she was still a little absent-minded so he didn't like her going out on her on, especially as she hadn't mentioned it to him. In addition to getting lost, there was the added problem that she tired easily and found walking any distance hard work.

As rain began to patter on the window he finished his tea and stood up. Probably she had gone along the road to look at how the work was progressing on her old home. It was the one little walk which she felt capable of doing on her own and most days she made her way there. Now, if she had gone out without a coat she was going to get wet.

Peter went out into the hall and pulled on his own anorak. He would go and meet her, he decided, as he took down her raincoat from the peg.

It was raining quite hard by the time he reached the almost finished house and the workmen were packing up. They all knew Betty, but they shook their heads when Peter asked if she was sheltering somewhere there from the rain.

'She was here earlier, about half an hour ago or perhaps a bit more,' one of them said.

'She's gone for a ride,' one of the others called out.

Peter's heart thumped. Surely Tim hadn't taken her out without letting him know, he thought startled. If it wasn't Tim then who was it, he wondered.

Trying not to let the men see how worried he was, he asked, 'Do you know what sort of car she went in?'

'Car? She didn't go in a car, mate, she went on that old bicycle that was in the garage.'

'Bicycle?' Peter looked blank. 'What bicycle?'

'The one that was at the very back of the garage, hidden behind all our bits and pieces. We've been clearing up in there today because we've almost finished the outside work here and the carpenters and decorators will need the garage to store all their equipment in.'

'And you say there was a bicycle in the garage.'

'There was, and she asked us to get it out for her, didn't she, Sam?'

'That's right,' Sam agreed. 'She said it was hers. It was as old as the hills, should have been in a museum.'

'It was one of those "sit up and beg" sorts,' Jimmy said with a broad grin.

'You mean she's taken it home?' Peter persisted.

'She's taken it away, mate. She said she was going for a ride on it. We warned her not to get caught speeding and not to take it on the motorway,' Sam chuckled.

'Which way did she go, she certainly hasn't brought it home because I've been there all afternoon,' Peter said, a hint of panic creeping in to his tone.

'No, she didn't wheel it towards your place, she went the other way, toward the hill,' Sam confirmed. 'She said she wanted to try it out there.'

'Heavens above,' Peter groaned. 'It's probably so old and rusty that it will fall to pieces if she gets on it.' He pulled up the collar of his anorak and shivered. 'I'd better go and see if I can find her. She'll be wet through by now,' he muttered, more to himself than to Sam and Jimmy.

'Well the rain's almost stopped so I wouldn't worry about that,' Jimmy said.

'No, the rain has stopped but I think you are probably right about the bike,' Sam agreed.

Peter wasn't listening. He was thinking of the bicycle. Betty had ridden it as a young girl. She couldn't possibly remember how to still ride, he thought worriedly as he hurried along the road in the direction the men had said. He knew all too well the hill they'd mentioned. Many years ago, he and Betty had ridden their bikes down it; gathering speed, their legs spread wide, refusing to put them back on to pedals until the very last minute, or even using them to help stop when they reached the main road at the bottom. In winter they had dragged their sled as close to the top of the hill as they could, and then they had come hurtling down. It had been dangerous then but nowadays, with so much more traffic, it was lethal because of the busy main road that ran along the bottom of the hill.

Betty was reliving the past so much these days that Peter was sure she was planning to ride down the hill like she'd done in the olden days. He broke into a run. He must get there before she started down the hill and reached the main road. He wasn't sure that she would have the sense to stop in time.

As he started to climb up the steep hill he looked upwards to see if there was any sign of her, but there wasn't. He breathed a sigh of relief. She walked so very slowly these days that she had

had probably been breathless after pushing the bike to the top of the hill and had needed to take a rest. With any luck he'd reach her before she tried to ride down.

Even as the thought went through his head he saw a movement above him, and a sixth sense told him it was Betty. He tried to shout out a warning but she was too far away to hear him.

In a split second she was heading straight down the hill, screaming with fright as the bike gathered speed. As Peter watched in petrified horror, he noticed that she was wobbling dramatically. It looked as though her skirt had caught in the spokes of the back wheel. When she realized this, and tried to apply the brakes to slow down, it was apparent they had no effect at all. Peter wasn't sure whether it was because her skirt was preventing the brakes from being effective or whether it was the brakes were useless because of their age.

Either way, he felt sick. Then he did the only thing he could do. He stepped directly into her path. It was all he could think of to try and stop her careering down onto the busy main road.

Her speed made it impossible for him to retain his balance as the bike, and Betty, impacted with him. They went down in a twisted mass of metal, arms and legs.

Peter felt a searing pain down his right side and at the same time he heard an ominous crack. For a moment, as they lay in a breathless heap, he didn't know if it was one of his bones, or one of Betty's, or part of the bike's metal frame.

He lay where he was for a moment, trying to regain his thoughts. The rain had stopped and, although the sky was no longer so dark, he knew it must now be quite late in the afternoon.

Recovered from his pause, Peter tried to extricate himself and immediately he was once again aware of the searing pain in his right shoulder and arm, as well as the fact that he couldn't move his arm. It wasn't trapped in the bicycle frame, yet it felt as though there was a dead weight preventing him from lifting it. When he finally managed to free himself from the tangle of metal, his right arm hung useless, and even the smallest movement caused excruciating pain.

Betty was alternatively sobbing and screaming, and he had no idea whether it was merely from fright or whether she was injured as well.

The sound of an approaching vehicle filled him with even greater dread. It sounded like a lorry. Surely it would see them and move its course, Peter thought. There was absolutely no way they could get out of its path.

To his surprise, and relief, the driver cut his engine and the lorry stopped. It was so close to them that another yard and they would have been under its wheels.

Then he heard voices, ones he recognized, and he realized that the workmen he'd been talking to earlier, who had found the bike and told him that Betty was planning to ride it, had come to look for them.

'You all right, mate?' Jimmy asked, coming over to where they lay.

'I think I've broken my arm or my shoulder,' Peter said. 'The pain is sheer hell and I can't seem to lift it.'

'What about Betty?'

'I don't know,' Peter told him. 'She's trapped by the bike. She was screaming her head off before but hasn't made a sound for ages. I think she's passed out; though whether it's from shock or from some sort of injury, I don't know.'

'Yeah, we know she's been screaming from time to time, we could hear her from Clover Crescent,' Sam said. 'That's why we thought that perhaps we'd better come and see if everything was OK with you both.'

As the younger man, Jimmy, approached to see if he could help to disentangle them, Sam stopped him. 'No, don't touch them, you might do more harm than good,' he warned. 'I'll phone for an ambulance,' he said, taking his mobile out of his pocket and dialling.

It only took him a minute to give the directions of where they were.

'The ambulance will be here as soon as possible, probably about ten minutes or so, depending on traffic conditions,' he assured them when he'd finished.

'Fair enough,' Jimmy said. 'Shall I get the tarpaulin out of the truck and put it over them to try and keep them warm until the ambulance gets here?'

'Yes, that's a thought, we could do that,' Sam agreed. 'I'll help you. It's reasonably clean and at least it will keep out the wind.'

Nineteen

Sally Bishop looked at her watch and frowned. It was later than she thought. She had been so engrossed in tidying her cupboards that she hadn't noticed how quickly the afternoon was slipping by. There had been a short, sharp rain shower earlier on that had stopped now but it had left the sky clouded over.

She checked on the time again. She had promised to go round to Clover Crescent to see Betty Wilson, but she'd probably left it too late now to do so.

Still, a quick walk in the fresh air would do her good, she told herself. A ten-minute chat and she'd be home in time to prepare her evening meal and watch the six o'clock news.

She put a comb through her hair, pulled on her heavy warm coat, picked up her gloves, found her keys, and set off.

To her surprise Peter's house was in darkness. When she went to ring the bell, she found the door was unlocked. That was strange, she thought. If they had gone out together then Peter would have been sure to lock the door; he was very careful over such matters.

She stood on the path wondering what to do. Surely they couldn't both be asleep. Betty often took a nap after her lunch but, as far as she knew, Peter never did. She went round to the side of the house to see if Peter was out in the garden or in his shed, but there was no sign of him.

Sally went back to the house and again rang the bell and rapped on the door, then stepped inside and switched on the hall light. She was so familiar with their home that in no time she had checked that there really was no one at home.

She wondered if Tim Wilson had come round to take his mother and Peter somewhere, but he certainly wouldn't leave the place unlocked. It felt like déjà vu and it was making Sally nervous.

She looked at her watch again. It was five o'clock so Tim Wilson's estate agency office would still be open. She decided to walk to the high street and find out if he had taken them out,

or if he knew where they were. If he wasn't there then someone
in the office might know his movements and be able to help the
pair, she decided.

Tim Wilson was there, but he was as puzzled as Sally that
neither his mother nor Peter were at home.

'Are you quite sure,' he pressed.

'Quite sure,' Sally Bishop said decisively. 'If you don't believe
me then come back with me and look for yourself.'

'OK I'll do that. I'm about to leave for the night anyway and
it will set both our minds at rest. We'll go in my car and then I
can run you home afterwards.'

Five minutes later Tim was agreeing with Sally that neither
Betty nor Peter were at home.

'Maybe they've both walked up to Mum's old house to see
how the work is getting on. The builders are due to finish tonight
and the carpenters and decorators will be coming in next week
to finish off the interior.'

Sam and Jimmy were packing up things into their van when
Sally and Tim arrived.

'Hi, governor!' Sam greeted him. 'We're just putting the last
of our stuff into the van. We've cleared all our clobber out of
the garage and left everything spick and span for next week.'

'How's your mother, Mr Wilson?' Jimmy asked.

'I don't know at the moment,' Tim answered with a frown.
'We're looking for her, have you seen her?'

The two workmen exchanged glances. 'You mean you don't
know that she's had an accident and been taken to hospital?' Sam
said.

Tim frowned. 'An accident; what sort of an accident?'

Again, the two men exchanged glances before speaking. Then
Jimmy said, 'It was on that old bike.'

'Old bike? What are you talking about?'

'We were clearing all our stuff out of the garage and she was
by the gate watching us,' Sam explained. 'She saw the bike at the
back of the garage and asked us to get it for her.'

'It was old, must have been sixty years old or more,' Jimmy
interposed.

'I know what they're talking about,' Sally Bishop said when
she saw Tim was utterly bewildered by the conversation. 'It's been

at the back of the garage for years. Betty wouldn't get rid of it. I got rid my mine about thirty years ago, but she hung on to hers. She must have left it in the garage when she moved in with Peter after the fire,' she added.

'You mean you let her take it away,' Tim said slowly.

'Well, she asked us for it and it was hers so what else could we do,' Sam said defensively.

Tim nodded understandingly. 'Of course,' he murmured. 'So, what happened then? Did she take it back to Peter Brown's house?'

The two men exchanged glances once again.

'Well, no,' Sam said. 'She went off with it the other way. To the hill—'

'What!' Tim shouted. 'Was she thinking of riding it?'

Both men nodded.

'And that's when she had the accident?'

'She got to the hill it seems and began to ride it down,' Jimmy told him. 'Mr Brown came here looking for her and when he heard what had happened he went to try and stop her. She'd reached the hill before he could stop her and she was already on the bike and coming down the hill hell for leather. He knew he had to stop her before she reached the main road at the bottom so he stepped out in front of her.'

'The bike bowled him over,' Sam said, taking up the story. 'The pair of them and the bike crashed to the ground. We went to look for them and saw what happened but we were too late to do anything. We found them in a heap almost at the bottom of the hill. Mr Brown seemed to be badly hurt—'

'And what about my mother?' Tim interrupted.

'Not too sure. She seemed to have passed out by the time we got there.'

'We phoned for an ambulance.'

'So where is she now?' Tim said, pulling at his stiff collar as if he was choking.

'In hospital. That's why I asked how she was,' Jimmy said.

'Are you feeling all right, missus?' Sam asked as he looked at Sally and noticed that the colour had drained from her face; she looked as though she was about to faint.

'Yes, I'm quite all right, thank you,' Sally murmured, but she clutched at Tim's arm as though she was about to fall.

'I had no idea about any of this,' she told Tim in a choking voice. 'It's all my fault.'

'How can it be your fault?' he said sharply.

'I promised to go round there about three o'clock for a cup of tea and I got so engrossed in what I was doing at home that I didn't set out until well after four. If I had been on time she would probably never have left home, and never got hold of the bike, and none of this would have happened.'

'Don't blame yourself,' Tim told her. 'I don't hold you responsible any more than I blame these two for letting her have the bike. It's one of those unfortunate set of circumstances that have combined with very disastrous results.'

The workmen nodded. 'Hope she's alright,' Jimmy added. 'Lovely lady.'

'Yes, we shouldn't have let her have that old bone-shaker, I can see than now,' Sam admitted.

'Never mind about all that. Will one of you kindly see Mrs Bishop home and I'll go straight to the hospital and find out what the news is.'

'I can't go home, I'll come to the hospital with you. Please let me, Tim,' she persisted when she saw he was about to refuse. 'I'll wait in the car but I won't be able to rest until I know that they're both going to be all right.'

It took Tim almost half an hour to ascertain that both his mother and Peter Brown had been admitted less than an hour ago, but he was not allowed to see either of them.

'They are still being assessed,' he was told. 'Come back tomorrow, or phone later this evening and we might be able to give you some news then.'

'The elderly lady is my mother,' he said worriedly. 'I understand that she was unconscious when she was brought in. Is she . . . has she regained consciousness?'

The receptionist frowned, then rather reluctantly she made a couple of phone calls and was able to tell him that Mrs Wilson had not regained consciousness. They had her under constant observation but could tell him nothing more at the moment.

'She doesn't appear to have any broken bones but the man with her has a broken arm and dislocated shoulder.'

Tim wasn't satisfied but thanked the receptionist for all her help.

She smiled kindly. 'Ring later tonight, about eight o'clock. You might get more information then.'

Sally was very concerned when Tim reported the information to her.

'I'll take you home and then try and find out more this evening. I'll phone you and let you know how my mother is as soon as I find out,' he told her as he drove her home.

'You promise you will let me know,' Sally begged as he stopped at her front door. 'Don't worry about what time it is. I won't be able to sleep until I know that she is all right.'

It was late afternoon the following day before Tim came to tell Sally that his mother was fully conscious, but completely unaware of where she was or what had happened.

Peter was also fully conscious. They had set his shoulder and he had his right arm in a plaster cast.

'Can I visit them?' Sally asked.

'Not today. I suppose they might let you see Peter, but when I left, Peter was heavily sedated and they wouldn't let me stay for more than five minutes with my mother as they insist she must have quiet. Try tomorrow.'

Twenty

Betty made a surprisingly good recovery. Apart from some scratches and bruises she was physically unhurt. Peter had taken the brunt of their impact.

The first time Sally visited them in hospital she was amazed at how well Betty looked and how bright she was in herself and how incredibly upbeat she appeared to be.

After saying how sorry she was that Peter had been so badly hurt, she startled Sally by saying what a lark it had been riding down the steep hill on her old bike; that was until her skirt became entangled with the back wheel and the brakes seemed to fail.

She wanted to be at home, and kept repeating a list of all the jobs that needed to be done there.

'You make the most of it while they keep you in here,' Sally told her. 'You are well cared for, have regular meals and no worries.'

'Oh, but I have,' Betty insisted and again repeated all the things she wanted to get back home to do.

'They won't keep you here any longer than they think necessary because they'll need your bed,' Sally told her.

When Sally went to see Peter, it was quite a different story. He was pale and seemed to be exhausted. He complained about the pain in his shoulder and the discomfort in his plastered arm and he never once mentioned going home.

A week later a smartly dressed woman wearing an identity tag around her neck, who told Betty that she was a health visitor, came and asked for her house keys so that she could inspect her home.

'Inspect my house!' Betty exclaimed in an incredulous voice. 'I'm not having you or anyone else poking around in my home while I'm not there!'

'We have to ensure that it is safe for you to go back there; if not, we need to see if there's anything we can install to help you,' the health visitor told her.

Betty remained adamant, but in the end agreed that the woman could visit if she was accompanied by Sally.

Three days later Betty was told that a package had been arranged for them.

'What sort of a package?' Betty frowned.

'A carer who will come in each morning, to help you shower and dress, and one will come in at midday to prepare your meal, and another each evening to help you undress and get to bed.'

'I don't need anyone to do those things,' Betty told her indignantly.

'You may think that you can manage, but you will find when you get home that you tire very easily and will be glad of the help. Mr Brown will certainly need help with dressing both night and morning,' she added as she saw that Betty was about to start protesting again.

Betty's lips tightened and her jaw set aggressively, but she said nothing. She didn't want strangers fussing round in their home but if it was necessary because of Peter's injuries then she'd try and put up with it, she resolved.

The first few days that they were back at home was tortuous to Betty. Three different people came each day and, although she tried hard, she couldn't accept their interference. They didn't do anything the way she liked it done. What was more, they put all the things they used back in the wrong places which irritated her greatly.

For Peter's sake she stuck it out, but when she discovered that he felt the same way as she did about the carers, and that he hated having them there, she decided to take a stand.

'You do realize that it will take me much longer than them to do things for you,' she warned Peter.

'That's all right. I'm not in any hurry,' he told her. 'You'll be gentler than them and not constantly rushing me because you have to get off to the next job.'

'Well, I'll do my best,' Betty agreed, 'but I'm not used to dressing anyone and getting your bad arm and shoulder into your clothes I might hurt you.'

'If you do then I'll stay in my dressing gown all day,' he said complacently. 'What about the shopping though?' he asked after contemplating what life would be like without carers.

'I'll ask Sally if she can do it for us. If not then Tim's wife, Brenda, or my Mary will have to help for a couple of weeks until we are both strong enough to do it for ourselves.'

'They won't like that,' Peter warned.

'If they don't want to do it then we'll get one of them to order our groceries online and have them delivered to the door,' Betty said firmly. 'Probably that is the best thing to do anyway.'

On their own at last, Betty and Peter developed a routine that was more to their liking. They overcame the problem of shopping by getting it ordered for them online and if they had forgotten anything then Sally would always pick it up for them the next time she went to the shops, which she did most days.

Sally found them a cleaner who came in twice a week to wash the floors in the kitchen and bathroom and vacuum the rest of the rooms. This suited Betty fine. She quite enjoyed dusting and automatically plumped up the cushions and straightened the curtains each morning. Peter barely moved out of his chair so he didn't make any mess or cause any untidiness. They adjusted their diet; buying more ready meals. They were utterly content.

Betty seemed to have regained much of her old sprightliness, both physically and mentally. It was almost as if her accident had brought her a new lease of life.

It had the opposite effect on Peter. A month later his shoulder was still so painful that he could barely lift a teacup and his broken arm either had shooting pains or ached.

'I think we need to go back to the hospital, like the surgeon told you to do if you were at all worried, and get you checked out,' Betty told him.

'How are we going to get there?' he asked. 'I can't drive and its too far to walk. Do you think your Tim will take us?'

'I'm not even going to ask him to do so, we'll get a taxi,' Betty said firmly.

Next morning, she phoned the hospital and explained the situation. She was given an appointment but it wasn't for another week.

When the day came, Peter was very shaky walking from their front door down the garden path to the taxi. He sat in the front next to the driver, because it was easier than climbing into the back of the cab.

When they reached the hospital, Betty asked the cabby to wait while she asked a porter to help them get Peter inside. The porter brought a wheelchair and Peter stiffened when he saw it.

'I'm not going to get in one of those,' he protested.

'Oh yes you are,' Betty told him. 'I can't help you and you certainly can't walk all the way to the clinic.'

Scowling, Peter let them transfer him from the taxi to the wheelchair, his face twisted with pain as they did so. Betty went for a coffee while Peter was being examined, X-rayed, and treated. When he was finally ready for home they were told that he needed physiotherapy and would have to attend a clinic twice a week for at least a month.

It was a blow for both of them but Betty tried to make light of the situation as best she could.

'Well, it will be an outing for us each week,' she commented brightly.

'I'd sooner have my outing going out into the garden and digging over the borders and pruning the bushes,' Peter grumbled.

'Well, at the moment you can't do any gardening at all but after you've had a session or two of them manipulating that shoulder of yours then you might well be able to do so,' Betty told him cheerfully.

Peter sighed but said nothing as he looked out of the window shaking his head dolefully at the amount of work that needed doing out there.

Betty mentioned the fact to Tim when he called and he promised to find someone to come in for a few hours each week and sort the garden out.

'I'll come round and take you to the hospital for Peter's treatment, too,' he told them.

'That's good of you, Tim, but there's no need. Once we get there there's always a porter with a wheelchair to help Peter.'

'No, I'll take you,' Tim insisted. 'I won't wait, when he's had his treatment, phone me on your mobile and then I'll come and pick you up.'

'What about if you are with a client?' Betty asked.

'If I am then I'll send one of my staff,' he said firmly.

It was the ideal solution and Betty was more than thankful that Tim had offered. Peter didn't mind Tim helping him into the wheelchair whereas, for some reason, he had resented the taxi driver having to do it.

The treatment was very effective. At the end of the month most of the stiffness in Peter's shoulder had gone and even his arm was no longer hurting, as long as he was careful.

'That means no gardening or lifting anything heavy,' Tim warned.

'I know, I know,' Peter said impatiently.

'Your garden is looking fine, all neat and tidy so sit back, relax and take things easy.'

'It looks OK,' Peter said grudgingly, 'but nobody does things the way you do them yourself.'

'Perhaps they do them better,' Tim said.

'Humph!' Peter muttered, but he didn't pursue the matter. He guessed that Tim was joking but he couldn't bring himself to rise to the occasion and retaliate. It was all right for Tim, he was young, he could still drive his car and do his garden if he wanted to do so. Tim wasn't old and decrepit like he was.

He wandered down the garden to his shed and looked with distaste at the state it was in. The man who came in might keep the garden in order but he certainly didn't bother to do the same with the tools. Spades, fork, hoes and even the shears were all jumbled up in a heap, not hanging on their respective pegs.

Exasperated, Peter began to sort them out. A stab of pain is his shoulder brought him up sharp, and the physiotherapist's warnings about what he could and could not do came rushing back. He flung down the shears in disgust and walked out of the shed, slamming the door so hard that it bounded back open and he had to shut it properly.

That was the last straw, he thought rebelliously. He couldn't even tidy his shed. He walked down to his garage and stared in at his car. It had been sitting there for months now and looked so dejected that he felt sorry for it.

Hearing Betty's voice calling his name, he came out of the garage closing the door quietly behind him. He hoped that she hadn't seen where he was. If he said that the car looked abandoned she might take it into her head to go for a drive in it and he remembered what had happened the last time she'd done that.

Betty could see that, although he accepted the situation, Peter was not happy about someone else doing the jobs outside that he preferred to do himself.

She tried to console him by saying that it would only be a short time now before he could potter out there, but she knew he didn't believe her.

She didn't believe what she was saying either and decided that she would have a talk with Tim, if she could manage to get him on his own and take him into her confidence. She would tell him that the house was becoming a burden to both of them and see what he thought was the right thing for them to do in the future.

Twenty-One

Peter became more and more fractious as time passed and, although his arm and shoulder had both healed, they continued to cause him considerable discomfort.

He couldn't bear to wear a formal jacket and instead opted for cardigans that were light and loose, yet warm for the greatest comfort. Whenever he tried to do anything manually, like lifting, digging, pruning and even mowing the lawn, they were out of the question. The gardener that Tim had found for them was a steady worker but the hours he was doing each week were nowhere near enough to keep everything in order now that spring had arrived.

Although Betty sympathized with Peter whenever he made this point, she always reminded him they really couldn't afford to pay out more for the care of the garden. She always added that if they could afford to spend more on help then she would like to have the cleaner come in more often. Although the house looked to be in order, Betty knew that the beds were never moved out from the wall, or the corners behind the furniture in the sitting room ever cleaned.

Often Betty found that she had to clean the windows herself and use a brush and dustpan to clean the carpet on the stairs. She'd tried to use the vacuum cleaner on the stairs but it was an old cumbersome model, and it was far too heavy for her to manage.

More and more Betty knew that sooner or later they would have to move away from the cottage and street they both loved to a place that was more manageable. She had been aware of this ever since she had discovered that Peter often went up the stairs on all fours because he hadn't the strength in his right arm to use the banister rail to pull himself up. Coming down was equally perilous for him and he was scared of slipping or falling and damaging his shoulder again.

Moving into a bungalow seemed to be the obvious solution

but when she spoke to Tim about it he had looked doubtful. 'There's not all that many on the market but I'll check through our lists and let you know,' he promised.

He brought her a folder of leaflets containing details of all the bungalows on his books. She picked out two that she thought might be suitable but when she showed them to Peter he wasn't interested.

'I don't like bungalows and I wouldn't want to live in any of those,' he told her.

'Then what about turning the dining room here into a bedroom for you to save you struggling to get up and down the stairs?' Betty suggested.

'What, and take our meals upstairs to eat?' he said sarcastically.

'No, of course not.' Betty said crossly. 'We'd eat in the kitchen; there's certainly plenty of room and we already have a table in there.'

'Sit at the kitchen table on a couple of hard wooden chairs, where's the comfort in that?' he asked in a withering tone of voice. 'What happens if someone comes to dinner,' he added when Betty said nothing.

'We don't have folks to dinner any more. I'm not up to doing the cooking. Anyway, who would we ask? If it was Sally then she'd be happy enough to join us in the kitchen.'

'What about if it was your Tim or Mary, or one of their lot,' Peter argued petulantly. 'Or even if they dropped in one day while we were eating our meal.'

'They'd have to take us as they find us. They're family. They'd understand.'

'Perhaps they would but I wouldn't like it,' he muttered.

Betty said nothing, but she carefully gathered up the details and pictures of the bungalows that Tim said were on the market at the moment and put them away. I'll leave it for a few days and then try again, she told herself. He may come round when he's had time to think about it.

Although they both avoided the topic, Betty noticed that Peter seemed to be studying what space there was available in the kitchen. Several times too, when she was busy doing something else in the house, he would be checking out the dining room as if contemplating using it as a bedroom.

A couple of nights later, just after she'd undressed, got into bed and turned the light out, she heard him moving about downstairs. She listened, wondering what he was doing.

Smiling to herself, she pushed back the bedclothes, wondering whether to go down and join him. It might be an ideal time to talk over the idea of them moving. She moved quietly because she didn't want him to hear. She didn't switch on a light, but pulled back her bedroom curtains so there was enough moonlight coming in through the window for her to see what she was doing.

She reached for her dressing gown and went out on to the landing.

To her surprise, there was no light coming from anywhere downstairs. She waited a few moments, then decided she'd been mistaken and that she might as well go back to bed. She had her hand on the door handle and was about to open it when she heard Peter coming up the stairs.

She hesitated. Was it too late now? Had she missed her chance, she wondered. Would it be better to do it in the morning over breakfast?

She decided to leave it for the morning and went back to her room. As she began to take off her dressing gown, Betty saw her bedroom door was very cautiously being opened. She smiled to herself. So he did want to talk about it and he was looking to see if she was still awake. She switched on the bedside light as she didn't want him stumbling over anything and falling.

As she started to speak her words ended in a shrill cry. It wasn't Peter standing there; it was a man in black jeans, black T-shirt and a black balaclava hood hiding his face.

Betty took a deep breath and let out another scream.

'Shut up, you silly bitch,' he snarled in a rasping voice. 'Where do you keep your money and your jewellery. Give us them. Hurry!'

Instinctively, Betty grabbed up the polished wooden jewellery box that had pride of place on her dressing table and clutched it to her. Jeff had made it for her when they had become engaged.

'No, you're not getting them,' she yelled at the intruder.

He grabbed at the box but she clung to it, refusing to let him have it. He was so much stronger than her that he grabbed even more aggressively. Betty heard Peter come into the room and shouted at him to stay away. 'You'll get hurt otherwise,' she warned.

'I'll phone for the police,' he said shakily.

The man let go of the box and grabbed Peter by the scruff of his neck and pushed him hard against the wall.

'You damn well won't,' he snarled and banged Peter's head against the wall again so hard that Peter groaned and dropped to the floor.

The burglar turned back to Betty, who was desperately trying to hide the precious box.

'Oh no you don't,' he spat and tugged at it harder and harder.

The box was at least fifty years old and, although well-constructed, the wooden hinges were fragile from constant use and came away, scattering the contents of the box in a heap onto the floor.

The burglar made a random grab at the rings and necklaces that lay in a pile at their feet, but Betty was having none of it. She grabbed what she could, stuffing them back inside the box. Once again, he grabbed at the box but, even when he twisted her wrist until she screamed out with pain, she refused to relinquish her hold on her precious keepsakes.

She looked round for Peter, but he had managed to crawl away and she heard the ping of the receiver as he replaced the phone in the hall.

The burglar heard it too and the next minute he had abandoned everything and was making for the Betty's window to escape. Betty struggled to stop him, grabbing at his ankles, but he managed to kick himself free and was off before the police arrived.

When Betty tried to straighten her dressing gown and take the curlers from her hair before facing the police, she found she was unable to do so because of the pain in her wrist. It was now very red and had swollen to double its normal size.

When Peter came into the room and said the police wanted to speak to her, she was horrified to see that he had a gash down the side of his face and that his shirt and cardigan were soaked in blood.

'What happened?' she gasped, touching his face very gently with the fingers on her sound hand.

'It was when he hit me,' Peter told her. 'He had a ring or something his hand and it scraped down my face.'

The policeman who was taking down the statement from them took a closer look at Peter's face, then spoke into his mobile.

'I've sent for the paramedics to take a look at that,' he told them.

'You'd better ask them to have a look at Betty's wrist at the same time. She says it's just been twisted by that brute, but I think there might be a broken bone in there,' Peter observed.

The paramedics agreed that Peter might be right and that Betty did have a bone broken in her wrist.

'We're taking both of you in to hospital,' one of them said. 'That wrist needs an X-ray and that wound needs proper attention. They'll probably send you both straight back home,' he added cheerfully.

'We can't be too careful at your age,' the other paramedic told them when Betty protested that she was sure it wasn't necessary.

'I'll have to phone and tell my son,' she stated as they said they were ready to leave and told her to put on the warmest coat she had, although they would wrap them both in blankets once they were in the ambulance.

'Why don't you leave it until after you've been examined rather than disturb him at this time of night,' the paramedic suggested.

'It's three o'clock in the morning, he'll be fast asleep and there is nothing he can do so why not wait until you can give him a full update.'

'Sounds a good idea,' Peter agreed.

'What are you going to do about the burglar?' Betty asked.

'Well, he'll be long gone, but we will have our men looking for him.'

He walked over to the window, slammed it shut and secured it. 'He won't come back here again, so you can rest your mind about that. Where are you going to put that box?' he asked nodding towards the jewellery box that Betty was still clutching. 'Don't forget to go through it again in case there is something missing that you haven't reported.'

'Yes, I'll do that,' Betty promised. 'While I'm out now at the hospital I'll put the box in my bed. An intruder would never think of looking there.'

'Good thinking,' the paramedic said with a smile. 'Come on

then, let's get moving. Are you both able to walk to the ambu-lance or shall I get a chair?'

'We can walk,' Peter assured him. 'You might have to help me down the stairs though.'

'Perhaps you should get them to take a look at that shoulder of yours while you are in A & E,' the man advised when Peter winced with pain as he took his arm to help him walk down the path to the ambulance.

Twenty-Two

The long wait before they were seen by a doctor seemed endless to Peter and Betty after the paramedics had left them in the A & E department of the hospital.

Finally, a doctor came and he attended to Betty first because she was in considerable pain with her wrist, which was now so swollen that they had to cut open the wrist of her nightdress in order to examine it.

While she was having her wrist X-rayed, another doctor attended to Peter's shoulder. He manipulated it, making Peter cry out with pain and finally decided that he, too, ought to be X-rayed.

By the time Tim came to the hospital that afternoon, they had both been told that they were being admitted overnight. Tim was told that a decision about when they would be discharged would have to wait until the next morning.

When Tim talked to his mother and Peter they were both adamant that they did not want carers back helping them once again.

'So how are you going to manage?' Tim asked. 'You won't be able to use your hand, Mother, for several weeks and Peter won't be able to look after you until his shoulder improves. You're becoming regulars here at the hospital, something has got to be done!'

After a great deal of argument, when Tim found that they refused to reconsider their decision, he suggested that in that case they had better go into respite for two or three weeks.

'What's that?' Betty asked with a frown.

'A nursing home. You'll be waited on, no cooking or cleaning to do and I'll know you are safe and well looked after.'

Although neither of them wanted to do this, they admitted that it probably was the best solution, at least for a couple of weeks.

It was a new experience for both of them. They had anticipated that they would be going to the same nursing home and would be able to see each other from time to time, but discovered that this was not possible. Not only were they in separate homes, but they were too far apart to be able to visit each other.

'Never mind, think of it as a holiday on your own and you'll be able to compare notes when you meet up again. Give you something to talk about,' Mary told her mother when she came to visit her.

'Peter will feel isolated, he'll have no one he knows to talk to until then,' Betty said worriedly.

'He's bound to find someone else in there to talk to,' Mary assured her. 'You've found people here to chat to, haven't you?'

'Mm! But I would much rather talk to Peter,' Betty told her.

Betty made the same comment to Tim when he came in to see her, and Tim promised to drop in and see that Peter was settled and to let him know that she was all right.

Although Betty found it was preferable to being at home with carers, she didn't really like being in the nursing home. Their routine was quite strict, they expected everyone to be in the dining room on time for meals and also ready to go to bed at nine o'clock at night, which she found ridiculously early.

A further irritation was that at least once during the night someone came in to see she was alright. Because she was a light sleeper she found that not only did this disturb her, but she couldn't get back to sleep afterwards.

'Stop doing it,' she ordered crossly. 'If I die in the night I'll still be here in the morning.'

'Supposing you don't feel well, wouldn't you like to tell someone about it and perhaps have them bring you a warm drink or something?' the night sister pointed out.

'I have a bell, if I want you during the night I can ring for you,' Betty argued.

The daytime was busy; there seemed to be something happening all the time and although she had her own en-suite room, there always seemed to be someone coming in to check on what she was doing or to make her bed, change her towels, collect her laundry, or open or close the windows.

She ate her breakfast in her own room but she went to the communal dining room for her lunch and evening meal. She had looked forward to this, hoping it would give her an opportunity to meet other residents. There were about twenty people gathered there each day but most of them were very frail or disinclined to talk, and after the first few days she no longer looked forward to meal times, even though the food was excellent.

As she waited between courses, she wondered how Peter was doing in his nursing home and whether, like her, he was at this moment sitting there waiting for the next course to be served and eager to get back to the sanctuary of his own room.

Betty had never expected to miss Peter as much as she did. He wasn't a great conversationalist but he was always there and ready to listen to anything she had to say. It was more than that, she reasoned. There was a happy atmosphere between them, she never felt lonely. He didn't interfere with anything she did in the house; he even left her to choose the meals she prepared and always expressed a favourable comment about them afterwards.

Here in the nursing home, although there was plenty going on around her, life seemed to be empty without him. She couldn't wait for her respite to end and to go home again to Peter's house in Clover Crescent.

On their first evening back at home they talked about their separation and Betty was both surprised and pleased to learn that Peter had missed her as much as she had missed him.

'We won't do that again in a hurry,' he agreed.

'No, and let's hope we never have another burglary,' she said. She was sitting in her armchair with the jewellery box on her lap, checking through the items to make sure that none of them were missing.

'You were right, of course,' Peter admitted, 'we can't go on living here. We need a lot more help, far more than we can afford.'

'So what is the answer?' Betty asked, putting her trinket box to one side and looking at him questioningly.

'I don't really know,' he admitted. 'I certainly don't like the idea of a bungalow.'

'Nor do I, not after what happened,' Betty said quickly. She suppressed a shudder, 'So what do we do?'

Peter shook his head from side to side and Betty was aware of how much older he looked. His hair was thinner and almost completely grey, and there were wrinkles in his clean-shaven cheeks that she had never seen before. The incident with the burglar, and the time they'd spent apart, had certainly taken it out of him, she thought reflectively.

'I'll have a word with Tim,' she promised. 'He's sure to have some ideas.'

'Yes, you do that, but remember I don't want a bungalow.'

'Don't worry, we're both agreed on that point,' Betty said with a wry smile.

Tim looked thoughtful when Betty broached the subject.

'I've been giving it a good deal of thought too,' he told her, 'and I think the answer is sheltered housing.'

'You mean some sort of old people's home?'

'No, not exactly. You buy your own flat but it is in a specially built complex. You have your own front door but in order to get to it the caller has to ring your door number from a panel in the entrance and say who they are. That means you don't get unwanted callers because you know who it is before you even let them inside the building, and if you don't want to see them you simply tell them to go away.

'When you admit them to the reception area they either wait there for you to come out and meet them, or you direct them to your flat and then, and only then, do you answer the door to them. In fact, not even then if you are not expecting them. You can check through a peephole in the door who is actually there.'

'Well that sounds secure enough,' Peter said with a nod of satisfaction.

'If anyone else comes to your door unannounced, for example someone living in another flat in the complex, you could still check if you know them or not by looking through the peephole,' Betty murmured.

'Quite so,' Tim agreed. 'The flat is one hundred per cent safe.'

'A burglar could still come in through the window,' Betty pointed out.

'Highly unlikely because there are outside alarms fitted to the building and connected to your flat and the place is well lighted, inside and out all night.' Tim assured her.

'So where do we find a place like that?' Peter asked.

'There are several nearby and there is one that is adjacent to the high street within a short distance from the shop in the village.'

'It gets better and better,' he agreed. 'Is there a long wait?'

'No,' Tim said slowly, 'they are always coming available. They are for the over-fifty-fives and there's a steady turnover; people die, go into nursing homes and so on. There are both one-bedroom and two-bedroom versions. They are very modern inside and the reception areas and passages and stairs, the windows, including the exterior of the windows to all the flats are regularly cleaned.'

'What about a garden?'

'Ah!' Tim hesitated. 'There is a very nice courtyard garden to all of them but you are not allowed to do anything to it.'

'There is an annual service charge to cover the cost of a professional gardener who comes in regularly to mow the lawn and trim the bushes and trees.'

'You mean you can't even have your own corner?'

'That's right. No pot plants of your own out there,' Tim said firmly. 'No pets either,' he added knowing they didn't have a cat or a dog, and hoping this might soften the blow for them.

'Have to give that some thought,' Peter said. 'Leave it with us for a couple of days to mull over. It sounds a solution though, I must admit.'

For the following week Betty and Peter talked of nothing else. Tim had left them useful details about the size of the rooms and, most important of all, what the flats cost.

'The two-bedroom flats are quite a bit more expensive than the one-bed flats,' Betty pointed out.

'Well, they would be now wouldn't they,' Peter reasoned. 'Probably cost more to heat and light and so on as well.'

'That's true,' Betty agreed. 'One thing we save on is that we don't need car parking, neither of us is fit to drive now.'

Peter looked gloomy when she said this but, as she went on to point out, they could do most of their shopping in the village and if they went by bus to one of the nearby towns a couple of times a month they could pick up all the extras they needed and come home by taxi.

'It will be an outing to look forward to,' she stated.

'Mmm. The taxi fares will eat up whatever else we can economize on. Of course, it would make things much cheaper if we had a one-bedroom flat.'

There was a silence. Peter quickly filled it by saying, 'We could get one those bed settees and we could use it as a settee during the day and I could sleep on it at night.'

Betty looked aghast. 'Oh no you couldn't; that would be dreadful. It might be all right for the occasional night if we had a visitor, but to do it all the time would be like camping out and living out of a suitcase.'

'So what do you want me to do; sleep in the bath?' he joked.

'We could share the bedroom, I suppose,' Betty murmured. 'Twin beds . . .' Her voice trailed off.

'I'm quite happy to do that,' Peter told her. 'I don't think you would like it though!'

'It does go against my principles,' Betty told him mockingly.

'In that case then, shall we get married?' Peter said thoughtfully.

He waited for Betty's adamant refusal and was amazed when, instead of turning the idea down like she usually did, she said, 'Yes, we could do that.'

'Get married?' his mouth gaped in surprise.

The next minute, he was out of his chair and was at her side, taking her hand and asking her formally if she would marry him. 'I can't go down on one knee these days because I might never get up again!'

Betty looked into his eyes; saw the love and eagerness in them as she assented.

His arms went round her, his lips on hers and he was hugging her ecstatically.

'So that means we will be taking a single-bedroom flat, does it?' he said as he released her.

She smiled happily. 'Shall we tell Tim our piece of personal good news first, or tell him we'll take a one-bedroom flat and see the expression on his face when he realizes what we've said?'

'We'll have to think about that,' Peter said with mock severity. 'I don't think we should risk him having a heart attack.'

Twenty-Three

It was almost two weeks before they told Tim that they had decided to go for a one-bedroom flat in one of the complexes that he had told them about.

'A one-bedroom flat?' He looked at them questioningly with raised eyebrows.

'Yes that's right,' Betty told him, the colour flooding her cheeks.

'We're getting married,' Peter added quickly.

Tim started at them in disbelief. 'Well, congratulations. I'm very pleased to hear that,' he said with a smile. 'When's the big day, or have you already sneaked off quietly and done the deed without telling any of us?'

'No, we've been talking it over though for the past week or so. We wanted you to be the first to know, but please don't say anything for a day or two. I'd like to be the one to tell Mary. After that you can tell whoever you like.'

Tim nodded his understanding. 'Let me know if you want to discuss all the implications or me to help you with any of the legalities,' he said rather formally.

Betty looked surprised. 'What do you mean, Tim?'

'Well, there's the date to be settled and where you want the wedding to take place and—'

'We want something quick and simple,' Peter interrupted. 'No fuss, no frills. A quiet wedding at the register office and then a dinner for all the family afterwards.'

'Right, that sounds feasible. You will probably have to change your will, Mother, and you, Peter, will have to see about selling your house in Clover Crescent.'

'Yes, we've talked about the house,' Peter said, 'and about the contents. We'd like to see the flat, or one like it, to decide what we should take and what to get rid of. It's going to mean getting rid of quite a lot of our stuff, I imagine. I'll have to get rid of all my tools and gardening equipment, too,' he added with a regretful sigh.

'Yes, it will be a new start for you both,' Tim agreed. 'Are you sure you're ready for it?'

'We can't afford to go on living at my house and paying out for a cleaner and gardener. A flat sounds the sensible answer and, from what you've told us about security, that's going to be another problem solved. I know they say that a burglar never visits the same place twice, but we're not taking any chances. He mightn't come back but he may tell one of his mates and they might pay us a visit!'

'Right.' Tim took a black leather-bound notebook out of his pocket and began to make a list. 'After you've told Mary we'll start setting things in motion,' he stated. 'Inform the register office and get a date. Check the number coming and book the venue for a meal afterwards. Help you to change all your documents to your new name, Mother.'

'Just a minute,' Peter interrupted. 'First things first. Take us to see these flats you are talking about so we can go inside one even if it is not the one we eventually buy. Then put my house on the market.'

'Wouldn't you sooner do that after you've moved?' Tim asked. 'You don't want people coming to view while you are still deciding what you want to take with you and what you want to sell.'

'It's all a question of money,' Peter pointed out. 'We need to sell the house to buy the flat.'

'Look, it's going to be yours jointly so let Mother put down the deposit.'

Peter looked dubious.

'The flat will be in your joint names,' Tim pointed out.

Peter shrugged. 'You know more about these things than I do, we'll just get into a muddle. You know what the house is worth and I am happy to let you see my bank statements and sort the money side of things out.'

'Stop worrying,' Tim told him. 'That's why I said that I will help you. Buying and selling can be something of a minefield.'

'Well, let's start by taking a look at one of these flats.'

'Right, I'll pick you both up at two o'clock today and take you to see one.'

Tim was as good as his word. The flat he took them to see was in a quiet road off the high street, and the flat was on the first floor. It only had one bedroom but it did also have a balcony.

'That would be big enough to take two or three big pots as well as a chair, or two,' Peter mused.

'Yes,' Betty said brightly, 'that would mean you'd have a garden after all.'

'True, and no hedges or trees to worry about,' Tim commented.

'Well, there is a tree outside,' Betty pointed out to the small tree with wide branches at the edge of the balcony.

'Yes, but you don't have to worry about it or keep it pruned; all that comes under the general maintenance,' Tim told her.

The living room faced south and was bright and sunny and looked out onto the courtyard garden.

'I'd say we were getting the best of both worlds,' Betty murmured. 'A lovely garden to look at, our own flower tubs and a sunny aspect.'

'The bedroom isn't very large,' Tim warned.

Peter and Betty nodded, but they were more interested in the large living room and the outlook from there. Neither the bathroom nor the kitchen had windows and the kitchen was rather small yet beautifully fitted out, in fact far better than the one in Peter's house.

They looked at each other and smiled.

'It seems to be very nice,' Peter commented.

'Is it vacant?' Betty asked, looking round at the various items of furniture and the curtains at the window.

'Yes, it is on the market,' Tim assured them. 'They will be leaving carpets and curtains, the fridge-freezer, the washing machine, the dishwasher, microwave oven, and any of the other items still here that the buyer might like.'

'The price?' Peter mumbled.

When Tim told them, they were both pleasantly surprised. 'There will be plenty left over for our moving expenses and any new items we might need,' Betty said happily.

'Shall we take it?' Peter asked.

Betty nodded. 'I think it will suit us fine. The only problem is how long it will take to sell your house. We can't afford to move until we do, and the people selling this may not want to wait.'

'Don't worry. I've already told you several times, Mother, that I can arrange a bridging loan.'

'Is that very expensive?' Peter asked dubiously.

'No, well within your means. Now, are you going to take it or not?'

Betty and Peter exchanged glances but neither spoke.

'Do you want more time to think about it and talk it over between you?' Tim asked looking from his mother to Peter, and then back again.

'No!' They spoke in unison, both of them smiling and nodding their agreement. 'It's ideal, we couldn't ask for anything better.'

'Good. Then don't worry about selling the house,' he told them as he shepherded them back to the lift.

When they reached the reception area, Tim stopped at the high counter and greeted the smartly dressed woman sitting there. She was in her mid-thirties and had a sleek cut and alert blue eyes. She was wearing a light navy suit with a pretty flowered blouse, and looked very smart and efficient. Betty was glad that she had taken the trouble to put on her best dress and matching coat and that she had persuaded Peter to wear a jacket, even though he still complained that it hurt his shoulders to put one on.

The woman greeted Tim as if she knew him well and he introduced her to his mother and Peter as Chelsea Brownlow. He then explained to Chelsea that they were about to buy the balcony flat on the first floor and that he was showing them around.

'Chelsea is the receptionist here and she will answer any questions you may have after you've moved in. If you have any problems concerning anything inside the building then she will help you deal with it, or find someone who can do so. Chelsea will also take in parcels if you are out or intercept anyone who comes to see you if you are not sure about them. She is a fountain of knowledge about all the social activities that are scheduled and makes sure that this place runs smoothly.'

They stood and chatted to Chelsea for a short while and she was able to tell them a great many things about living there that Tim didn't know about.

Afterwards, instead of walking straight to the front door, Tim took them to another door that opened into a spacious room furnished with easy chairs and low tables.

'This is a beautiful room,' Betty breathed, 'and such a lovely view of the garden.' Peter nodded his agreement then walked round the room, studying the tastefully displayed works of art and pictures strategically placed to enhance the room.

'This way,' Tim told them and guided them towards the far end of the room and into a glass conservatory extension that had double doors leading out into the garden.

'You haven't seen the garden properly, only the view from your flat,' he said as he opened the door and ushered them outside.

They both expressed surprise. The garden was a riot of colour with rose bushes in full bloom, lavender, geraniums, and countless flowers that Betty had never seen before but were both colourful and scented.

'It's bigger than I thought it was,' Peter observed as he studied the lawn edged with paving, the bird bath and the water feature, as well as comfortable wicker chairs, two wooden benches and a number of fancy iron tables.

'You can sit out here on warm days whenever you feel like it, you don't even have to walk to the park.'

'Can we also use the main room whenever we want to sit in there? It would be very relaxing to sit in one of those easy chairs at the conservatory end of the room looking out onto the garden,' Betty asked.

'Yes, you can use the room at any time unless someone has booked it for a private party.'

'What do you mean?' Betty frowned.

'Well,' Tim explained, 'it would be difficult to hold a family party in your living room, wouldn't it. So if you want a family gathering on the occasion of your birthday or something of that sort then you could hold it down here. You can book it for three hours provided it is not booked for any other function, but you have to let Chelsea know in advance and then she puts a notice on the door to make sure people know and won't come in and disturb you. At other times the Community Room is where they hold functions from time to time; like a coffee morning once a week, birthday tea parties, and social events.'

'It gets better and better,' Betty smiled. 'You've done us proud, Tim.' She slipped her arm through his and hugged him as they walked along the many little paths that made up the perimeter of the cleverly landscaped garden.

'Don't say a word anybody, not even to your Brenda, about what we've told you about us getting married. I want to break the news in my own way, and to Mary first of all. You do understand.'

'Of course I do, Mother, and we'll do it whatever way you wish. I am pleased, both by your decision to finally marry Peter, and that you have decided to move here. I am sure that the rest of the family will be happy for you as well.'

'I'm not so sure about that,' Betty said with a sigh. 'That's why I feel it is so important to tell them myself when I think it is the best moment to do so.'

Twenty-Four

Betty had suspected that breaking the news to her daughter, Mary, was not going to be easy, but it was much more difficult than even she had anticipated.

Ever since she'd been a small girl, Mary had had an opposite viewpoint to that of her mother on most things. She had seemed to take a delight in being disobedient and would stamp her foot or sulk at the slightest provocation.

Betty had tried reasoning with her, explaining things in detail, even pleading with her but all to no avail.

In the end, Betty had found that the easiest way to get Mary to do something, or agree with any changes she made, was to approach her through Jeff. Mary had been a daddy's girl and would walk through fire to please him. If he asked her to do something she obeyed with a smile. No matter what the occasion, she was always eager to be in his good books. Betty knew that it was not the right way to go about things, but it was both practical and peaceful to work that way and invariably it was a ploy she used.

Since Jeff's death, Mary had become critical and resentful of everything Betty did that affected the family. She rarely visited her mother and never did anything to help her. Betty tried to shrug off any resentment she might feel over such treatment and to be as tactful as possible if she was doing anything that affected the family.

She was pretty sure that Mary would disapprove of her marrying Peter, but she had no idea of just how resentful Mary turned out to be. Betty understood how she must resent her father being replaced by Peter, but she was shocked at her reaction.

'You're going to marry that awful old man, let him take the place of my beloved father,' she said in a rasping voice, glaring at Betty as if her mother was about to commit a crime. 'How can you bear to be with him? He's grey haired, wrinkled and shambles along as if it's too much trouble to stand upright.'

'Yes, Peter is old and grey,' Betty admitted, 'but then so am I. At the moment he is recovering from not being well, and I must admit he does tend to shamble along but give him a few more months to regain his strength and he will be as upright and as brisk as he ever was.'

Mary made a face and shrugged her shoulders.

Betty bit her lip. She didn't know what to say to placate Mary. In her heart she knew that whatever she said it would be the wrong thing. Mary obviously didn't like Peter, but then there weren't many people that she did like.

'So, when is the wedding?' Mary asked. 'You're not expecting me to be a bridesmaid, I hope.'

'The date isn't finalized yet,' Betty said, ignoring Mary's quip. 'We are going to move into a flat, in that new block just off the high street and we want to finalize the date for that first.'

Mary shook her head. 'You won't like it there. He'll miss the garden and I've heard they're very pokey.'

'I don't agree,' Betty protested. 'We've already decided on the one we want; it has a balcony that is big enough to take reasonable sized pots so we will be able to grow flowers. There's a lovely courtyard garden too where we can sit whenever we want to do so.'

'I suppose Tim has pushed you into buying that. Commission for him when you buy the flat and then more when he sells your house. Good old Tim, always has his eyes on the prize.'

'Tim has been most helpful,' Betty defended.

'I bet he has! He can be quite charming when he is lining his own pocket,' Mary retorted.

'What do the rest of the family think about you marrying Peter Brown?' Mary asked.

'I've no idea what they will think; I haven't told anyone except you,' Betty told her.

'Oh, and Tim!' Mary said caustically. 'He's always the first to know everything, always has been, always will be.'

Betty ignored her remark.

'So, when are you telling the rest of the family?' Mary pressed.

'Well, now that I've told you I don't mind who else knows. It's bound to be public knowledge in due course. I simply wanted to be sure that you were the first to hear about it and that you heard it from me and not from anyone else.'

'I bet Brenda will have plenty to say about it; in case it affects her inheritance,' Mary said waspishly.

Betty didn't answer. She wasn't looking forward to telling Tim's wife about the forthcoming wedding, and she rather hoped that Tim would do it. With any luck he would also tell Graham and his wife, Shirley. She was sure though that her grandson and his wife were modern enough to accept such a happening and barely comment on it. These days, since he had married Shirley, she saw very little of her grandson or of his little daughter, Anna, who would be eight years old in a couple of months' time.

She still had to break the news to her two oldest friends: Sally Bishop and Hilda Marsh.

Sally knew more or less what was going on, and Betty knew she would have her full support. Hilda would be cynical but Betty was sure she would wish her well. Probably both of them would be slightly jealous of the fact that she would now have company for the rest of her life and even envy her the opportunity to move into a modern, easy-to-look-after flat, instead of living in houses as old and decrepit as they were themselves.

Betty decided to invite them both to tea so that she could break the news to them. She told Peter what she was planning to do and he promised to keep out of the way while they were there.

Sally arrived first, her face wreathed in smiles. 'So, you have some special news, have you?' she greeted Betty.

'Yes, but wait until Hilda gets here and then I can tell you both together to save repeating myself,' Betty told her. 'You are looking very summery,' she commented, admiring Sally's light green floral dress.

'It's not a colour I usually go for,' Sally admitted, 'but it was in the sale and I couldn't resist it.'

Before Betty could comment further Hilda arrived. She was the exact opposite to Sally; she was small and nondescript, her grey hair drawn back in a bun, and her face almost devoid of make-up. As usual she was wearing trousers and a white blouse.

'Well?' she said in a disapproving voice. 'What have you been up to now?'

'I'll tell you over a cup of tea,' Betty told her. 'Come along in, Sally is here and you can talk to her while I make the tea.'

She took Hilda through to the sitting room and left the two women together while she went into the kitchen. The kettle was boiling and she already had a tray ready with cups and saucers, sugar, milk and a plate of fancy biscuits.

She carried the tray through, set it down on the low coffee table and then went back for the teapot.

'So why have you asked us both to come and see you at the same time?' Hilda asked, her narrow lips pursed.

'I have some news and I wanted you two to be the first to hear it, outside of the family that is. I'm getting married!'

'Wonderful! Great news,' Sally beamed. She put down her cup and saucer and moved so that she could hug Betty and kiss her on both cheeks.

'Risky step to take at your age, isn't it,' Hilda frowned. 'I thought Peter was ill.'

'He has been but thankfully he is better now.' Betty added, 'It's one of the reasons why we want to get married. I never realized how important he was to me until we were in separate nursing homes. I know he missed me as well.'

Hilda wiped her lips on the silver-edged serviette Betty had given her. 'Well, it's your business, of course, but I wouldn't want the responsibility of taking on an old man at my age. I don't want to end up having to nurse him. Enough to do looking after myself.'

Sally laughed. 'No more long, lonely evenings wishing you had someone to talk to.'

'I'd sooner watch television,' Hilda said. 'When you have only yourself to please you can watch what you like when you like. You'll end up watching football or golf when you would rather watch *EastEnders* or *Holby City*.'

Betty said nothing. She had been so right about their reactions, she thought.

'Another cup of tea,' she asked as both of her visitors seemed to be engrossed with their own thoughts.

'Yes, we'd better make the most of it,' Hilda said. 'I don't suppose you will be able to have us round here for a gossip once you're Mrs Brown.'

'I certainly won't be able to invite you here anymore,' Betty said as she refilled their cups. 'We're moving.'

'Away from Clover Crescent?' Sally exclaimed.

'Away from the village?' Hilda asked.

'No.' Betty found herself smiling at the look of shock in both their voices. 'No, we're moving to one of the flats in that new block that they've built just off the high street.'

'The old people's home,' Hilda exclaimed, her mouth curling in disgust.

'It's not an old people's home, it's a block of fifty individual, privately owned flats and it's for people over fifty-five.'

'Same thing,' Hilda retorted. 'Boxes, all of them.'

'Not at all,' Betty told her. 'They're extremely modern, and practical, and extremely well equipped. The one we've picked has a balcony.'

'Sounds ideal,' Sally said before Hilda could come up with an adverse criticism.

'It is, and there is a lovely courtyard garden where we can sit out whenever we want to do so and, when it isn't warm enough to sit outside, there is the community room which is spacious and well furnished. Anyway,' Betty added as she handed the biscuits around again, 'you'll both be able to judge for yourselves when we've moved in.'

'Are all the family pleased?' Sally asked.

Betty gave a little shrug. 'Tim certainly is, he understands how impossible it is for Peter to keep the garden as he likes it to be. It's all the bushes, hedges and trees,' she explained looking towards Hilda. 'I find I need help with the cleaning as well.'

'You'll still have to keep the place clean if you move into a flat,' Hilda reminded her.

'Yes, but not nearly so much work as it is only half the size. It's got one bedroom, a large living room and dining room combined and a very small kitchen.'

'Sounds very pokey for two people,' Hilda sniffed.

'It sounds ideal to me,' Sally contradicted her.

No wonder I rarely see them both together, Betty thought wryly. They still bicker and fight the same as they did when we were all at school together.

Deciding it was time to break up the party, Betty said, 'I'll see if Peter is awake. He was going to have an afternoon's sleep.'

She went to the bottom of the stairs and called out his name.

'Coming,' he called back. 'Be right with you.'

By the time Peter came down, Hilda was ready to leave. 'Hello Peter, I've heard the news,' she said bluntly. 'Got yourself a good catch.'

'I have indeed,' he smiled, reaching out and taking Betty's hand.

'Well, let's hope it turns out well, seems to be madness to me at your age. Anyway, I must go,' she commented, picking up her handbag.

Betty walked with her to the front door and watched as Hilda scurried off down the road. She was shaking her head from side to side as if disapproving of the news she'd just heard.

Peter and Sally were laughing and talking quite happily, so Betty went out to the kitchen and made a fresh pot of tea and brought in a clean cup and saucer for Peter.

The moment Sally had finished her tea she said she must be leaving. Once again, she congratulated them and said that she thought it was wonderful news.

'Keep me up to date on progress,' she said with a warm smile as she said goodbye. 'I think you'll both be very happy so don't listen to what anyone says. You both know in your hearts that you are doing the right thing.'

Twenty-Five

For the next few weeks Betty had so many other things occupying her time and thoughts that she had no time to worry about the family's reaction to the news of her getting married.

Tim was handling the sale of Peter's house and he was anxious to get the viewings under way while the summer weather still held and the garden was a picture.

'It all helps to sell the place,' he told them. 'I'm sorry about the upset, but it is the only way. I will come myself with any prospective clients and show them around. You won't have to do anything except keep the place tidy and I will always telephone you in advance to let you know when I am bringing somebody around.'

It all sounded so pleasant and so easy, but both Betty and Peter found it excruciatingly difficult to keep silent when people were commenting about their home and garden in a disparaging manner. Some of the comments about how old and shabby the place was hit them hard. It also made them look at their home with fresh eyes.

'I suppose we could replace the three-piece suite,' Peter said. 'It is beginning to look shabby. My armchair is almost threadbare on the arms.'

'But you find it comfortable,' Betty said thoughtfully.

'I know,' Peter agreed, 'but remember; we are moving to a modern flat and this is rather too big for that living room. Perhaps we should sell it and get two matching armchairs.'

Betty nodded. 'If we are going to do that then I'd like one of those chairs that recline and have a footstool that pops up whenever you want to use it.'

When they tried to sell the suite, however, they found no second-hand shop would take it because it was so old that it did not have a fire certificate and was considered a fire risk. 'Without a certificate it is against the law to sell it,' they were told.

'Perhaps we can give it away, to some charity organization,' Betty suggested.

'Not unless it has a fire certificate,' they were told again.

'So what do we do with it?' Peter pondered. 'We can't sell it, we can't give it away.'

'Get the council to come and take it away,' Tim advised.

'What will they do with it?'

Tim shrugged. 'I don't know, burn it probably. It's old, shabby and dangerous; what else can they do with it?'

Betty didn't know, but to her it seemed a dreadful shame. She was sure that some needy family would be glad to have it.

The dining-room suite came to much the same fate.

The table was far too big for the flat they were moving into and the matching dining chairs had padded seats and backs which rendered them unsuitable for resale.

'Never mind, we'll buy either a small round table or a drop leaf one and that will give us more room in the new flat,' Peter promised.

'It looks as though we are going to move in there with all new furniture,' Betty commented.

'Not such a bad thing,' Peter smiled. 'A new start for us in every way.'

Even though she quite looked forward to the prospect of buying new, it still irked Betty when she heard people criticizing items in their home as they walked around the place.

'Take no notice,' Tim told her. 'Very often they are only doing it because they think it will help to make you agree to a lower price than what you are asking.'

'I don't understand that,' Betty argued. 'It's the house they are buying not what's in it.'

'Leave it all to me,' Tim told her. 'Why don't you go out when you know I am bringing people around then you won't hear their comments.'

He said the same to Peter, who was mortified when they made detrimental remarks about the garden he had lavished so much care and attention on.

'I think the sooner we buy the new furniture we need for the flat and move there the better it will be.'

'Yes, it's silly to get upset about what other people think,' Peter agreed.

With Tim's help, they found this was possible. 'Have it

decorated throughout before you move in,' he advised. 'It is not only easier for the men to work in an empty place, but it means that you won't need to have it done again for a few more years, perhaps even longer.'

He also suggested that they had new carpets and curtains; ones which would be more to their choice than those the previous owner had chosen.

When all the work was finished it looked so bright and clean that Betty fell in love with it all over again. They had already ordered their new furniture and a week later it was delivered so they made the move.

Betty had known that it was going to be smaller but the difference was greater than she had imagined. She'd been used to plenty of cupboards, especially in the bedrooms, now she found storage space very restricted.

There was only one thing for it, she decided, and that was to be ruthless with her own wardrobe. She knew she was a hoarder, but now she went through all the clothes she possessed and divided them into two piles; those she wanted to keep and the ones she was prepared to take along to the charity shop.

Once again, Betty was shocked to find that even the charity shop turned down most of them as being too old and too old-fashioned.

'Unless you want them to go for storage the only thing I can suggest is that you put them in the Salvation Army box. There's one in the park. I won't guarantee that they will be able to use them but at least you will have tried to find them a home.'

When she told Peter, he hugged her and told her not to worry, and said that perhaps she should throw them all out and go and buy some new clothes.

'The way we're carrying on I don't think we can afford to do that,' she said grimly.

'Oh, I don't know, according to your Tim we will be able to pay for all the changes we've made and have a nice little nest egg left over once the house deal is completed.'

'I'll believe that when the money is in the bank,' Betty stated. 'We've still got to buy those special flower pots for the balcony and the plants to put in them.'

'That's already done,' he told her.

'When? You mean you bought the pots without letting me see them first?'

'I had to! Tim said that our buyer was about to sign and that once he put pen to paper then everything in the garden was his and I couldn't touch it. I wanted to take some of my favourite plants, ones I knew would thrive in pots, so with Tim's help I got hold of the pots, planted them up and they're safe and sound in Tim's garden until I can move them to the flat.'

'Behind my back,' Betty repeated, but she was smiling and so was Peter.

'You were too busy sorting out your clothes and stuff to be interested in anything to do with the garden,' he smiled.

Although the new carpets and curtains were now in place and also the two new armchairs and dining room pieces, the day of their move was still one of upheaval.

Finding things in the kitchen was the worst. Although Betty had labelled the boxes with which room they were to go in, she hadn't put on labels stating what was in each box.

'Never mind, as long as we can find the kettle and a couple of cups or mugs, we'll manage,' Peter told her as the removal men left.

'Let's do that first; find them, make a brew, and sit in our new armchairs and weigh up what has to be done.'

As they drank their first cup of tea in their new home, Betty felt a glow of satisfaction. Her new armchair was lovely and comfortable, the flat looked clean and sparkling, and the sun was pouring in through the open French doors and shining on the colourful display of flowers in the pots on the balcony.

'Happy?' she asked, looking across at Peer.

'Extremely!' he said, raising his cup of tea in salute.

'Only one hurdle remains and then everything will be perfect,' Betty smiled.

Peter looked puzzled. 'What's that?' he asked.

'The wedding.'

'Aah, I'd forgotten about that. If it's bothering you then let's forget about it,' he suggested. 'I'm quite happy as we are.'

'Living in sin!' Betty tried to look shocked, but she didn't manage it for very long.

'I don't think folks think about it like that these days,' Peter observed. 'Look, if you're worried about all the to-do and fuss then don't let's bother, or else let's just go off quietly on our own and get the deed done.'

'Too late for that now. We've set a date and told all my family when it is. They all assume that they've been invited.'

'Even those who don't approve!' Peter said, the smile on his face softening the scorn in his voice.

'Yes, even them. What I thought was we could book a room at a restaurant or hotel for the meal afterwards. One big table. After all, there will only be nine of us, including little Anna, that's if they let her take the day off from school, and Sally Bishop.'

'Sounds a good idea. What about your friend Hilda, aren't you asking her?'

Betty took a deep breath. 'I suppose I ought to do so but I think she may be jealous when she finds that I have asked Sally to be one of the witnesses. Sally and Tim, you only need two witnesses,' she added by way of explanation when Peter gave a puzzled frown.

'You seem to have it all wrapped up and it looks as though there's nothing you want me to do,' he commented.

'Not at the moment there isn't, but I do expect you to arrange a car to get me there and to bring us back home afterwards from the restaurant.'

'Don't worry I'll attend to that,' Peter promised. 'I'd better cheek first that your Tim hasn't got that all in hand. He's pretty hot on organizing things. Takes after his mother,' he added with a chuckle.

'There's one other thing,' Betty told him. 'You need to get a haircut, I want you looking spruce.'

Peter groaned. 'Must I? Does that mean I am going to have to wear a suit?'

'Of course it does, and a collar and tie and a buttonhole,' she told him with mock severity.

She studied him, he looked so happy and relaxed in his comfortable cardigan and open-necked shirt. So relaxed that even his wrinkles seemed to have vanished.

'I suppose you will be all dolled up in a new outfit,' he stated and his blue eyes seemed to be clearer and brighter than ever as they met hers.

'You'll have to wait and see, won't you,' she said teasingly and was rewarded by a warm smile.

Peter sat deep in thought finishing his tea, then he said, 'What about afterwards? We can hardly call it a honeymoon, not at our age, but do you want us to go away somewhere on holiday?'

Betty looked round their comfortable sitting room and settled back in her new armchair. 'I don't think so. It's so lovely here that I don't want to go anywhere else. All I want to do is come straight back here and get on with our new life. What about you?'

Peter put down his cup, stretched out his hand and took hers. 'This is perfect for me, too,' he murmured contentedly as he squeezed her hand.

Twenty-Six

The actual ceremony was very short and formal. Tim gave his mother away, and the rest of the formalities were completed in next to no time. Tim and Sally Bishop signed as witnesses.

Betty could hardly believe that she was now Mrs Brown as she and Peter drove to the restaurant to preside over the meal to celebrate the fact with the rest of her family.

The meal was excellent. As she looked round, Betty felt proud at how well turned out they all appeared to be. The men were all in smart suits, white shirts, ties and sporting buttonholes. The women all wore smart summer dresses and striking hats or pretty fascinators. Even little Anna had a concoction of flowers entwined around a hairband that looked very pretty with her pale pink floral dress.

Betty herself was wearing a pale lilac dress, teamed with a light jacket in a deeper shade of lilac and a wide-brimmed straw hat in two shades of lilac.

Brenda looked so glamorous in her white dress and hat that when they had entered the restaurant the manager who came forward to greet them had mistakenly thought that she was the bride and escorted her to the top of the table.

He had apologized profusely to Betty when he discovered his mistake, but Betty only smiled and told him not to worry. She was feeling far too happy to let something as trivial as that spoil her special day.

Although Brenda had given in gracefully, and moved from the prominent position at the head of the table, she continued to organize the meal as if she really was the one in charge.

Betty could see that it was annoying Tim so nudged Peter and whispered, 'Take over before she upsets everyone.'

He tried valiantly to do so but Brenda was having none of it. She was enjoying herself, issuing orders to the waitress, saying what wines they would have, and generally taking charge.

Tim eventually intervened. He ordered champagne and at the

end of the meal he asked who would prefer port to a liqueur, completely ignoring his wife's attempted intervention.

He even quietly murmured to his sister, 'Mary, I think you have had enough to drink,' when he saw her motion to the wine waiter to refill her glass for the fourth time. Mary's eyes were shining, her face was flushed and she was chattering so loudly that no one else could be heard. Betty was glad that they had a private room. She was sure Mary had drunk far too much and she suspected she wasn't used to drinking so much wine.

It was good to see her so happy and relaxed but Betty could see, just as Tim could, that one more glass of champagne would send her right over the top.

Betty had also become very aware that her grandson, Graham, and his wife, Shirley, were highly amused by what was going on, which was another reason not to let Mary become too inebriated.

The family were very surprised when they learned that Betty and Peter were not going away afterwards, but returning to their new flat.

'We love it there,' Betty told them, 'so why go away and stay at a hotel.'

'Celebrating! Change of scenery. You've got the rest of your life to live there so take the opportunity to have a super holiday.'

Betty shook her head and smiled at Peter. 'We're very happy there, aren't we?'

'Absolutely perfect,' he confirmed. 'We've the most beautiful balcony to sit out on, comfortable chairs in the living room, a bed that suits us, and we know where everything is. We can do what we like when we like. We don't have to stick to a time table and if we want to go anywhere we know exactly how to get there, and we can understand what everybody says.'

'Take the opportunity to travel while you are still fit enough to do so,' Graham admonished.

'Go on a cruise,' Shirley prompted. 'I know I would, given half a chance.'

Prompting and banter went on during most of the meal, but Peter and Betty remained unmoved. They'd already talked the matter over and they knew exactly what they wanted to do.

'Perhaps next year, when the novelty of living in our flat has dimmed a little we might think about a holiday,' Peter told them, bringing the matter to a close.

'In that case,' Tim said, as the dessert plates were cleared and coffee and liqueurs served, 'can we have the speeches?'

'There wasn't a best man, so who is going to make a speech?' Shirley asked. 'I know Graham has made some notes,' she added pointedly.

Embarrassed, Graham stood up and made some complimentary remarks about how Peter had helped his grandmother after his grandfather had died and how pleased he was to welcome him into the family.

Tim followed with glowing tributes to his own father and to Peter and the hope that his mother would be happy with her new husband.

Betty felt a wave of relief sweep over her as Peter thanked them all for coming and welcoming him so warmly into their family. Surely now, she thought, the event was over and she and Peter could go back to their new flat and relax.

Peter looked tired and, although he was smiling, she was sure that, like her, he wanted quiet and rest. She was dying to take off her new shoes which were pinching and rest in her comfortable chair. That, she soon discovered, was out of the question.

As the staff helped them into their coats, Tim announced, 'I'll take Mum and Dad in my car and you can follow us, Graham.'

'Where are we going?' Mary asked.

'To Mum and Peter's flat, of course,' Tim told her. 'I have all the wedding presents in the boot of my car.'

'You take Aunt Mary in your car, Graham,' he said, 'and I'll take Sally in mine.'

'You don't have to come back,' Betty protested with a smile. 'It's been wonderful being all together but I feel we have already taken up too much of your time.'

She waited hopefully but it was pointless. They all insisted that they wanted to see the flat and also wanted to see the wedding presents.

'It will be rather a squash,' she warned them but no one took any notice.

On the drive home Betty worried about whether she had

enough cups to go round, whether they would want tea or coffee and where would they all sit. She knew she was being selfish but she was tired and she didn't like the idea of their flat being invaded by so many all at once.

As she had thought, there were really too many people for such a small space. Anna bounced on Peter's new chair, Mary put the foot rest up and then put it down half a dozen times, and the men stood in a cluster on the balcony.

'Tea or coffee?' Betty asked.

'Oh tea, of course,' Mary said. 'Where are the cups, shall I put them on a tray for you?'

Betty switched on the kettle. She wasn't sure how many tea bags to put in the teapot, she'd never entertained this many people before. She remembered the old saying, one for each person and one for the pot, but decided that if she put that many in there would be no room for the water.

She took a chance and put in four. She could always make a fresh pot if this didn't work, she thought.

She felt very flustered and when the kettle boiled her hand was shaking so much that she had difficulty pouring the water into the teapot.

'Can I do that for you, Gran,' Graham offered. Reluctantly, but very grateful, she put the kettle down and stood back so that he could do it.

'Why don't you go and sit down,' he suggested. 'Shirley will help me.'

'I must find the biscuits first,' she protested.

'Biscuits! No one wants biscuits after what we've eaten today,' Graham told her with a chuckle.

'I do, I want a biscuit, a chocolate one,' Anna protested.

'You go and sit down and behave, and then you can have a piece of the wedding cake,' her mother told her.

'Wedding cake? I haven't got any,' Betty apologized, her face turning red with embarrassment.

'Don't worry, we've brought one with us,' Brenda told her. 'It's on the table along with all your presents.'

'I'll help you open all your presents,' Anna told her.

'You'll go and sit down and be a good girl,' Brenda ordered.

'I want a drink, a glass of milk,' Anna stated.

'I'll see to it,' Shirley offered. 'Where do you keep the glasses, Grandma?'

Once again Betty felt waves of panic sweeping over her. There were so many people, so much to do and all she wanted was some peace and quiet and time to reflect on what had been happening that day.

The afternoon seemed to go on forever. Opening the presents took another hour and Anna was more hindrance than help in unwrapping them. She tore off the paper so quickly and tossed them aside that Betty was afraid she would never remember who had given her what.

'Don't worry,' Tim said quietly. 'I have a list and we can go through it tomorrow or sometime when you feel like it.'

She smiled at him gratefully. She didn't know how she and Peter would have got through the day without him. He seemed to think of everything and he seemed to be able to bring control to the most confused scene.

The presents were all lovely and very practical but Betty did wonder where she was going to find space for the new tea set, the matching dinner service and the set of assorted glasses.

Anna gave them a furry dog and she told then that it was a guard dog to keep them safe.

'I know you can't have a real one,' she said stroking and hugging it, 'so this is a toy one instead. Can I come and see him and play with him, Granny Betty?'

'Of course you can, whenever you like,' Betty told her.

'Every day?' Anna asked.

'No, of course you can't come every day,' Brenda told her sharply.

Anna looked at her grandmother and pulled a face. 'I'm going to ask Daddy if I can,' she said stubbornly.

'You can come whenever she has time to bring you,' Betty intervened, as she saw tears flooding into Anna's eyes. 'Don't worry, Granddad Peter and me will take great care of him, I think he is lovely. Has he got a name?'

'Of course he has,' Anna said indignantly, scrubbing at her eyes with the back of her hand. 'His name is Woof Woof.'

'Oh, we'll have to remember that,' Betty told her and was relieved when Anna nodded happily. Betty suspected that although she was almost eight years old she didn't really want to part with the toy dog.

Finally, they all said their goodbyes and wished them well for the future. Betty and Peter thanked them all for coming and for their presents. One by one they left, Anna making a great fuss of Woof Woof before she exited.

Betty wondered if she ought to suggest that she took it home with her, but decided that would probably bring a sharp reprimand from Brenda. In a few weeks' time she could probably ask Anna to look after Woof Woof so that the child could have the dog back.

When they had finally gone, Betty went into the kitchen to clear up but she found it had already been done for her. Everything had been washed, dried and piled up on the worktop so all she had to do was put them away.

'Leave that, my dear,' Peter said, taking off his tie and undoing the top buttons of his white shirt. 'Come and sit down. I feel shattered so I am sure you must be weary as well.'

'Yes, it's been a wonderful day,' Betty agreed, 'but all I want to do is take my shoes off, put my feet up and enjoy the peace and quiet of being on our own.'

'And nod off for half an hour like I am going to do,' Peter smiled.

He waited until she had sat down and then gently removed her tight shoes and massaged her feet.

'Now, have a little sleep,' he told her, as he kissed her softly and moved away to his own chair.

Twenty-Seven

Betty and Peter had a very quiet time the following week. The excitement and so many people fussing around them had left them both exhausted.

They took their time over everything, did the minimum amount of shopping possible and spent most of the day sitting out on their balcony enjoying the September sunshine.

The days were already getting shorter and very soon the flowers would be fading as the colder weather took over. Betty didn't like the short days and long dark evenings of winter, but here was still the last few days of summer and the prospect of a colourful autumn to follow.

When winter does get here, she consoled herself, I have the most comfortable chair in the world to sit in, Peter for company, and the television and radio to enjoy.

Yes, life was good, she told herself, and now that she had adjusted to the size of the flat and the close proximity of living there with Peter she was really appreciative that they had made the move.

As Christmas approached, she was even more happy to be in their cosy flat. It was easy to keep it warm and with its well-fitting door and windows there were no draughts or cold spots, no matter how hard the winds were blowing or how low the temperature was.

Then, a week before Christmas, they had snow. It wasn't very deep but it made the pavements icy and treacherous.

Peter insisted on doing the shopping and Betty didn't argue. She hated walking in snow. Nevertheless, she did decide to venture out because she had her heart set on buying a bottle of special single malt whisky for Peter as a Christmas present, and it would be no surprise if she asked him to buy it.

She waited until Peter was having his afternoon nap, then wrapped herself up warm and put on her fur boots.

'You'd think I was planning an Arctic trip instead of simply going across the road,' she told herself aloud as she looked in the mirror before leaving the house.

The pavement outside the block of flats had been treated with salt and was reasonably easy to cross, but when she reached the stretch of pavement outside the store it was a different matter. So many people had walked along it that the snow had turned to slush and as the temperature had dropped it had iced over, and walking on it was very tricky.

Betty knew she was walking like a crab, afraid to put one foot in front of the other, but inwardly she was pleased at the progress she was making.

Then, when she was within almost touching distance of the door, her feet went from under her and she struggled to stay upright. Instead, she felt herself sliding, and although she put her hand out to save herself, she slid, crash landing with one foot twisted underneath her.

She lay there for a couple of seconds, her face resting on the frozen slush, afraid to move because her foot was throbbing and she didn't know how to get up. If she could only use one foot then would she manage to stand up without falling again, she pondered.

Before she could determine what to do, she felt a pair of strong hands grab the top of her arms.

'Relax and I'll soon have you on your feet again,' a deep voice told her.

She turned her head but all she could see were two dark brown eyes peeping out from a black balaclava hood.

Memories of the burglar when she'd been living at Clover Crescent flashed through Betty's mind, filling her with terror. Had he come back? Her mind swirled. Where was she? What was she doing on the ground and why was it so hard and cold. Had he pushed her over and was that why she was lying on the ground, she wondered in panic.

She tried to struggle but she had no strength, no option but to do what he told her. Her body slumped. She felt his hands move from the top of her arms to her waist. She wanted to call out for help but, although she opened her mouth, no sound came out.

She closed her eyes and gave in. The next minute she was

on her feet and several other hands were supporting her; brushing the slush from her coat, picking up her shopping bag and offering to see her home.

In a shaky voice she thanked them all and looked round for the man in the balaclava but he had already gone on his way.

Someone came out from the supermarket with a glass of water and said if she would come inside she could sit down until she felt better.

Betty nodded gratefully as several people began to help her in through the automatic doors and one of the staff brought over a chair for her to sit on.

She sipped at the water and slowly her feeling of panic ebbed away, she was able to breath normally and once again she thanked everyone round her for their help.

As one by one they drifted away she handed the glass back to the assistant, who had remained with her, and told her what she had come in to buy.

'You sit there and I'll get it for you,' the girl told her, taking the notes that Betty held out. 'Let me have your shopping bag and give me time to put on my coat and I'll walk you back to your flat,' she told Betty.

'Won't you get into trouble with your boss if you do that?' Betty asked.

'Not at all. You are one of our regular customers and I've seen you and your husband in here many a time.'

'Well, thank you very much, I would be grateful. It would be terrible if I dropped the bottle and it broke! I want it as a Christmas present for my husband,' she added with a warm smile.

Betty's wrist was aching. When she pulled up her left trouser leg a little way and started to unzip her boot to find out why her ankle was hurting so much, she was worried when she saw that it had swollen up to double its usual size.

She quickly pulled her trouser leg down over it when she spotted the girl returning. She didn't want to make any more fuss. She'd wait until she got home and then take another look at it. Probably a cold compress on it would soon take the swelling down and ease the pain.

'Give me your arm and let me carry your shopping bag,' the girl said.

'Are you going to tell me your name?' Betty asked.

The girl smiled. 'It's Lucy, Lucy Peterson.'

'Well, I am most grateful to you, Lucy. I feel rather shaky,' she said as they went through the doors into the street. 'Look, can I take hold of your arm instead of you holding mine. I feel safer that way.'

As they moved off down the street Betty tried to keep up with Lucy but it wasn't easy because every step she took was painful.

'Do you think you could walk a little slower,' she asked breathlessly.

Lucy walked Betty right to the door of the flat but wouldn't accept an invitation to come in.

'Sorry, but I must get back,' she explained. 'Another time perhaps,' she said with a smile as she handed over the shopping bag with its precious contents to Betty. 'Have a nice Christmas.'

'I will now,' Betty smiled as she took the bag from her. 'A very Happy Christmas to you, Lucy, and thank you for all your help.'

Betty closed the door behind her then peeped into the sitting room. Peter was still asleep. He had raised the footstool on his chair and was reclining back, looking relaxed. Betty stood there watching him for a moment, thinking how lucky she was and what a wonderful companion he was.

As quietly as possible she went into the bedroom and she squirrelled the bottle away in the bottom of the wardrobe, smiling to herself at the thought of how pleased he would be when she gave it to him on Christmas Day.

As she took off her bedraggled coat the pain that shot through her ankle was like a knife turning. It hurt so much that she had difficulty getting her out of her coat. When she did get it off, she sat down on one of the dining chairs. Seeing once again how swollen her ankle was, she felt alarmed.

She'd known it was swollen when she'd tried to look at it in the supermarket but now it was far worse. So was the pain. Every time she moved her foot tears sprang into her eyes.

She was going to have to tell Peter about it, she'd have to get some treatment. Perhaps it would be better to tell Tim and ask him to take her to hospital. If she did that, though, she'd have to tell him that she'd been out and he'd already warned her not to do that.

She'd have to tell both Tim and Peter how foolish she'd been, so perhaps the best thing was to ring for an ambulance.

She was downstairs still sitting on the dining chairs when Peter woke up.

'What are you sitting there for?' he asked. 'What's wrong with your armchair?'

'Nothing. I was—'

He stared at her. 'What's happened. Why are you crying?'

'I'm not crying,' she protested as she rubbed at her eyes.

'Something is wrong. What have done to yourself,' he said, bringing his chair into an upright position and coming across to her.

He noticed her swollen ankle and went to touch it, but she let out a scream which made him move back instantly.

As he did so he noticed the state she was in. 'Have you been outside?' he asked, his forehead creasing into a frown. 'Whatever for?' he demanded before she could answer. 'I bought everything we need this morning.'

'There . . . there was something I needed,' she said lamely.

'Then why didn't you ask me to go for it?'

'You . . . you were asleep.'

'If you were in such a hurry then why didn't you wake me up,' he said in a bewildered voice.

He looked at her again and noticed the mud and wet of her skirt. 'You've been out to the shop and you've fallen over,' he said accusingly.

'Yes, but I'm all right,' Betty said defensively.

'Are you? Then why are you holding your foot off the ground like that?'

He went to touch it again but she pulled away. 'Don't. It hurts.'

Going down on his knees he gently examined it, letting out a low whistle when he saw how swollen it was.

'You need to get this X-rayed,' he said in a worried voice.

'I was about to ring for an ambulance,' Betty told him.

'I'll do it.'

She heard the concern in his voice as he spoke to someone on the phone and heard him say, 'She's almost eighty, can you hurry?'

It was almost an hour before the ambulance arrived. Peter made a cup of tea and suggested she should take a painkiller.

'I don't think I had better do that, if I am going to hospital,' she told him.

'You're in pain,' he pointed out.

'I'll grin and bear it. It's not so bad if no one touches it.'

The X-ray revealed that nothing was broken but it was very badly strained. Betty was warned she must keep her foot elevated and walk on it as little as possible for the next week or more, until the swelling was gone down, then they would check again to see if she needed any physiotherapy treatment.

'It will probably be weak for quite some time so you may find you need the support of a walking stick for a few months,' she was told.

She wasn't admitted, so Peter wondered how they were going to get home. He couldn't decide whether it was best to ring for a taxi or phone Tim and ask him to come and collect them.

'I think it is probably best to ring Tim because you will need someone, as well as me, to help you from the car to the flat at the other end,' he said at last.

He made the call on his mobile. 'He'll be here in about twenty minutes,' he told Betty. 'Let's go and have a cup of tea in the restaurant. I've told him that's where we will be.'

'I'm not sure that I can walk that far,' Betty said hesitantly.

'Wait here then. I'll get a wheelchair and take you there in that, and we can use it to take you out to Tim's car when he arrives.'

Twenty-Eight

It was the quietest Christmas that Betty had ever known. She had made no special preparations whatsoever. She hadn't bought any presents, she hadn't put up any decorations.

It didn't matter because, as far as she knew, there would be no visitors. Tim and Brenda were going to Paris for the holiday, Mary was going to stay with friends and Sally and Hilda would both be with their own families.

She had sent Christmas cards to the family, to Sally and to Hilda but they were not of her choosing; they were a packet that Peter had bought at the supermarket.

Shirley had sent a message to say she would be sending Graham round on Christmas morning with their Christmas dinner. She had invited Betty and Peter to come to them for the day but Betty had declined because she felt she was so clumsy and she didn't want to be in the way.

The only other bright spot on Christmas Day was that Betty was able to give Peter the bottle of whisky she had bought for him.

He looked at it with a smile in his face. 'This is very special,' he told her. 'I shall never forget the story behind it.'

'Neither will I,' Betty said wryly. 'By the look of things, I will still be hobbling about next Christmas.'

'No, you won't,' he told her. 'Another couple of weeks and you'll find that ankle is as good as new.'

'I certainly hope so,' she said fervently. 'I hate seeing you do all the shopping and cleaning.'

'Well, I won't be doing any cooking today, that's for sure.' he said with a broad smile when Graham arrived with plates of turkey, roast potatoes, sprouts and all the trimmings that made a social repast. To follow, there was a serving of Christmas pudding for each of them, together with a carton of double cream and mince pies to follow that, or for them to have later on in the day.

'I will probably sleep all afternoon,' Peter said as he regarded the piled-up plates. 'It looks good and smells great,' he added, sniffing appreciatively.

'I hope you enjoy it. I can't stop, Shirley wants to dish up ours,' Graham said as he made a hasty exit.

They enjoyed their meal and then, as he had warned, Peter fell asleep. Shortly afterwards Betty did the same.

When they woke up it was four o'clock so Peter made a pot of tea and they ate the mince pies that Shirley had sent over for them.

'I don't think we will need anything else to eat today,' Betty murmured as she brushed some crumbs from the front of her dress.

Early in January they had more snow, so they took a taxi to go to the hospital for Betty's check-up.

'It's coming along nicely, all the swelling and inflammation has gone, so I think you can start putting some weight on it. I am giving you some crutches. Take your time, practise using them at home before you go out, and don't rush things. You still need to keep the foot elevated when you are sitting down.'

Once they were home Betty wanted to try out the crutches but Peter persuaded her that she'd been on her foot enough for one day.

'You can't go outside on them until the snow has cleared so there is no hurry,' he told her.

Three days later Betty tried them out. She didn't go far, just a short distance up the road and back again, with Peter at her side, fearful that she might fall because she was so wobbly.

At first, she used them alternatively, as though they were a pair of sticks, but after a little practice and under Peter's guidance she could use the two together to take her weight and move her forward.

'Only put the tip of your toe down on the ground to help you keep your balance,' Peter warned. 'The crutches are intended to help you take the weight off your ankle.'

It was almost two months before Betty felt confident. Winter was almost over and weak spring sunshine was brightening their days. As Peter watched her hobbling down the road he was afraid she might do more damage than good to her ankle, which still ached when she walked too far. In the end he suggested that she might like to try using a Rollator.

'A Rollator? What's that?'

'A three-wheeled trolley, some people call them a walker,' he told her.

'Oh, I've seen people using those and I always feel sorry for them. They look as though they've got a small pushchair and forgotten to put the baby in it. How long do you think I'd have to use it if we do get one?'

'Until your ankle feels stronger. You will know when the time is right and then you can go back to using your stick,' he told her. 'It might be worth giving it a try,' he suggested. 'We could hire one, then, if you didn't like it, we could take it back. It would have a shopping bag on it,' he pointed out. 'So it would be very useful when we went to collect groceries,' he persisted when he saw she was reluctant to do as he suggested.

Finally, Betty agreed to try one out and, to her surprise, she found it was much easier to use than the crutches but it gave her as much, if not more, support. The fact that she was evenly balanced with a hand on both handles was a great asset.

Peter encouraged her and, as her confidence grew, decided they ought to buy one for her.

Whey looked at the price Betty shook her head. 'It's not worth paying that much when in a couple of months' time I will be able to walk with no help at all or perhaps just a walking stick,' she stated.

'Nevertheless, it would be useful for you to use when the weather is bad and the roads are a bit slippery, or when we wanted to go shopping to save me having to carry heavy bags.'

They were still arguing about whether or not to buy or hire when Peter saw one outside a charity shop. The price was only a quarter of what they would have to pay for a new one and worked out far better than if they hired one.

He took Betty along to see it and they studied the trolley very carefully. It looked to be in reasonably good order so they decided to buy it. When they got home, Peter adjusted the height to make it more comfortable for Betty and the next time they went out she used it and declared she was quite satisfied with it.

It gave them both a new lease of life; Betty had found walking to the park was too arduous on her crutches but pushing the walker she found it was a pleasant stroll. Once more it was a pleasure for both of them to go out and enjoy their favourite walks. The only drawback was that, even though she seemed to have no problem walking, Betty was rather slow and Peter found that restricting himself to her pace made his back ache.

He tried to ignore the discomfort but it didn't take Betty long to spot that something was wrong.

'Are your shoes hurting you, or have you sprained your ankle now?' she asked when several times he put a hand on the handlebar of the walker as if to give himself some support.

For a while he managed to make excuses but finally, when he was finding that he could no longer stand the back ache, so much so that he didn't want to walk with her, he confessed as to what was wrong.

'Why ever didn't you say so before,' she muttered.

'I like going out with you to the park and so on,' he told her.

'Well, I can't walk any faster than I do but we can still have our outings. You walk at your own pace and I'll catch you up.'

Peter looked dubious but, in the end, he agreed and for while it seemed to be the perfect solution.

The first mishap came when Betty made a short cut when she was meeting Peter by the pond in the park. The route she took ended in a steep little path down to the edge of the pond. As she started to go down it Betty applied the brakes of the walker and then found that nothing was happening. No matter how hard she tried she couldn't make the brakes work. In the end, she let go of the walker and let it make its way straight into the pond while she remained stranded halfway down the path.

Peter was sitting on one of the park benches by the pond and was alarmed when he saw the walker rush past him followed by the splash as it ended up in the pond.

For one heart-stopping moment, as he saw a blue cardigan on the surface of the water, he thought Betty was in there with it.

His relief when he heard her voice calling out to him to come and help her down the hill was so great that, for a moment, he couldn't move. He found it was difficult to breath because his heart was thudding like a sledge hammer.

He looked at the walker, which was slowly sinking and then at Betty stranded on the hill and, not for the first time, realized that she was the most important thing in his life.

Once he had helped her down the hill and settled her on the

park bench he went over to the pond to see if there was any
chance of recovering the walker.

By the time he reached the edge, a youngish man had already
fished it out. It looked intact but the contends of the shopping
bag on the front of it was soaked and sodden.

The man who had rescued the walker was studying it with a
frown on his face.

'Those brakes need attention, mate,' he said as he handed the
walker over to Peter. 'They're perished. Get them done before your
missus has another accident or next time she might be the one
who's perished!'

Peter nodded. He felt too shaken to discuss the state of the
walker but he knew what the man was saying.

'We'll get rid of that thing, it's a death trap,' he stated when
they reached home.

'Oh no we won't. It's a great help to me,' Betty told him

'We're getting rid of it before you have another accident. You
could have ended up in the pond, don't you realize that?'

'Only if I'd tried to keep up with it,' she laughed. 'The moment
I knew it was running away with me and the brakes weren't
working I let go of it.'

'Thank heavens you did. Even so, it's going. That's the second
near accident you've had with the damn thing.'

'Second?' Betty frowned and looked puzzled.

'What about the day it folded up on you and if I hadn't been
walking at your side and managed to grab your arm you would
have ended up on the ground and probably smashed your face in.'

'That was partly my own carelessness,' she said, her colour
rising in embarrassment. 'I forgot to make sure it was locked after
I'd folded it so that I could get past a car that was parked on the
pavement.'

'Yes, and that could happen again at any time, there's always
obstructions on the pavement with all the advertising placards the
shops stick outside as well as parked cars.'

'Then why don't you start a campaign to make them stop
doing that,' she said spiritedly. 'It would be a much better idea
than depriving me of my walker and plenty of other people would
benefit as well as me.'

Twenty-Nine

Peter couldn't sleep. Over and over again, the thought of what could have happened to Betty that day went through his mind. He was determined to get rid of the walker, but how was he to do that without depriving her of the means of getting around.

He went over in his mind what might be possible. He didn't think a walking stick was enough support. She didn't need to use crutches, and anyway he was sure she wouldn't go back to using them, so what was the answer?

He woke up the next morning with the perfect solution: an electric scooter.

He said nothing to Betty, but the first thing he did after breakfast was to search the web to find out what was available. There were many types, but they were all expensive. Perhaps hiring one would be the best, at least until he knew she was going to be happy about using it. She had driven a car, he told himself, so it should be second nature. Then he remembered her car accidents and he wasn't quite so confident.

Still, he told himself, this was quite different and if he bought her a scooter then he would make sure that it was one that she could only use on the pavement, so that it wouldn't be powerful enough for her to do any damage.

Perhaps he ought to have a word with Tim first of all, or with young Graham. They might have more knowledge about how safe such vehicles were. There was such a variety he was bewildered. He didn't think a two-wheeler was the answer, because she would need to balance one of those, but whether a four-wheeler was safer than a three-wheeler, well, he wasn't sure.

The three-wheeler looked more manoeuvrable and that was important because of the size of their flat and because she would need to get it in and out of the lift every time they went out. He was wishing now that they had taken a flat that had a garage space, then there would be no problem about storing it when they were at home. The only place he could think of where they could keep it was on the balcony.

There seemed to be an awful lot of problems to overcome but he was sure it would be worth it once they found the right vehicle for her.

Tim seemed to be very knowledgeable when he mentioned it to him. 'Make sure it is a Class 2, that is one that can only be driven on the pavement and has a maximum speed of four miles an hour. We don't want to risk her taking it on the road. You won't have to register it but be very careful about buying a second-hand one. If you do, then do make sure it has been well maintained and that the brakes are in good working order before you let Mum use it.'

'I wondered about hiring one first to make sure she wants to use one,' Peter told him.

Tim frowned. 'Why don't you take her along to one of the big garden centres or one of the supermarkets where they have mobility scooters for customers to use, then you can see how she copes with one of those?'

Peter nodded his thanks. 'Good idea.'

When he put this suggestion to Betty she was quite scornful. 'I don't need to try out one of those. I drove a car most of my life, I know how to steer and control a vehicle.'

'Right, then in that case we'll go ahead and buy one.'

'Do I really need one? I'm sure I can manage with my walker.'

'It's for my benefit as much as yours,' he told her. 'You know that walking at your pace gives me backache. Well, if you had an electric scooter that will do up to four miles an hour, then I could walk along with you.'

'Can you walk that fast these days?' she asked with a teasing smile.

'Well, we'll soon find out and if I can't then you can be the one going slower, but at least it won't give you backache.'

Once the idea had taken hold, Betty couldn't wait for the vehicle to arrive.

Peter was afraid it mightn't live up to expectations, but when the three-wheeler was finally delivered, and he saw the pleasure on Betty's face, he felt it was worth every penny of what it had cost.

Betty wanted to go out on it right away but Peter was more cautious. 'Let's leave it until the morning and wait until the children have all gone to school and the pavements will be quieter.'

'You have to go to the doctors first thing tomorrow morning,' she reminded him.

'Yes, but it's only for a blood test so that won't take long and we can go for a run on it the minute I get back.'

Betty nodded but she was already scheming in her head. She'd go down to the surgery on it in time to meet him coming out and that would prove to him that she was quite capable of handling it.

It was a lovely sunny morning and the minute Peter had left the house Betty manoeuvred the scooter out from the balcony, through the living room to the front door, then along the corridor to the lift. The scooter had been on charge all night, so there was no worry about how far she could go, so she decided to go into the high street first and then onto the doctors.

At first, she found it a bit scary at how light a touch she needed to make in order to accelerate but the brakes were good and after a slightly erratic stop-start she was on her way. The steering was a little stiffer to manoeuvre than she had expected but it was manageable. At least it was until she reached the newsagents. She thought she had swerved far enough away from the paper stand that was outside the door to avoid it but one of her back wheels caught in one of the legs of the stand. Suddenly there was an ominous crash as the stand came down and newspapers scattered everywhere.

For a moment, she wanted to accelerate away but she was too late. The newsagent was outside his shop, waving his arms in despair as he saw the newspapers scattered in all directions on the road.

Passers-by stopped to help pick them up but a great many of them were dirty, soiled and crumpled and so unfit for sale.

Betty felt like crying but, remembering that it was better to attack than be attacked, she reprimanded him for having his stand jutting out on the pavement and making it difficult for pedestrians.

'Pedestrians manage all right,' he shouted back. 'I've never had anyone complain before. It's that contraption you are driving. Motor vehicles should be on the road not on the pavement.'

'This vehicle is not allowed on the road,' Betty retorted. 'It is designed to be driven on the pavement. You are the one at fault because your stand is taking up too much room on the pavement.'

They were sill glaring at each other when Tim appeared. His estate agency office was only a few doors further down the road and he had been on his way to buy a newspaper at the shop before he started work.

He quickly took in what had happened as he saw the state the papers were in, and was trying to apologize on behalf of his mother, but neither the newsagent nor his mother would listen to him.

In the end, Tim told the newsagent to send him a bill for any newspapers that were unsalable and steered his mother away from the scene.

'It is all right, Mr Wilson, very kind of you but why should you recompense me for the mistake made by this silly old woman,' the newsagent declared.

'Because the "silly old woman" as you call her is my mother and this is the first time she has been out on her new three-wheeled scooter.'

Peter had returned from the doctors by the time Tim had escorted Betty back home, and he was frantic when he found she had gone out on the scooter on her own. He told Tim that he had planned to take her out and make sure she could use it the moment he got home.

Tim said he understood, but he still looked very disconcerted as he hurried away to start his own day.

'I think we'd better go inside,' Peter said as he laid a hand on the back of the scooter.

'No, let's got for a coffee,' Betty suggested. 'I really do need one.'

Peter smiled. 'Very well, something to settle your nerves? Now take it easy,' he went on, not waiting for her to reply. 'Keep your speed down, there's no hurry.'

They made their way to the coffee shop, Peter advised her where to park. She was still shaking a little when she dismounted so he held her arm as they walked to the door.

'Coffee or chocolate?' he asked.

'Coffee please, and ask them to make it a strong one,' she told him with a grin.

They sat for some time enjoying their drinks and until Betty was feeling more her old self.

'Home now?' Peter asked.

'I suppose so,' Betty agreed. 'There are one or two things we need at the supermarket though. Perhaps we should get those on the way home.'

Peter mused. 'You can wait outside while I pop in for them,' he told her.

He listened to what she said they needed, repeated the list to make sure he remembered everything, and then hurried off.

As he was disappearing inside the door she remembered something else. She called him back but the automatic doors had closed and he didn't hear her. She gave a resigned sigh, then decided to try her luck. It was silly to go without something when they were on the doorstep, and she really had had enough for one day and she didn't want to come out again.

She toyed with the idea of leaving the scooter where it was parked and walking into the store, but the scooter wasn't insured so imagine if someone took it while she was inside.

No, she couldn't risk doing that, she told herself, she'd be extremely careful and only move at a snail's pace then she couldn't possibly do any harm.

She switched it on and approached the automatic doors which immediately opened and she was inside before she knew it. She looked for Peter but couldn't see him so decided to go and pick up what she came in to buy and wait for him at the checkout.

She drove very slowly down the aisle, found what she wanted, and then reversed to go back to the checkout. As she did so there was a loud crash; she turned her head in horror to see that she had backed into a pyramid of cans that had been on display just behind her and that they had crashed to the ground and were rolling everywhere.

Betty felt so mortified that she couldn't think what to do next. She wanted to call out to Peter and ask him to come and help, but she felt that would be making a spectacle of him as well as of herself. When several assistants and the store manager came rushing over towards her she tried to think rationally of what to say but she felt so stunned that she could have made the same mistake twice in such a short space of time that she couldn't speak.

To her surprise, and relief, the manager didn't seem angry about the accident but instead was very conciliatory and anxious to know if she was all right and not hurt in any way. He apologized for where the display had been and started to berate one of the assistants for putting it there.

Betty tried to stop him and explain it was her fault, when Peter appeared. He had heard the commotion and a sixth sense had told him that Betty was involved in some way.

He was quite angry with her, telling her she should have waited outside like he told her and refusing to accept her explanation of why she had come into the store.

'I could always have popped back in for it,' he told her.

Betty felt like crying but then she noticed that the manager was smiling and that some of the staff were laughing when Peter relayed her earlier mishap.

'We only got the scooter yesterday and she hasn't had a chance to try it out,' he explained.

His remark set them off into fresh fits of laughter.

'I think she has given us an excellent demonstration both on how not to drive a scooter and on how we should think carefully before erecting pyramids of cans as an advertising gimmick,' the manager said.

'Don't let this little incident put you off coming in here again,' he said addressing Peter and Betty. 'Think of it as a valuable lesson for all of us.'

Thirty

As Betty became more and more used to handling the scooter their walks and shopping trips became more pleasant.

Peter was able to walk at his own pace and Betty had no trouble adjusting her speed. They also found it ideal when they went for their milk, bread and other groceries. No more heavy bags for Peter to carry; everything slipped neatly into the bag on the scooter.

They had also found a way to park it on the balcony so that it didn't stop them enjoying the time they spent out there and allowed them still to have a small table and two comfortable chairs outside. Peter had arranged for a long cable to run from the living room out onto the balcony, and as soon as they came home the scooter was plugged in ready to use the next time Betty wanted to go out.

The only diversion from this was if it was raining and then, sometimes, they kept the scooter indoors not only to keep it dry but also because Peter had a dislike of plugging it in when it was raining.

'Might be dangerous,' he mumbled. In truth he was remembering some of his own accidents that had involved electricity and he was taking no chances.

The idea that the scooter was always ready for use made Betty eager to go out, but above all she wanted to go out on her own. Peter didn't like the idea at all.

The opportunity for her to do so came one afternoon when she found that they had run out of milk. Peter was asleep and it seemed heartless to wake him simply to go across the road to get milk. Betty debated with herself whether to try making the journey with a stick, with her walker, or with the scooter. Common sense told her that the walker was the safest and most manageable, but she chose the scooter.

She would be very careful, she told herself, smiling as she recalled the incidents she'd been involved in the first time she had used the scooter.

Very cautiously she backed the scooter off the balcony and though the living room, hoping desperately that she wouldn't wake Peter. Once outside the flat she let out a sigh of relief as she pushed it along the corridor to the lift.

Out on the pavement she had a real feeling of achievement. She drove carefully, especially inside the supermarket. She collected the milk and, as a treat to celebrate the success of her adventure, she added two chocolate éclairs to have with the cup of tea she was going home to make.

She was almost halfway home when the scooter stopped dead. No matter what she did it wouldn't move. The only thing she could think of was that the battery must have run out of power. She frowned. How could that have happened when it had been plugged in all night, she wondered.

She sat there for a moment wondering what to do. There was only one thing she could do and that was get off and push it. She found that wasn't too difficult until she came to the small hill that led up to their flats. Suddenly the scooter seemed to have doubled its weight and after half a dozen steps she found her heart was racing and she felt so breathless she had to stop.

She was still panting when a youngish man approached.

'Trouble?' he said.

'I think my battery is dead although it has been plugged in all night.'

He looked amused. 'Let go,' he told her. 'I'll give it a push to the top of the hill for you. Have you far to go after that?'

'No, only across the road,' Betty told him.

He walked so fast that for one frightening moment Betty thought he was stealing her scooter. Desperately she tried to walk faster. If only she had brought a stick with her, she thought as she slowly made her way up the small hill, her breath rasping with each step.

'Are you alright now, missus?' he asked as she reached him. 'There you are then. Sure you can make it the rest of the way?'

She nodded her thanks, almost too breathless to speak. 'Very good of you,' she gasped, as she took the scooter from him and leaned heavily on it, trying to calm down.

She was still panting when she got back to the flat and, as she wheeled the scooter out of the lift, she began to think it was going to be too much of an effort for her to wheel it along the corridor to their flat.

As she bumped her way through their front door Peter woke up and was immediately alert when he saw the state she was in.

'What's happened, have you had an accident?' he asked struggling out of his chair to come over and help her.

Betty shook her head, she was beyond speaking, all she wanted to do was sit down before her knees gave way. Peter helped her into a chair and then went into the kitchen to make some tea. It didn't take him a minute because the water in the kettle was already hot. When he looked for the milk he realized what had happened.

'You went out for milk,' he said accusingly.

Betty nodded.

'Wait until you've got your breath back and then tell me,' he said. He finished making the tea and brought her a cup. 'Mind it's not too hot, would you like me to put a splash of cold water in it?'

Betty nodded. They sat there in silence while she drank. Peter kept looking at her in such a worried way that as soon as she had her breath back Betty gasped, 'There hasn't been an accident; I'm not hurt. I'm puffed out from pushing that damn scooter.'

'What were you pushing it for, have you forgotten how to drive it?' Peter asked with a puzzled frown.

'It conked out on me,' Betty told him in an exasperated voice. 'Just as I came to the hill. A chap came to my aid and pushed it up the hill for me but I still found it hard work getting it home.'

'What do you mean that it conked out?'

'It stopped dead. Nothing I did was any good. The only answer was to get off and push.'

'That's strange,' Peter muttered. He put down his cup of tea and went over to the scooter. He tried to switch it on but it was completely dead.

'Flat battery, but I can't understand why that is,' Peter mused. 'It's been on charge all night.'

'That's what I told this chap and he said it might need a new battery as it wasn't holding the charge.'

'Rubbish! Didn't you tell him the scooter was less than a year old?'

'Well, I suppose it could have been used a lot while it was still in the showrooms, demonstrating it and that sort of thing.'

Peter didn't answer. He picked up the cable, examined the plug and the socket and then began running his hand along the cable to see if there were any breaks in it. When he reached the room plug he stopped with a loud exclamation.

'Something wrong?' Betty asked.

'Wrong! I'll say there is. It wasn't plugged in!'

They looked at each other for a moment then both of them burst into laughter.

'You plugged it in,' Betty told him.

'Yes, but I must have knocked it out when I was using the vacuum cleaner,' he told her.

Again, they laughed. 'Another lesson to be learnt,' Peter said. 'From now on we check the plug before we go to bed.'

Betty agreed, but even though they had both laughed about the incident, she did wonder which of them was responsible. Had she accidentally unplugged it in order to use the socket for her iron, or had Peter done it when he vacuumed earlier in the day. They would probably never know, but it worried her than neither of them could remember changing the plug over at any time that day.

Were they both becoming forgetful? Was this the next stage in growing old? She knew she sometimes had trouble remembering where things were when she had put them away safely, or being unable to recall people's names when relating something to Peter, but then so did he. He blamed it on the fact that he no longer had a shed or workshop when it came to remembering where a certain tool was and had to hunt through the drawers in the kitchen to try and find it.

Betty sighed. There was not a lot either of them could do about their memories going, even young people couldn't remember names or where they'd put things, she told herself.

Neither of them mentioned the incident again but, nevertheless, she paid attention to where she did put things for the next week or two so that she wouldn't be caught out again as she didn't want Peter to think she couldn't remember. From the concentration on his face when he was putting tools away after using them, she thought he was probably doing the same.

They made the most of the summer sunshine although their walks became shorter and shorter. Peter blamed it on the heat but Betty suspected that he was slowing down.

If she asked him where he'd like to go when they went out on one of their walks he more often said either the park or the library, and she suspected that it was because at both places he could sit down for ten or twenty minutes to regain his breath and energy.

She was so tired of these trips that some days she longed to go for a really long ride on her scooter on her own. After all, she told herself, that was one of the reasons for getting it; so that she could go further afield than was possible with the walker.

She even began hoping that perhaps one of these days Peter would say that he felt too tired to go for a walk and then she would have the perfect excuse to go off on her own.

As his walking became more limited she suggested that he might like to use her walker. At first, he refused to even consider the idea.

'Think how daft we would look me pushing a walker trailing after you riding the scooter.'

'Then you use the scooter and I'll use the walker,' she told him. 'I don't mind trailing behind you. Or you could adjust your speed so that I walked in front and you followed me.'

Again, Peter scorned the idea of them going for a walk in that manner.

Then, one day, when he complained his leg was hurting, he did. He agreed that it made walking far easier but he wanted to go out on his own.

'Of course I don't mind,' she told him when he asked. 'You can walk down to the park using the walker and I'll follow you on the scooter. Or we'll do it the other way round, which-ever you prefer.'

They agreed that Peter should go first because it would take him longer and that Betty would follow.

The moment he was out of sight Betty set out. Elated by her freedom, she decided she wouldn't go straight to the park but have a little ride around first.

It was wonderful to be able to explore roads she hadn't been down before, and also along roads that she used to know quite

well but hadn't visited for a long time. After about a quarter of
an hour she decided she had better go to the park or Peter would
be getting anxious about why she hadn't joined him.

At the end of the road she was on she paused to try and decide
which was the quickest way to get to the park. To her annoyance,
she couldn't think where she was. She went to the next turning
and felt equally lost. This is crazy, she told herself. She knew all
these roads well, knew where they led and should have known
the best route to take to the park – but suddenly she didn't.

Finally, in desperation, she stopped a passer-by and asked
if they knew the way.

The moment the woman gave her directions she knew at once
where she was and felt annoyed with herself that she had needed
help.

She drove as fast as she could, hoping Peter wouldn't be worried
and trying to think of an excuse as to why she was late. She
certainly wouldn't tell him that she had lost her way and couldn't
remember how to get there.

Thirty-One

When she arrived at the park Peter didn't seem to notice she was late. In fact, he said nothing when Betty parked the scooter alongside his walker and sat down beside him on the wooden park bench.

'How are you?' she asked as she unbuttoned her coat to make herself more comfortable.

He stared at her and then frowned. 'Fine and yourself?' he said politely.

'Yes, I'm OK. Sorry I took so long to get here.'

'There was no need for you to come at all. I only came out for a breath of fresh air,' he said in a slightly irritated voice, avoiding her eyes and looking straight ahead into space.

Betty didn't answer. His moods puzzled her. Some days he was bright and talkative; others he was morose and could barely take the trouble to answer when she spoke to him.

She studied his face. He had uneven stubble, as if he hadn't taken the trouble to shave properly. His blue eyes had a faraway look in them and, although he was staring straight ahead, they didn't seem to be focused on anything.

She sighed and looked away, then back again because something else was worrying her about his appearance. This time she saw that his shirt was buttoned up unevenly causing it to crumple up around his thin neck.

She wondered if he had buttoned it up incorrectly or whether it was her fault and there was a button missing. She itched to put it right, but was afraid of irritating him by doing so while they were in public view.

They sat there in silence for about a quarter of an hour. Betty studied her surroundings; signs of approaching autumn were everywhere. Even some of the trees were beginning to shed their leaves or show signs of turning colour.

She was on the point of suggesting they went for a coffee to pass the time when Peter stood up, stretched, squared his shoulders and with a polite nod in her direction prepared to leave.

Betty decided to give him a few minutes to get ahead of her before following him when, without warning, he mounted her scooter and was away down the path and out of the park heading towards the main road. Betty felt nonplussed. She didn't mind him taking the scooter, didn't mind the fact that she would have to use the walker to get home, but it was the way it had happened.

Peter had seemed to think that he didn't need to ask her if she would mind if he took the scooter; he acted as though it was his.

She sat there for a moment considering what to do for the best. Normally if he had said he wanted to ride on the scooter she would have thought nothing of it knowing that he was as capable of doing so as she was, but in his present mood, was he safe? Supposing he decided to drive on the road instead of staying on the pavement, she thought worriedly.

Pulling herself together she stood up, fastened her jacket and set off after him.

She knew she couldn't possibly catch him up because she had to use the walker but was also aware that there was nothing else she could do.

She was almost halfway home and still hadn't caught a glimpse of him when she saw a small crowd gathered ahead of her and knew at once that Peter was in some way involved.

When she reached them, a smartly dressed man was shouting at Peter and telling he was a madman.

'If I hadn't been able to jump out of your way there could have been a more serious accident. As it is, you knocked me to the ground and look at the state I'm in!' Betty heard the man say as she reached the edge of the crowd. 'If it had been a child in your path then you could have seriously injured, or even killed it.'

'You should have got out of the way a bit quicker,' Peter told him. 'Walking in the middle of the pavement, who do you think you are?'

'Who do you think you are careering along at the speed you were doing?' the man told him. 'You should be on the road in that vehicle not on the pavement.'

'You don't know what you're talking about. This vehicle isn't designed for the road only for riding on the pavement,' Peter retorted.

Betty pushed her way through the small crowd. 'I'm very sorry, what's happened?' she asked the man.

Now that she could see Peter more clearly, she saw that he was very dishevelled; his coat was covered with dust and dirt. It was obvious that he had been knocked over but managed to pick himself up again.

'Who are you?' the man demanded, 'his wife or his carer? Whichever, you need to keep him under control; he is a menace.'

'Wife? She's not my wife? What makes you think a man of my age would have a woman as old as that as my wife?'

'Wife, mother or carer, I don't give a damn,' the man said angrily. 'I want your name and address, I'm going to sue you.'

'Please,' Betty intervened. 'He's old and frail . . .'

'You speak for yourself,' Peter said loudly. 'I'm forty-five, if it has anything to do with any of you, and I have my own business and I have just bought a house in Clover Crescent. This woman,' he added, looking straight at the man who had knocked him down, 'is my mother!'

Turning back to Betty he said angrily. 'What do you think you are doing following me, that's why I was going so fast and had the accident. I was trying to get away from you.'

The man looked from one to the other in bewilderment. 'You are his wife, aren't you?'

'Yes, I'm his wife,' Betty confirmed, 'and he shouldn't be on the scooter; it's mine.' She indicated the walker. 'This is his.'

The man dusted down his coat, shaking his head all the time. 'I think he's mad,' he muttered. 'Take him home and don't let him out on his own again because, believe me, he's going to do some serious damage to someone or something.'

Betty bit her lip and nodded. She couldn't think what was the right thing to say. She had never seen Peter like this before. He was bristling with anger and so aggressive.

'Under the circumstances,' the man went on, 'I won't take this any further because I can see you are very upset.' He laid a hand on Betty's shoulder. 'I feel sorry for you, I really do; having to live with that madman.'

There were amused titters from some of the crowd then, one by one, they drifted away leaving Betty standing on her own with Peter.

'What was all that about?' Peter asked, frowning. 'All that shouting and carrying on. Was that man out of his mind?'

'Don't worry about it,' she said as soothingly as possible. 'I'll take the scooter,' she said, pushing the walker towards him. 'Come on, take this and you walk ahead.'

'Where are we going?'

'Home,' she said wearily. 'We won't be going out again until I am sure that you are better,' she said, but Peter didn't hear her. He was already pushing the walker ahead and heading for home.

Betty put the kettle on as soon as they went indoors. She needed a cup of tea, her nerves were jangling as she contemplated what had happened.

She had never seen Peter in such a mood before and she simply couldn't understand it. She didn't know whether she ought to take him to see the doctor or not. She'd have to speak to Tim about it and see what he thought.

By the time she had made the tea and taken a cup into Peter he was fast asleep. She put the tea down on the table and sat down and drank her own. His would be cold if he didn't wake up soon, she thought, but it was so peaceful with him snoring away that she decided not to disturb him until she had finished drinking her own tea.

When she did, he woke up, stared around, picked up his tea and drank it and said, 'Are we still going out for a walk?'

His voice was so normal that Betty wondered if she had imagined what had taken place only a short time earlier. For one moment she wondered if she was the deluded one.

'No', she said, 'it's too late for us to go out now.'

'That's a pity,' he sighed. 'I was dreaming about us walking down to the park. Still, never mind, we can always do it tomorrow.'

Over the next few days Betty was on tenterhooks, watching his behaviour and listening carefully to what he said, but there was no sign at all that he was in any way unwell.

The incident in the park, taking her scooter and colliding with someone, was never mentioned. Peter seemed to have completely forgotten that it had ever taken place. It was as if it had never happened at all.

Betty mulled over whether or not to mention it to Tim. Would he understand? Would he think she was making a fuss about nothing? What could he do about it anyway, she asked herself. He would only tell her to take Peter to see a doctor and, somehow, she didn't want to do that.

I'll do the same as Peter and forget it ever happened, she told herself. But, it wasn't that easy. Every time they went out Betty made a point of parking the scooter behind Peter's walker so that there was no chance of him taking it by mistake.

It hadn't been a mistake the day he took it when they'd been in the park, she reminded herself. He had done it deliberately. Yet he had never even ventured to use it since, she thought. It puzzled her. In the end, because she could stand the worry no longer, she spoke to Tim about it.

'It sounds serious,' he told her. 'I think you should task him to see a doctor in case it is the start of Alzheimer's. These days they have all sorts of medication and they may be able to give him something to slow the process down.'

'I don't want them putting him in a hospital or something like that,' Betty said worriedly. 'He's quite healthy and been perfectly all right ever since. He's never once mentioned what happened. He hasn't shown any interest in riding the scooter again either.'

Tim shrugged. 'I don't know what else to suggest. It may never happen again, just "one of those moments",' he laughed. 'I wonder what he thought he was doing; had he been drinking?'

'Of course not. He never goes to the pub, you know that.'

'I meant drinking at home,' Tim said. 'He has the occasional glass of wine, doesn't he?'

'Very rarely. He might have a hot whisky toddy before going to bed if he thinks he has a cold starting. That nips it in the bud, he always says.'

Betty came away feeling none the better for taking Tim into her confidence. She even wondered if he had been laughing at her for making such a fuss.

She had two choices, she decided. She could either put it all out of her mind and forget it ever happened or she could try and persuade Peter to go and see a doctor.

That would be very difficult, she mused, because she wasn't sure how he would react if she told him the reason she wanted him to do so.

I'll be going out of my head myself if I don't stop worrying about it, she told herself. It was one isolated incident. There may never be another. The best thing to do was to forget about it.

Thirty-Two

Betty watched Peter carefully for the next couple of weeks but he showed no further tendency to anything out of the ordinary. She even went as far as to test him out by suggesting that he might like to take turns with her on riding the scooter and using the walker.

'You like the scooter still, don't you?' he asked anxiously.

'Of course I do but I sometimes feel mean about riding it and you having to walk,' she said with a warm smile.

'That's ridiculous. I've got the walker and that suits me fine. I get my daily exercise by walking, which is more than you do.'

'Oh, I get plenty of exercise,' Betty assured him.

'Well, I wouldn't want to ride the scooter as it's such a poor replacement for the car,' he went on, with a teasing smile. 'If you've got to have a change then make it a good one,' he added with a laugh.

Peter seemed to be so normal that Betty decided to put the entire episode out of her mind. There was something far more important in the offing, she told herself. In a couple of weeks' time it would be her eightieth birthday and she thought it would be a good opportunity for a celebration; a party or an evening out that included not only all the family but her friends, Sally and Hilda, as well.

When, where and at what time; midday or evening? Perhaps it would be better to have it at midday, she mused, because of little Anna. She wanted her to be there but she knew that Shirley didn't like her being up too late at night because she had to go to school the next day. If they had the party at midday, Anna would be at school, she frowned. Unless they had the party at the weekend, of course. Yes, that seemed to be the best idea.

The trouble was that restaurants were usually very busy on the weekend and it would be a fairly large party. She could have it at home of course, but she didn't think their flat was big enough for so many people. There would be ten of them so there weren't enough chairs to go round for a start and she wasn't sure that she had enough dinner plates and cutlery for so many people. It would be very crowded to try and sit them all round their small dining table. Unless they had a buffet . . .

Betty thought about it for several days but decided holding a party at the flat was out of the question. For one thing, even if they all gave a helping hand, she would still find it more work than she could manage. She'd not be able to enjoy their company because she'd be too anxious making sure that everybody was being looked after.

When she mentioned the idea to Peter he was most definitely in favour of them going out.

'If you try to do it yourself, even if you buy in most of the food, it's still going to make you sick with worry,' he told her. 'If you hire someone to come in and take over there won't be room for any guests,' he said with a laugh when she was about to argue with him.

'No, let's have a real party and let someone else do all the hard work. You're the one who is supposed to be celebrating this special birthday, not killing yourself trying to make it enjoyable for other people.'

Betty mulled over the idea for a few more days, made lists of where they could go and the number of people there would be and then decided to ring round and ask and find out if they were prepared to cater for such a party. Was it best to do that or would it be more sensible to make sure that all the family could be there on whatever date she chose. First things first, she told herself. But which was the first thing she ought to do? She couldn't even make her mind up about that.

'If they can't come to the party then that's their loss,' Peter said when she faced him with the problem.

'Yes, but when I book they will want to know how many are coming.'

'Give them an estimate, nine or ten, or something like that.'

Betty nodded thoughtfully. 'I suppose they will be happy with that,' she murmured.

'So, where shall we go? Where do you fancy, Peter?'

'Where do I fancy!' he laughed. 'Don't ask me, I've only been out for that sort of meal about a dozen times in my life and I wouldn't know one place from another. Pick the one you fancy; or find out what price they are charging and judge by that.'

Betty raised her eyebrows. 'Yes, of course, I suppose that is the clever way to do it.'

Afterwards, as she thought about it more carefully, she wasn't at all sure that it was the best way to set about organizing things. After a couple of sleepless nights, when she lay awake trying to work out where to go and what to do for the best, she made up her mind that she would have a talk with Tim about it.

Tim would know exactly where to go because he was so used to wining and dining clients and attending functions organized by other estate agents.

She settled on a definite date before she talked to him. She checked the calendar, noted down the Sunday nearest her birthday, and put on her coat to make sure she was looking her best as she went along to his office.

'I'm afraid Mr Wilson said he didn't wish to be disturbed this afternoon,' the receptionist told her. 'Would you like to make an appointment?' she asked, pulling a ledger towards her and scanning through it to see when he would be free.

'No, I'll see him now,' Betty said firmly. 'It's very important but it won't take long.'

The girl was about to protest when an older woman walked into the office. She greeted Betty warmly. 'Hello Susan,' Betty said with a friendly smile. 'I wanted to see Tim but this young lady has said he's too busy,' Betty sighed.

'I'm sure he is never too busy to give you a few minutes of his time, come along, I'll take you through to his office.'

'Is there something wrong, Mother?' he said anxiously when she was shown into his office.

'No, no,' she said quickly, 'I just need a spot of advice from you.'

'Oh, in that case sit down and I'll arrange for a cup of tea to be brought in for us both.'

'Please don't bother, Tim. I don't want to take up your working day and this won't take a minute.'

'I was about to have my own cuppa so it only means that they have to bang in another cup. Sit down, you look all hot and bothered.'

Betty sank gratefully into the chair he indicated and looked around at the smart office, the display of properties which had SOLD marked on them and all the other paraphernalia that were part of his working day.

When the tea came she asked, 'Are you free the Sunday after next?'

Tim pulled his desk diary towards him and opened it. 'Is something happening then?' he said, his lips pursed as he sipped the tea. Then he looked up, shaking his head. 'No, sorry, I am doing something that day.'

Betty bit her lip. 'It's so difficult to get you altogether,' she said, and there was a tinge of both sadness and irritation in her voice.

'Really!' He sounded surprised. 'Who else have you tried?'

'No one, not yet. I thought I would have a word with you first.'

'Is it important?'

Betty frowned and looked thoughtful. 'It could be the following Sunday, I suppose,' she said thoughtfully.

'Does it have to be a Sunday?' Tim asked.

'Well, yes, because I wanted little Anna to be there and on other days she's at school.'

'So why do you want us all to meet?' he said.

He sounded as though he was laughing as he closed his diary abruptly and looked at her. Betty felt annoyed when she saw the huge smile on his face.

He was laughing at her. She wondered if he was even telling her the truth when he said he couldn't manage that date. He had guessed what she was trying to do and he was teasing her.

She took a long sip of her tea so as not to let him see how annoyed she was with him.

'OK,' he said when she put her cup down. 'Is this anything to do with your birthday?'

'You know it is.'

'A rather special one, if my arithmetic serves me right,' he said in a deadpan voice.

'I was trying to arrange a family party but I wasn't sure where to start, or which was the best place to take you all, so in the end I decided to come to ask your advice,' she admitted.

'Go home and forget about it until Sunday week arrives,' he told her. 'We all know it's your eightieth and you don't think we would let such an important milestone pass without doing something about it, now do you? It's all booked. All you and Peter have to do is be ready by midday, dressed up to the nines, and ready to go out. The car will be waiting outside the flats.'

'Where are we going?'

'Aah, somewhere quite special; somewhere you've probably never been before.'

'So where is that?' Betty persisted.

'Wait and see. It's all arranged, you don't have to do a thing and we will all be there, including young Anna.'

Betty knew it was a waste of time trying to get Tim to tell her where it was but she would have felt happier if she had known. It would have given her a better idea of what she and Peter ought to wear.

She tried to approach it from another angle. 'I intended to invite Sally and Hilda . . .'

'That's already been done.'

She looked relieved. 'So, they know where we are meeting?' she commented.

'No. I didn't tell them because I knew you would immediately try and get them to tell you if they knew.'

'That's not very fair on them,' she said with a frown.

'They seemed to be happy enough with the arrangement,' he said blandly. 'Now, don't worry, they'll be there and we've even arranged transport for both of them.'

'Oh, Tim!' she exclaimed and spontaneously got up, went round the desk and hugged and then kissed him.

'Steady on,' he admonished her. 'What would my secretary, Susan, say if she walked in and found you with your arms around my neck?'

'I think she would understand,' Betty told him. 'If she didn't then I would soon enlighten her by telling her that I had the most wonderful, thoughtful son in the world.'

'Don't put all the blame on me,' Tim said, straightening his jacket and making sure that his tie was in place. 'The others have all done their share and I'm more than surprised that it hasn't already leaked out. I was sure someone would accidentally mention it to you!'

'No, no one has said a word. If I'd heard even a whisper then I wouldn't have spent so many sleepless nights wondering what to do,' she told him.

'Well, you don't have to worry anymore. Everything has been taken care of,' he told her, as he escorted her to the door. 'Catch up with your sleep otherwise you will be feeling so worn out you won't want to party.'

Betty felt light-hearted as she made her way home. All she had to do now was decide what dress she was going to wear and make an appointment to have her hair done, she thought with an inward smile.

Thirty-Three

Betty was dressed and ready at midday.

She inspected Peter, adjusted his shirt and tie, brushed the shoulders of his dark-grey suit and then went into the bedroom to fetch him a clean handkerchief.

'We'll put that one in the laundry basket, put one in your trouser pocket and the other in your jacket pocket,' she told him when he protested that he already had one.

'Why don't you sit down and have a glass of wine until they get here. It might help you to relax,' Peter suggested.

'Start drinking now at this time of the day! Most certainly not. I had enough trouble fastening these pearls as it is. If I have a drink I'll be incapable of doing anything.'

'You'll be having a drink with your meal,' Peter pointed out.

'That's different, I'll be having some food then so the wine won't affect me. To drink now, on an empty stomach—' she shook her head – 'that's out of the question.'

'Well, sit down anyway and let me have a look at the fastening on those pearls. The jeweller told me it was a magnetic catch and that all you had to do was simply hold the ends together and they'd join up.'

'Well they've done that, nearly jumped out of my hand when they did it, but I'm not sure a catch like that will stay firm. It's not like a screw, or a slip rind and holder.'

'He said it was safer and no fuss doing up,' Peter told her. 'If you don't feel comfortable then don't wear it.'

'Not wear it! The loveliest set of pearls I've ever owned and given to me by the man in my life,' she admonished.

'Let's look at it.'

'Mind my hair, it's only just been set,' she warned as he lifted the hair from the back of her neck and checked the pearls.

'They're as sound as rock,' he assured her, 'and they look lovely on that dark red top you're wearing.'

'So they should, I picked it specially to show them off,' she told him.

She put her arms around his neck, hugged and kissed him. 'The most wonderful present ever and something I've always wanted,' she told him.

He returned her kiss, holding her face between both his hands. 'This is what I've wanted, so we are both happy,' he said, his blue eyes bright with affection and love.

She pulled away. 'Now look at me. I'll have to go and do my hair all over again because now it's all messed up.'

'You look lovely whether it is messed up or not,' he told her gallantly and patted her on the shoulder as she made for the bedroom to restore her hair.

She had barely finished when she heard their door buzzer. 'That will be Tim, let him in,' she called as she hurriedly tidied her dressing table and came back into the sitting room.

'They're on their way up, where's your coat? Let me help you with it.'

Peter was already in his coat and, by the time their internal doorbell rang, Betty had her coat on and they were ready to go.

Tim was wearing a dark suit and a white shirt that was partly hidden by his white scarf, teamed with a dark topcoat.

'Brenda is in the car,' he told his mother and Peter as he escorted them to the lift.

'Have you got a new car . . .?' Betty started to say, then stopped short when she saw that there was a uniformed driver at the wheel. 'What's all this about?' she asked in surprise.

'We'll all be having a drink or two so I wouldn't be able to drive home afterwards, or see you home, so this seemed to be the best solution,' Tim told them.

He settled Peter and Betty into the back with Brenda and took the passenger seat next to the chauffeur himself.

Brenda greeted them effusively and helped Betty with her seat belt and by then they were already moving. Ten minutes later they were drawing up in front of a magnificent-looking stone building that Betty had never seen before.

'Where are we?' she asked leaning forward and staring out of the window.

'Branwell Court, if I'm not mistaken,' Peter said, looking very impressed.

'Beautiful, isn't it?' Brenda commented. 'Wait until you see inside.'

'Is it a hotel?' Betty asked.

'Well, yes, in a way. It was a private house many years ago but the late owner sold it to the National Trust and now it is used as a hotel and restaurant.'

'Whew!' Peter let out a low whistle. 'I bet it costs and arm and a leg to stay here,' he commented.

'Yes, and that's only for one night,' Tim said with a laugh. He guided them towards the wide stone steps that led into the entrance hall, which itself was so large that Betty thought it would have taken the whole of their flat and still had space left over.

There were three or four comfortable chairs, a high desk, ornate mirrors and deep pile carpet in a welcoming shade of red.

The girl behind the reception desk smiled warmly at Tim and greeted him by name, as if she knew him well. 'I've summoned a porter to take you and your party through to the dining room,' she told him.

'There will be four other people joining us,' he told her.

'I'll have them shown straight to your table,' she said with a smile.

The dining room was twice the size of the reception area. The round tables were well placed so that they were easy to manoeuvre, and far enough away from each other to ensure privacy when discussing anything private. Many of them were already occupied by men in business suits, some already eating, others enjoying their wine while waiting for the next course.

The waiter led them to a table placed in an advantageous spot near a window that looked out onto magnificently tended gardens. Place names had been set out and Betty was guided to a position with Tim on one side of her and Peter on the other.

As she sat down, admiring the beautiful table decorations, she noticed that the table was laid for eleven people.

'Tim,' she said in a whisper, 'there are only ten of us.'

'That's alright. I know its laid for eleven; it's because Clare is bringing a friend.'

'A friend? Clare!'

'Yes, someone she works with, I understand.'

'She works at the hospital so who on earth would she want to bring from there?'

'I don't know, but you can ask her yourself, she's here.' He nodded in the direction of the door.

Betty stared in surprise. She saw her granddaughter was wearing a well-styled turquoise blue dress with matching jacket and looking smarter than she had seen her ever look before. She was escorted by a tall fair-haired man who looked to be in his late fifties.

Tim looked equally taken back and Betty saw him whisper something to Brenda before he walked over to greet the newcomers and guide them to their places at the table.

Betty waited to be introduced, but the waiter who was hovering by them waiting to take their orders captured her attention. By the time Tim had told him that he could go ahead and serve their meal, Clare and her friend were already seated. Either side of them were Shirley and Graham, and they were so busy talking to them that the opportunity for her to speak to them was temporarily lost.

'As there are so many of us I thought it was simplest to make it a set meal and suggest if the dish being served is not to your liking then you mention it to the waiter and it can be changed for something else. I take it that you all drink champagne,' Tim added with a smile.

'Tim, who is that man who is with Clare?' Betty asked as he sat down.

'Oh, sorry, Mother, you haven't been introduced. I'll do that now.'

He was about to lean forward and interrupt the animated conversation going on between Shirley and Clare's guest, but Betty touched his arm and shook her head.

'Leave it for now, you can do it afterwards,' she said with a smile.

'Yes, very well but I do think Clare should have made a point of introducing him to you first when she arrived,' he said in a rather disgruntled manner.

The meal was excellent and the champagne flowed liberally. Tim made a toast to his mother at the start of the meal and made sure that her glass, as well as everyone else's, was kept replenished as they ate.

The party became very relaxed as the courses were served and the many incidents that they all remembered concerning Betty were aired. They were very varied. Tim recalled childhood episodes and Graham told stories about when he had been a small child.

Anna was enthralled. She seemed to be enjoying her glass of sparkling apple juice which she accepted was special champagne because it looked just like the champagne the others were drinking.

The pudding was greatly to Anna's delight too, a concoction of ice cream and strawberries topped by countless mini profiteroles and equally tiny chocolates filled with coloured cream.

With the meal over, Tim told them that they would all retire to a lounge that had been set aside for them where a birthday cake and coffee would be served and the presents they had brought could be given to Betty.

The room was smaller, but equally lavish, with a magnificent thick pile carpet in pale green, and deep-green velvet drapes at the window. The chairs and settee were luxuriously comfortable.

More champagne was handed round, more toasts were made and then, finally, Betty was given her presents. Before she opened any of them Betty proudly drew their attention to the double row of pearls that had been a present from Peter. Then, with little Anna's help, she began to unwrap her gifts.

These ranged from a wonderful collection of perfumes and soaps, to chocolates, scarves and flowers.

Each one had to be admired and the donator thanked. Glasses were replenished while this was going on.

When it came to the time for the coffee and for Betty to cut birthday cake, Peter was sound asleep.

They laughed, nudged each other and left it to Tim to wake him.

When he did, Peter was in an irritable mood and stared around him as if he had no idea where he was. Then, he struggled out of his armchair, pushing them all to one side as they tried to help him. Staggering wildly, he headed for the door.

Graham laid a hand on his arm to stop him, but Peter slammed a fist in Graham's direction. Luckily, the younger man was agile enough to sidestep and avoid the blow.

'Peter, whatever's the matter with you!' Betty exclaimed. 'Come and sit down here and enjoy a slice of my birthday cake,' she said, patting the settee.

'Sit down there? What the hell do I want to do that for? I don't know you and I don't want to know you or your horde of noisy friends.'

'Peter, you've been asleep and dreaming,' Tim intervened.

'Shut your damn mouth and don't interfere,' Peter told him. 'I've seen you around before, you and that old wife of yours,' he said, giving Betty a hostile look. 'She looks old enough to be your mother.'

'She is my mother,' Tim said quietly. 'She's also your wife.'

'My wife! I'm not married and if I was it wouldn't be to an old woman like that. Look at her! All dolled up with her crimped hair and powdered face. I'm not one of your kind, hanging onto the apron strings of any old woman who gives you a smile in the hopes that she'll leave you a fortune.'

'Peter!' Tim was incensed. 'Graham, help me to take him along to the men's room and get him to wash his face in cold water to help him regain his senses,' Tim ordered.

Before Graham could do as his father asked, Clare's companion stepped forward and took Peter firmly by the arm. 'Leave this to me,' he said in an authoritative voice. 'I know how to deal with it.'

Betty was shocked. Her eyes were full of tears. She had been enjoying her party so much and now, in a matter of minutes, everything was ruined.

Mary came over and put an arm round her mother's shoulders. 'Don't worry, Mum,' she said gently, 'everything will be all right. Rossiter is a psychologist, he knows how to handle him. He's in charge of the dementia ward at the hospital, that's where him and Clare met.'

Betty stared at her daughter in growing horror. 'Dementia,' she said frowning. 'Peter hasn't got dementia.'

Betty moved to her husband's side and took his arm. 'Come on Peter, it's time we went home,' she said in a cajoling voice.

He stared at her blankly for a moment and slumped to the ground.

'What do we do now?' Graham asked.

'Leave it to Rossiter,' Clare advised. 'He'll call an ambulance and take him to the hospital.'

'I think if you leave him for a while you'll find he comes round and that he won't remember anything about what has happened,' Betty told them.

She frowned. 'You mean this has happened before?'

'Yes, but only once and it was ages ago,' Betty explained. 'When he came round he thought he'd been dreaming and there's not been anything like that happened since.'

Thirty-Four

'Well, this is a birthday I am not likely to forget in a hurry,' Betty said as the ambulance drove away with Peter on board.

He was still unconscious, or so deeply asleep that it amounted to the same thing.

'Really there is no need for him to be taken to hospital,' she repeated. 'Leave him to wake when he is ready and he will be perfectly normal.'

'We can't be too sure,' Tim told her. 'Remember, Clare's colleague is a specialist in dementia and he appears to be concerned. He thinks that the champagne Peter has been drinking has brought on the attack. Drink has a strange effect on dementia, or so it would seem.'

The arrival of the ambulance had caused concern and questions from members of the hotel staff, and Tim was anxious to put their minds at rest.

'He'll be all right,' he told them. 'A little too much excitement, I'm afraid. He's merely gone for a check-up. At his age you have to be careful.'

They all nodded or murmured understandingly, but Tim was aware that there was whispering and he heard the word 'drunk' voiced a few times amongst themselves.

'Come on,' he said taking Betty's arm, 'we'll see you home.'

'You don't have your car here,' she pointed out.

'I know that but I've sent for the cab that brought us. It will be here at any moment.'

Tim and Graham, helped by Clare and Mary, began to gather up her birthday presents and the moment the car arrived the chauffeur took them and carefully placed them in the boot of his car.

Betty said goodbye to Sally and Hilda and promised to let them know how Peter was and when he would be home again.

Tim told them that he had arranged transport for them and thanked them for coming. This time, Tim sat in the back between Betty and Brenda.

'Don't worry,' he told his mother as they drove away. 'Rossiter will see that Peter is well cared for.'

'I'm more annoyed by all the fuss than I am worried,' Betty told him. 'As I have said before, if you'd left Peter to wake up naturally then he'd have been fine. This has happened before, remember, and when he had slept it off there was no reoccurrence, no after-effects at all.'

'A single seizure of this kind is one thing but to have another one is surely worrying,' Brenda intervened. 'Let Rossiter investigate the cause. Possibly there is medication available that will prevent it happening again.'

Betty's lips tightened but she said nothing. She could see it was useless to do so, and that whatever she said she would lose the argument. To her great relief, after helping the chauffeur to bring in all the presents from the car, Tim and Brenda said they were going.

'Are you sure you are going to be all right on your own?' Tim asked. 'Would you like to come and stay with us for a while?'

'No, I'll be fine,' Betty assured him. 'I might go in to see Peter later.'

'They won't let you see him today, not while he is still unconscious. His progress is being monitored and Clare has promised to let us know the moment there is any development.'

'I still might go and see him, even if I can only sit by the bed,' Betty repeated, her jaw set stubbornly.

'They won't let you see him, Mother,' Tim said firmly. 'Anyway, how would you get there?'

'By taxi, of course,' Betty told him sharply.

'Please don't do that,' Tim pleaded. 'You'll be turned away and that will distress you even more.'

'I will phone Clare the moment we get home and check what has happened so far and phone you and let you know,' he told her. 'I promise, the moment you can go to see him then I'll take you.'

'Yes, all right,' Betty murmured resignedly.

The flat seemed empty without Peter. Betty unwrapped her presents again, arranged the flowers in water, and put the other items and birthday cards somewhere safe so that she could look at them all again when she knew that Peter was going to be all right.

The rest of the day passed in a dream. Tim phoned twice to say that Peter was still in a deep sleep and so there was nothing really to report.

Late in the evening Mary phoned to see if she was all right on her own or if she would like her to come and stay with her overnight.

'No,' Betty said quite sharply. 'I'm relying on you and Clare to let me know when Peter wakens, and how can you do that if you are here with me.'

'We're not at the hospital, Mother. As I'm sure Tim has told you; they won't allow any of us to be there.'

'How about that Rossiter chap?' Betty asked.

'Rossiter Evans is a specialist and Peter's condition is being carefully monitored and reported to him. He will let me know as soon as there are any changes.'

'I see.' Betty's tone was cold and clipped.

'Look, Mother, why don't you take a sleeping pill and get a good night's rest? You'll feel all the better for it in the morning and I'll phone you early and tell you what the latest news is.'

Betty didn't take a sleeping pill. She avoided pills whenever possible and she didn't think that one of those was what she needed. What she did want was good news about Peter. She wanted to hear that he was awake, and none the worse for what had happened. She wanted to hear that he was perfectly well; the episode wiped from his mind and that he was waiting to come home.

It was three days before Peter was discharged. Tim brought him home from the hospital and Betty was shocked when she saw him. Peter looked so old and frail, and his balance was very bad. He moved round the flat clutching at doors, furniture and anything else within arm's reach, as waves of giddiness swept over him.

'For heaven's sake sit down and have a cup of tea,' Betty said.

He nodded and sank into his armchair with a heavy sigh. 'Keeping me in bed for so long has put years on me,' he grumbled. 'I'm shaking like a leaf and I feel as if I am going to fall over at any minute.'

Betty patted his arm consolingly. 'Don't worry about it. By tomorrow, after a good night's sleep, you'll be back to normal,' she told him.

He clutched at her hand and kissed it. 'I don't know what I would do without you,' he said. 'The best day of my life was when we got married. Sorry to be so much trouble.'

'You're no trouble,' she told him, kissing the top of his head.

'I ruined your special birthday party,' he said ruefully.

'Not to worry, we can always have another party. As long as you are all right, that is all that matters.'

They spent the next few days very quietly. Betty fed him all his favourite dishes but his appetite was poor and she began to despair that he was never going to be fit enough to walk as far as the park with his walker ever again.

It took half the morning to help him to get out of bed, showered and dressed. She was so afraid that he would turn giddy while under the shower and have a fall.

When she mentioned this to Tim he frowned and look worried. 'I'll give Clare a ring and see what that friend of hers thinks. You haven't phoned her about it?'

Betty shook her head. 'No, I don't think it's a good idea or he'll have him back in hospital under observation again.'

'No, no, don't worry about that. Hospital beds aren't that easily available. I'll just mention it to Clare and see what she says. I'll tell her to phone you so that you will know if she can advise you on what to do.'

Neither Clare nor Mary telephoned Betty, but a few days later they had a visit from someone from the hospital, who told her that they were sending along a carer each morning to help Peter to dress and shower.

Betty wanted to refuse their help because she knew that Peter would resent it, but she also knew that if Peter did slip or fall in the shower then she would feel responsible. She didn't think she would be strong enough to help him or get him up, so it seemed to be common sense to accept their help.

Peter didn't seem at all pleased by the idea. He accepted the carer's administrations for a week and then he rebelled.

'I can't stand this,' he told Betty. 'I'd sooner stay dirty than have strangers mauling me about.'

'You had strangers helping you when you were in hospital,' she pointed out.

'I had no option when I was in there, but now I'm in my own home and I'm not standing for it.'

'What happens if you have a giddy turn when you are under the shower?' Betty asked.

'I never have had one, now have I,' he pointed out.

'Well, you do seem very unsteady on your feet. You seem to need to hold on to the furniture when you're moving round the room.'

'That's different,' he told her. 'I'm crossing a wide area then. When I'm in the shower there's walls on three sides that I can lean on if I need to do so.'

They discussed it for several days without making any headway or decision. Then, one morning, Peter refused to get out of bed when the carer arrived.

'I'll get up and shower when I'm ready to do so,' he told her. She tried all sorts of persuasion but Peter refused to give in. The carer shrugged and looked apologetically at Betty. 'I'm sorry, there is nothing else I can do. We are not allowed to use physical force. I'll see you tomorrow morning.'

The carer came twice more, then said that the situation was impossible and that she would be notifying her superior of the position.

Betty said that she understood and thanked her for her help.

Peter breathed a sigh of relief when Betty told him the outcome of his stubbornness.

Tim grimaced when she told him and that was the end of the matter. Slowly, Peter seemed to regain his energy. As if to ward off the attention of carers, he forced himself to get up in the morning and to shower and shave before he had his breakfast.

Once or twice, he made the suggestion that he was going to grow a beard. Betty put a stop to that idea immediately.

'If you find shaving is too much for you then I'd better arrange for the carers to come back in each morning,' she told him thoughtfully.

There was no more talk of growing a beard.

Their life was far quieter, Peter seemed to tire easily. Betty did most of the shopping, leaving him watching the television while she went across to the shops nearby.

Sometimes she used the scooter, at other times she took the walker because she found it easier to manoeuvre.

Tim tried to persuade them to place a regular food order and have it delivered, but Betty insisted that she liked to see what she was buying.

'You could still buy the milk, bread, vegetables and fruit but have all the other things delivered,' he told her. 'After all, one tin of beans is very like the next and you can't see inside the can anyway.'

As the weather became colder and the days shorter, she agreed to give it a try. Tim set up the necessary arrangements and all she had to do was open the front door when the delivery man arrived.

Once she had agreed that this was a very satisfactory arrangement he suggested that they should have ready meals delivered in the same way.

'One delivery a month and they all go in your freezer and they're there when you want them,' he informed her.

He left her with an illustrated leaflet that showed main meals and puddings and she agreed to give it a try.

Once again, she found it was labour saving and she also decided that it didn't upset her anywhere near as much when Peter left half of his dinner on his plate, as it did when she had cooked the meal herself.

When Christmas came, Betty refused all invitations because she was sure it would be too much for Peter and she didn't want a repeat of what had happened at her birthday.

Instead, there was a repeat of the previous year and Shirley sent Graham round on Christmas morning with a home-cooked Christmas dinner, complete with Christmas pudding, a cake and mince pies.

Remembering Rossiter's warning about drink, they abstained over Christmas, but they did indulge in one drink a week later to welcome in the new year.

Thirty-Five

Betty was delighted to find that with the return of the better weather Peter improved daily. He wanted to be up and active as soon as it was light. His appetite improved and he began to look his old self.

Some days he seemed to have more energy that she had, Betty reflected.

She was still cautious about letting him do too much and encouraged him to have a sleep after he'd had his midday meal. This became an established pattern and she usually made use of the time he was asleep to go across to the shops for daily necessities like milk and bread or anything else they might need. When she arrived back she would make a cup of tea to greet him when he woke.

As spring approached she was beginning to once again really enjoy their flat. Opening wide the balcony doors, even if it was only for an hour on sunny days, seemed to bring the flat alive. She enjoyed looking down on the garden. It was waking up after the bleakness of winter; first the snowdrops, then the daffodils waved in the breeze, and then the crocuses began pushing up through the dark earth to shine like coloured stars.

As the days became warmer she found that Peter was already awake and had made her a cup of tea by the time she returned from shopping.

She was rather worried by this because some days he seemed to be a little shaky or unsteady on his feet and Betty was afraid he might have an accident with the kettle; missing the teapot and pouring the boiling water over his hand.

She had only mentioned it once because he had been so annoyed with her. 'Do you think I'm a fool or something,' he said angrily. 'Why should I do something as silly as that? You never pour the water over yourself even though you fill up the kettle so full that it's almost too heavy for you to lift.'

After that they seemed to be watching each other but neither voiced aloud their anxiety.

Betty knew he was right about filling the kettle too full and tried to remember to only half fill it. Peter was quite right, she didn't have the same strength in her wrists and hands as she once had. She often found that using the vacuum cleaner made her wrists ache afterwards. Now that Peter was so much better she encouraged him to do it.

While he had been ill she had even been tempted to employ a cleaner, but it seemed a waste of money when they lived in such a small space.

She cleaned the kitchen and bathroom every day, and in between made sure everything was clean and tidied away each time she used them.

After all, there were only the two of them and as Peter spent most of his day sitting in his armchair, a weekly vacuuming both for the living room and bedroom were adequate and she could easily manage that without help, she told herself. They had established a routine that was satisfactory so perhaps it was best to leave it like that.

As the days became longer she wondered when Peter would feel confident enough to restart their walks. At the moment she was the one using the walker, but she had a sudden urge to use the scooter instead. She tried it out once or twice telling herself that if she didn't start using it again she would forget how to drive it.

That was nonsense, of course. Nothing could be easier.

The next time she went out on it she decided that before she went into the supermarket she'd go for a little trip. Peter was asleep, so why not, she told herself as she set off on a journey around the block.

She felt exhilarated as she saw the gardens with their flourishing borders, and noted the green foliage appearing on bushes and hedges, and even some of the trees seemed to be about to burst into leaf.

She could have gone for miles, but her conscience told her she ought to get back to the supermarket, do the shopping, and go home. Peter would have the tea made and be wondering what was keeping her.

As she pushed the scooter down the corridor and into their flat she called out to alert him that she was home, knowing that he would be waiting to make the tea. By the time she'd unpacked the shopping and put it away the tea would be ready to drink.

To her surprise, Peter wasn't in the living room or the kitchen. In case he was in the bathroom she called out his name to let him know she was home and then went to make the tea herself.

The kettle was cold; Peter hadn't even laid out the cups ready.

Mystified, she tried to think where he could be. She checked the bedroom and the bathroom, but he wasn't in either.

As she went back into the living room she stopped to look out at the garden, wondering if he was feeling so much better that he had gone to sit down there for a few minutes and forgotten the time.

Peter was in the garden. Betty watched in horror as she saw he was messing around in the flower border. She couldn't exactly see what he was doing but whatever it was she knew he shouldn't be touching them. One of the rules they had been given when they bought the flat was that a professional gardener was employed and that under no circumstances must the residents interfere. They must not pick any of the flowers or put plants in, they mustn't even tell the gardener what they thought ought to be done.

Tim had laughed and pointed out that all their worries were over when it came to maintaining the garden.

'A perfect garden and you don't have to lift a finger,' he told them. 'You don't even have to water it in summer, it's all done for you. They've installed an efficient sprinkler system that keeps everything as it should be.'

Peter had eventually come around to that idea. He said he'd done enough gardening to last him a lifetime and disposed of all his tools. Betty had approved as well. She'd found the garden at Clover Crescent far more than she could manage, even with the help of a gardener to cut the lawn, bushes and trees. She had found that even the flower borders called for more work that she felt capable of doing.

So, what was Peter doing out messing around in the flowers borders, Betty asked herself.

She thought it might be best if she went down and reasoned with him, rather than call to him from the balcony. The fewer people who were aware that he was contravening the rules the better.

Peter refused to listen to her warning. 'Rubbish! I can't leave it in this state,' he told her.

She looked at the pile of plants by his feet that he had uprooted and she felt concerned. What would people say? What would the gardener say? It didn't bear thinking about.

As quietly as possible, she reminded him of the agreement they had made when they moved in but he merely shrugged. 'That was a long time ago, rules change,' he said.

'This one doesn't,' she told him.

'So, what are they going to do about it, turn us out of the flat,' he jibed.

'I don't know what they'll do but obviously we will have to recompense them for the damage you have done.'

Peter turned on her angrily. 'Damage, I haven't done any damage. I've simply tidied it up.'

'You have pulled up plants that are just starting to flower,' Betty told him, pointing to the handful of daffodils that were just coming into bud and that he was holding in his hand.

'Flowers! These are weeds. These borders are overrun with weeds.'

'Come on indoors and we'll talk about it,' she said gently. 'I've just made a pot of tea so we can talk it over while we have some.'

'I don't want to come indoors, I've just started on this job and want to get it finished before dark.'

'After you've had a cup of tea,' Betty insisted. 'You can bring it out here then and I'll finish mine while I work.'

Batty had never seen him so argumentative. It seemed that there was no way she could reason with him. She knew he was destroying the flower bed, but how was she to stop him?

'I don't think I can carry your cup of tea down here without spilling it,' she told him.

'Put it in a mug then,' he told her. 'Make sure you put two spoonfuls of sugar in it and stir it properly.'

'I think you'd better come up and do it yourself and make sure it has the right amount of milk,' she told him sarcastically.

'Yes, I probably had better do that,' he agreed. He dropped the plants he was clutching, brushed the soil from his trousers and walked off ahead of her.

Relieved that he had given up what he'd been doing, she followed him. Once in the flat she turned the lock and removed the key so that there was no way he could get out again.

He poured his tea and a cup for her, took his into the living room, settled in his armchair and said no more.

Betty took her own tea in there as well. She waited for him to say something about the garden but he appeared to have forgotten all about it. He sat drinking his tea, staring into space and then finally nodded off to sleep.

Betty washed up their cups, then went down to the garden to see if there was any way she could repair the damage he'd done. The plants seemed to be all right; the soil was quite moist so she replanted them to the best of her ability and hoped that no one would notice that they'd been uprooted. If they did, then she hoped they would think that it had been caused by a stray animal.

Several days passed and no one made any comment about the garden or seeing Peter out there messing around in the flower border. They had several sharp showers and she hoped that the moisture would help the border settle.

Surreptitiously, Betty watched the strip of border to see if the daffodils and other things she had replanted had died after being pulled out of the ground. To her relief, she saw that they were still alive and blooming.

That, she hoped, was the end of the incident although it did mean that she was going to have to be vigilant and make sure Peter never had the opportunity to do anything like that ever again.

Peter had forgotten the whole thing and Betty didn't mention it but encouraged him to start taking short walks, using his walker. Once the old routine was re-established, Peter lost all interest in going into the garden. It wasn't yet quite warm enough to sit out there and after his daily walk he seemed content to sit in his chair.

Tim came to see them once or twice a week, Mary phoned occasionally and Sally was a regular visitor. Shirley dropped in spasmodically, usually with some tasty dish she had made for them. If she was very busy then she sent Graham along with it. Neither of them ever stayed for more than a few minutes, but Betty was grateful that they came at all.

She tried to extend their daily walks but Peter had still not yet managed to walk as far as the park and so she set that as a target for their Easter weekend, which was less than a week away.

Thirty-Six

Betty and Peter agreed that they would try and walk to the park next day, so they were both disappointed when they woke up in the morning and found that the sky was overcast and there was a light drizzle falling.

'Never mind,' Betty said optimistically, 'you know what they say, if it rains before breakfast then it will be fine in the afternoon.'

'I hope you're right,' Peter told her, as he helped her to carry their breakfast dishes through to the kitchen. 'I was looking forward to going out and the chance to buy a newspaper.'

'We need some milk so I'll go across to the supermarket and buy you a newspaper,' Betty offered.

'You'll get wet,' he argued. 'I'll wait until this afternoon.'

'They may all be sold out by then,' she told him. 'It won't take me a minute.'

Peter was still arguing and saying that it wasn't necessary as Betty put on her raincoat, covered her head with a rain hood and wheeled the scooter out into the corridor.

'I won't be long,' she called as she headed for the lift.

'You are good to me, Betty,' he said appreciatively, as he closed the door behind her.

The supermarket was busy and it took her longer to get served than she had expected. This was partly because she stopped to buy two cream doughnuts for them to have with their morning coffee, as she knew how much Peter liked them and she hoped that it would cheer him up.

Outside, as she was starting for home she gaped in surprise. Surely it couldn't be Peter, she told herself, staring across the road where there were two men: one young, one old and using a walker, hurrying as fast as he could to keep up with the younger well-dressed man who looked to be in his late thirties. They seemed to be going in the direction of the high street.

Yet the older man did look like Peter and he was wearing a brown cardigan the same as Peter had put on that morning. It couldn't be him, Betty told herself, not out in the rain without a hat or coat.

She was so sure she must be mistaken, that she dismissed the idea from her mind as she went home.

She called out his name as she wheeled the scooter into the flat. There was no reply. The flat was empty.

She stood there wondering what to do next. It really had been Peter she had seen. But who was the man? The only man about that age that they knew was her grandson, Graham, and it was unlikely to be him at this time in the morning. He wouldn't have taken Peter out into the drizzle wearing only a cardigan; in fact, it was most unlikely that he would have taken Peter out at all, or that Peter would have gone anywhere without letting her know. They would have waited until she came home and then explained why they had to go out together.

No, she told herself, it didn't make sense.

She made another tour of the flat, to be sure she hadn't made a mistake about him not being here, and then she turned the scooter round and made her way back to the lift.

Peter obviously hadn't been looking for her because they had been going towards the high street. Was it someone from Tim's office, she wondered as she turned the scooter in that direction.

At the top of the high street she found Peter by the post office. He was standing there in the rain looking utterly bemused and when she got closer she was sure that there were tears, as well as rain, on his face but he was so wet and bedraggled that it was difficult to tell.

'Peter, where are you going?' she called.

As she touched his arm he looked startled and the expression on his face was a mixture of relief and guilt.

'Oh Betty . . .' He seemed to choke on the next words and stood there abjectly shaking his head as if unable to explain what he was doing.

'Come on, let's go home and have a hot coffee,' she said as calmly as she could.

She was about to take off her raincoat and wrap it round his shoulders, to protect him from the rain that was still falling, when she saw how wet he was already. She decided that would be useless, and the best thing to do was to get him home as quickly as possible so that he could take off his wet clothes and put on something dry, rather than get them both soaked.

As he walked alongside her she was more concerned than she would admit even to herself. Something had happened but what it was he obviously couldn't explain.

Once they were safely indoors she switched on the kettle and, while she waited for it to boil, helped him out of his wet clothes and into warm dry ones.

He was still shivering with cold so she fetched a blanket and wrapped it round him, before helping him into his armchair. Then she made the coffee and added a tot of whisky to his in the hope of warding off any chill he might be feeling.

She was halfway through her own cup of coffee before he spoke.

'It's dreadful,' he said in a shaky voice. 'So dreadful that I don't know how to tell you what has happened.'

It took almost an hour for Peter to reveal what had taken place.

A salesman had called within minutes of Betty leaving to go across to the supermarket and when he heard the door buzzer, Peter had thought that it was Betty and that she had forgotten her keys and had locked herself out of the building, so he let her in.

'I was standing at the door expecting it to be you but it wasn't. It was this young man,' Peter explained. 'He was a salesman, I think. Anyway, he had a case full of jewellery and I thought that it would be a wonderful opportunity to buy you a present. You do so much for me, Betty, that I was pleased at the idea of being able to buy something and surprise you.'

Betty squeezed his hand understandingly. 'So what happened?'

'I didn't have enough money,' he said pathetically. 'The necklace I wanted to buy you was thirty pounds.'

'Never mind, it's the thought that counts,' she told him.

'That's not the end of it though. The man said he would come with me to a cash machine to get some more money if I had a card, you know a debit card. Well, I knew where you kept yours and I knew what the number is so I thought that was a wonderful idea.'

'You went to the cash point with this man?' Betty said in alarm.

'That's right. My hand was shaking so much that I couldn't

put the card in the slot so he said he'd do it and that he'd get the money out for me if I told him the number.'

'So, you let him draw the money out for you?' Betty said, trying to keep her voice calm although inwardly her thoughts were in turmoil.

'Well, yes, but the trouble is he didn't give me the money or the card back, or give me the necklace I had chosen for you. He just made off and he was walking so fast I couldn't catch him up. Then a car drew up and it must have been someone he knew because he jumped into that and they were gone.'

Betty stared at him in horror. 'Never mind the necklace, you say he took my debit card and that he knows the number,' she exclaimed.

'I'm afraid so.'

Betty tried to think what they ought to do but her brain was numb. It was the sort of thing you read about in the newspaper. It was something that happened to other people, not to her. She was always so careful about keeping her card in a safe place, especially after her previous experience. She never carried it with her unless she was going to draw out money or they were going on what she called 'a big shop'. It was bad enough that he had already taken money from their account, but if he had the car he could draw out all she had, all her savings, unless there was a way of stopping him. Previously, when fraudsters had known her card details she had been lucky to not lose any money with the bank recompensing her. Betty had a feeling she wouldn't be so lucky a second time.

She couldn't think which was the best thing to do first, phone the police or phone the bank.

In desperation, she phoned Tim and tried to explain to him what had happened.

'Have you told the bank?'

'No, not yet, shall I do that now?'

'Of course! They can put a stop on your card. I'll come round and help you do it,' he told her.

The procedure took almost half an hour and Betty felt a wave of relief when it was completed.

'So I have nothing to worry about now,' she said to Tim.

'No, but the bad news is that when he first used the card,

when he was with Peter, he drew out two hundred and fifty pounds, the maximum you can get from the machine.'

'Oh my goodness!' Betty went white. 'He can't withdraw any more can he?'

'He probably intended doing the same thing tomorrow, and the day after, until your account was empty. I've told you before,' Tim said, 'you shouldn't keep that much money in your current account, you leave yourself open to losing it.'

'I know, I know,' Betty said, 'but I find that it is so difficult to make transfers from my savings account to my current account. You see, there are all sorts of standing orders to be paid out each month that I have to make sure the balance is enough to cover them.'

'Well, let me do it for you. You have only to ask,' Tim told her. 'Or you can add up exactly what the standing orders come to and ask the bank to transfer that amount from your savings account to your current account each month. That way you won't have a surplus lying dormant in your current account.'

'Oh dear, I find it all so difficult,' Betty muttered unhappily.

'Well, it doesn't have to be. I'll come to the bank with you and tell them exactly what you want to do, if you wish.'

'I would be grateful, Tim, if you would,' Betty told him.

'Very well, we'll do it tomorrow morning, and at the same time we can check if that rogue has tried to draw any more out.'

'Thank you. I feel I can put it all behind me now,' Betty told him.

'Not quite, Mother. We need to report what has happened to the police and give them details of the man and his accomplice and the car they were using. I don't suppose you managed make a note of the number plate?'

Betty shook her head.

'Or of the make of car?'

Again, Betty shook her head. 'It was a dark colour, that's all I can tell you. The man who took my card was in his thirties and smartly dressed, he was wearing a trench coat style, cream raincoat. Peter might be able to give you a better description.'

When he questioned Peter, Tim found he wasn't as helpful as Betty.

'I don't think we will take him along to the police station,'

Tim told her. 'The state he is in, they are not very likely to take his evidence seriously. I'll pick you up at ten o'clock. Is that all right?'

'I'll be ready,' Betty promised.

The desk sergeant took what they told him very seriously and asked them to wait while he consulted with someone higher. They were taken along to another room, where a plain clothes detective was waiting to interrogate them.

'Is it possible to speak to the man who was taken to the cash point?' he asked.

Betty shook her head and Tim explained, 'Mr Brown is very upset by the whole matter. He feels that he is responsible and, at the moment, we have persuaded him to rest. Perhaps you could leave it for a day or two.'

The detective frowned. 'We would like to have a full description of the man who came to your door and it would seem that Mr Brown had a better opportunity to notice his face and what he was wearing than anyone else did.'

'I really don't feel that he is fit enough to come to the station,' Betty protested. 'Anyway, he feels guilty about what happened as it is, and to have to come here would only make that worse.'

The detective nodded. 'I understand. What about if I came to the house? Perhaps if I walked back with you now he might regard me as a friend, and simply talk about the incident. My name is Bill Forest, by the way. Call me Bill.'

Tim and Betty exchanged glances. 'Very well,' Betty said.

She was still unsure about what the effect was going to be on Peter, but she could see that Bill Forest was very persistent so she thought the sooner they got it over with the better.

Peter was as cooperative as he could be and, by the time Bill left, he had a pretty accurate description of the man who had been involved and promised that his description would be circulated.

'Is there any hope that I will get my money back?' Betty asked.

Bill Forest looked dubious. 'I hardly think so,' he said. 'However, the good news is that your prompt action ensures that he can't draw any more money out of your account.'

Thirty-Seven

Betty found that Peter being interviewed by the police had left him in a very confused state.

He seemed to think that they believed him to be guilty of something and jumped nervously every time there was a knock on the door saying, 'Have they come for me?'

She tried to explain why they had interviewed him and to reassure him that he was in no way guilty of any misdemeanour, but her efforts had very little effect so she decided the best thing to do was completely ignore his signs of alarm. He would forget the incident in time, she told herself.

He did forget about it eventually, but it took him far longer to do so than it did to forget things he should remember. His memory was certainly playing tricks on him, Betty thought with a sigh. Sometimes what he said or did made her laugh, but more and more it left her annoyed or frustrated.

He had also taken to doing some most peculiar things. She found him one day, armed with the bread knife, filling away furiously at the railings on the balcony.

'Whatever are you trying to do?' she asked him as she tried to take the bread knife from his hand.

'I'm trying to get rid of the bars on this cage so that I can get out,' he told her.

'They're not prison bars, they are railings that have been put there to protect you, to save you from falling,' she told him, in disbelief.

'Don't be ridiculous, they're there to keep me a prisoner. I want to go out into the garden,' he protested. 'And if I can't remove them I'll have to climb over them.'

Betty was startled. If Peter attempted to climb over the railings then, without doubt, he'd have a very nasty fall and end up breaking his legs or his arm, or even both, as there was a drop of over twenty feet. Right below the balcony was a rockery which, though it might help to break his fall, would also cause additional injuries.

She could see he was in aggressive mood, so she tried to think of a way of mollifying him and distracting his mind from what he was doing.

'Let me have the bread knife to cut some bread for our meal,' she said holding out her hand but not attempting to take it from him.

He studied it for a minute then quietly handed it over. 'You have it, it's not much good anyway. I'll have to find something stronger.'

'Leave it until after you've had your lunch and then I will take you into the garden if that is where you want to go.'

He nodded as he walked past her, then sat down in his armchair and closed his eyes.

There was no mention of the garden when he woke up. He ate his lunch and then agreed that they should go for a walk. Betty wondered if they could get as far as the park, but decided that it might only disturb him if she mentioned it, so she merely turned in that direction and let him walk where he chose. To her delight, they managed to make it to the park.

They sat there for a while, enjoying the light breeze, and admiring the flower beds now ablaze with polyanthuses and daffodils. When school ended and the park began to fill up with children, their shouts and noisy screams seemed to upset him so she said it was time to go home for a cup of tea.

For several days this pattern was repeated. Peter seemed calm and quite content. He was eating well and sleeping soundly, and Betty thought that perhaps he had managed to put all the earlier worries behind him and hoped that from now on life was going to be reasonably normal.

As the days became warmer, they spent more and more time sitting out in the garden. Betty kept a watchful eye on Peter to make sure that he didn't tamper with any of the flower beds, but he seemed to show no inclination to do so.

Sometimes she took the newspaper down with her and read out to him any items she thought might interest him but, as he never commented on them or showed the slightest interest, she stopped doing so and simply enjoyed reading them to herself.

Peter didn't seem to notice. He seemed content to simply sit, drifting into a dream world, or half asleep.

When he sometimes got up and walked up and down the path, Betty felt that there was no longer any need to worry about him pottering in the flower beds. She even started to leave him on his down there while she went up to the flat to make them a cup of tea and bring it back down to the garden.

One very warm afternoon she was contentedly reading when she realized that Peter had been absent from the seat beside her for rather a long time. She looked round the garden but he was nowhere to be seen. Slightly worried, she laid down her magazine and walked round looking for him in case he had gone behind one of the many flowering bushes and was hidden from sight. Peter wasn't in the garden.

Slightly more concerned Betty went up to the flat. The door was locked. She put her hand in the pocket of her cardigan for her keys; they were not there and she realized that she must have left them on the table out in the garden.

When she went back down they weren't there either. Puzzled, she searched through her pockets, and looked under the table in case they had fallen out. Then she heard Peter calling her and looked up to see that he was out on their balcony and leaning so far over that she was afraid he would fall over head first.

Not wanting to alarm him she called up quietly, 'I'm coming up to make you a cup of tea.'

He shook his head, but she wasn't sure whether he meant he didn't want a cup of tea or was trying to tell her that he was coming back down. She wanted a drink herself so she went up anyway.

When she reached the door of the flat she found it was still locked. She called out asking Peter to open it but there was no response. As she stood there, wondering what to do, she realized that he must have taken her keys to get in. Why had he locked the door from inside? She recalled the way he had leaned over the balcony and she was worried in case he was having one of his 'funny turns', as she called them.

She tried to think of a way to persuade him to open the door and let her in but she couldn't, partly because she was so afraid that he might fall over the balcony that she could think of nothing else.

She tried two or three times to persuade him to open the

door, but all she got from him was a strange laugh. He sounded demented. He certainly had no intention of opening the door.

The only other person she could think of who had a key was Tim, but how could she reach him. Her scooter was inside the flat and she didn't even have a walking stick so she couldn't possibly walk as far as the high street. She wondered if there were any neighbours at home. Most of them were still of working age and out all day and the nice receptionist lady was nowhere to be seen and probably on a break.

She went out into the road to see if anyone was passing by so that she could ask them for help. The street was deserted. In the end she tried to flag a car down. They just stared at her waving her hands for them to stop and drove on. Eventually a delivery van stopped.

'Could you make a phone call for me?' she said to the driver. 'My husband has locked himself inside our flat and refuses to open the door to me. He's suffering from dementia,' she explained, 'and I'm afraid he is going to do himself some harm. He's talking about jumping from the balcony!'

The van driver stared at her for a moment, as if he was trying to work out whether she was telling him was truth or whether she was the one who was demented.

He shook his head; she looked sane enough; she reminded him of his mother, and he recalled the trouble they'd had with his father some years before he died.

'All right,' he said. 'What's the number?'

She told him Tim's number and said, 'He has the estate agents in the high street. The trouble is I can't walk that far.'

'Is he a tall guy with dark hair?'

'That's right. Do you know him?' Betty asked eagerly.

The driver nodded. 'I know him, we bought our house through him,' he commented.

As he spoke, he was dialling the number. When the girl who answered said she would put him through to Mr Wilson he handed the mobile over to Betty, so that she could explain things to Tim herself.

'Tim, can you come round. Peter has locked me out of the flat and . . . and . . . and he's threatening to jump from the balcony.'

'All right, all right don't worry I'll be straight round. Are you with a neighbour?'

'No . . .' She was so relieved that she was sobbing now and her voice was muffled.

'Don't upset yourself, Mother. Calm down, I can't hear what you're saying.'

The delivery driver took the mobile from her. 'Hello,' he said, 'this is Bert Jackson. Your mother flagged me down and asked me to help her. I'll stay with her until you get here.'

Tim was there in a matter of minutes. He recognized Bert Jackson and thanked him for helping.

'That's all right,' Bert told him, 'but I can't stay any longer. I've deliveries to get out before closing time.'

When he had driven off, Tim tried to get a more lucid story from Betty.

'Let's go up and see if the door is still locked or whether he'll let me in,' Tim said.

The door was still locked. Tim called out, 'Peter, it's Tim, can I come in?'

There was a silence and then Peter said, 'Is that woman with you?'

'You mean my mother?'

'That's her. She's not coming in here ever again,' he said. 'Understand?'

'Yes, I hear what you are saying, but you can let me in,' Tim said quietly.

'No, I don't trust you. You'll bring her with you and I'm not having her in my flat ever again.'

Tim placed a finger to his lips to warn Betty not to say anything, but it was no good. No matter what he said Peter would not open the door to him.

Tim drew his mother away from the door and down the corridor. 'Let's go out into the garden and see if I can talk some sense into him from there.'

Then they looked up and Peter was on the balcony.

'You think I'm going to jump, don't you?' he shouted down to them. 'You'd like me to do that; break every bone in my body but I'm not going to do it.' Again, he gave the strange wild laugh that Betty had found so frightening.

Tim didn't bother arguing with him. He got out his mobile and phoned the police, explained the situation to them and asked them what he must do. They agreed to come round but told him that they would also be alerting the fire brigade to the situation.

Within a very short while they were both there. The firemen had brought an extending ladder that they leaned against the balcony. Peter stood there watching them. When the ladder was in position he tried to push it away, but it was too heavy so that, with his limited strength, he was unable to move it.

'I'll go up and persuade him to come down with me,' one of the firemen said quietly to Tim.

As if alert to what was happening, Peter dashed back inside the room and they heard him lock the balcony doors.

'Now he's locked himself in completely,' Tim said with a frown. 'There's no way now of getting him out.'

'Have one more attempt at persuading him to open the main door,' the fireman suggested, 'and if that doesn't work then we can break one of the panels of glass in the balcony doors and get in that way.'

Peter was adamant that he wasn't letting them inside so the fireman went ahead with breaking in. As soon as he was inside he unlocked the main door so that Tim and Betty could enter.

By the time they did so, Peter was sitting down in his armchair, a rug over his knees already nodding off to sleep. He stared at them all in surprise.

'This is like the dream I just had about firemen shouting to me from the ground. What's going on? Is there a fire somewhere?'

Thirty-Eight

Tim stayed on after the police and firemen had left.

Peter had settled down quietly in his armchair and appeared to be asleep, but Tim was taking no chances. He drew his mother out into the corridor and closed the door behind them, to make sure that Peter couldn't overhear what he was saying.

'Look, Mother,' he said softly, 'I don't think that it is safe for you to stay here with Peter. He really does seem to be unwell and doesn't know what he is doing. I think he needs hospital-ization, you really aren't safe to be alone with him.'

'It's just one of the spells he has from time to time, he'll be all right now,' Betty assured him. 'You saw for yourself that he has settled down in his armchair and is asleep.'

'Is he, or is he faking,' Tim said in a worried voice. 'I really don't trust him, Mother. You don't know what he will be up to next.'

'He'll be all right now, I'm quite sure of it,' Betty said confidently. 'He was upset about the police taking him in for questioning, he thought they were accusing him of a crime.'

'Which proves that his reasoning has gone and he doesn't know what is going on around him. I think he is living in a fantasy world,' Tim told her. 'I'm really concerned about your safety, Mother. Shall I ask a doctor to come round and assess him?'

'No, certainly not. He doesn't need any more upsets at the moment,' Betty retorted sharply. 'Leave him alone, let him sleep and wake up when he's good and ready, and I know that he will be quite normal again.'

'Yes, but for how long and what will the crisis be next time,' Tim said grimly.

Betty patted his arm. 'Don't you worry, I know it will all be back to normal once he's had a good sleep.'

'Very well,' Tim said as he planted a kiss on her cheek. 'Remember, though, you are to ring me the moment there is any upset or trouble. Promise?'

'Yes, dear. I promise I will but believe me, Peter will be as right as rain when he wakes up.'

Betty was quite right, Peter woke up after a couple of hours of sleep, refreshed and ready for a cup of tea.

'Are we going for a walk when we've drunk this?' he asked.

'No, not today,' Betty told him. 'I feel rather tired so we'll sit in the garden today and go for a good long walk tomorrow.'

Peter accepted without any argument. After a few days their normal pattern of day-to-day living was restored. The only grumble Betty had was that Peter never seemed to want to go to bed at night, which meant that he was tired and wanted to sleep for most of the following day.

Although in some ways this was very convenient for Betty because it left her free to do the chores without any interruption, and even to go across to the supermarket for milk and bread if they needed them, it also meant that she, too, was tired because she couldn't settle to sleep at night until she knew that Peter was safely in bed.

She had a fear of him falling, or, even worse, that he might decide to go out for a walk, especially when it was a bright moonlit night.

Several times she thought about mentioning it to Tim but she knew that his answer would be to call the doctor. She did mention it to Sally.

'It's his body clock gone wrong,' Sally said. 'Not much you can do about that. It's another of the problems of old age.'

'Well, my body clock hasn't changed,' Betty replied, 'and neither has yours.'

'True,' Sally agreed. 'In your case it's a pity it hasn't because then Peter sleeping half the day wouldn't worry you because you'd want to do the same.'

'I often do, not because my body clock has changed but because I'm so tired; sometimes I stay awake until two or three in the morning waiting for him to go to bed.'

'Well, don't do that,' Sally said. 'Go to bed and go to sleep. Leave him to sleep when he's good and ready. If he has a fall then that's too bad. I don't suppose he'll hurt himself and he'll probably stay where he is and go to sleep. He won't catch a cold, not at this time of the year.'

'What about if he decides to go out for a walk,' Betty murmured.

'Keep all the doors locked and put the safety chain on the door at night. He probably wouldn't manage to get that undone, if he does you will probably hear him anyway.'

Sally's advice seemed to make sense but sometimes, when she followed it, Betty felt guilty about leaving Peter up but she was so tired herself that the moment her head touched the pillow she was asleep.

Peter was always in bed when she woke in the morning. Sometimes he was fully dressed, even wearing his slippers as he had been the night beforehand when she'd left him still watching television.

Sometimes in the morning she even found that the television was still on. When she mentioned to him that he ought to turn it off before he went to bed, he scowled at her. 'You always go to bed and leave it on,' he reminded her.

Betty said nothing in response to this. She knew it was true, but if she started the argument that if he went to bed at the same time as her then she would turn it off it would go on for days.

Betty was finding more and more that, although Peter's memory was now extremely bad, if he launched on a subject then he would keep the same topic going for several days, worrying at it like a dog with a bone until she was almost at screaming pitch.

Lately, she mused, his look as well as his character had changed so much that there were times when she no longer recognized the placid, sweet natured man, with lovely blue eyes that she had known for so many years. Now he was becoming more and more aggressive and ill-tempered; his skin was like crinkled-up tissue paper and his hair was thin and almost white.

He hated Sally coming round. 'What do you want that woman in here for, chattering away like a bloody monkey. Whole load of nonsense she talks, tell her to push off. If you don't tell her then I will.'

Betty warned Sally of his funny moods and described them but Sally only laughed.

'Don't let it worry you, I can take whatever he has to say. Poor fellow, he's going out of his mind. Some of them talk like that. They don't like anybody, not even themselves. It's you I'm concerned about, Betty. You are beginning to look cowed. Are you afraid of him?'

'Good heavens, no. I'm tired Sally, that's my trouble.'

'Then why don't you put him in respite for a couple of weeks and have a holiday? I'll come with you. We'll go wherever you like, do whatever you like. What about a short cruise or a couple of weeks in Bournemouth or somewhere like that? You choose, I'm game.'

The more Betty thought about Sally's suggestion the more attractive it became. It would be heaven to get away, somewhere peaceful, no worries about Peter and his odd behaviour. No shopping or cooking and regular hours.

When she mentioned it to Tim he was very enthusiastic, 'Good old Sally, it is exactly what you need. I'll have a word with her and fix things, and I'll make arrangements for Peter to go into respite for a couple of weeks. Fabulous idea.'

Peter didn't like the idea but Tim told him he had no choice. At first Peter thought that Betty was going with him but when he found out that she wasn't he became very angry.

'Trying to get rid of me, aren't you?' he accused, his brows drawn together in an angry scowl. 'Bundle me into one of those places and then forget me. I've seen it happen countless times. Take all my money and go wild spending it while I'm shut-up in prison.'

'No, Peter, it's not like that at all. You will probably enjoy the break just as much as I will. It must be a strain for you living with someone when you've been a bachelor for most of your life.'

Several times, because he was so upset, Betty tried to pull out of the arrangement or postpone it for a later date when Peter was stronger.

'He's not going to get any stronger or better and you know it,' Tim said sharply. 'You need a break, Mother. Go ahead with the arrangements that Sally has made; it will do you the world of good. Stop thinking of all the drawbacks and concentrate on packing. It's less than a week away. Do you want to go and see the nursing home where Peter will be going?'

Betty hesitated. She didn't want to offend Tim by saying she needed to see that it was all right, because she knew Tim would have been very careful to choose the most appropriate one. Tim had made a booking that meant Peter left home three days before she was due to travel. This gave her time to leave the house in order and do her packing.

She had already put some clothes into a case but, now that she was on her own and could think about what she was doing without interruption, she decided they were all wrong and started all over again. She so enjoyed the peace and quiet of the flat that she would have been quite content to stay there and not do anything else for the time that Peter would be away.

Once she and Sally set out, though, she felt excited at the thought of two weeks somewhere she hadn't been before.

The hotel Tim had chosen was a perfect escape. It was very comfortable, they were both thrilled with the choice. He'd booked them adjacent rooms, and Betty found that this was a perfect arrangement. It gave her an opportunity to be on her own whenever she felt like it.

She had Sally's company at mealtimes, for taking strolls along the promenade, or going further afield on arranged trips and for visits to the smart shops. She was even tempted to buy a new dress and some tops, and persuaded Sally into buying a new dress as well.

'I don't really need it,' Betty admitted, 'but I simply couldn't resist it.'

'You do need it,' Sally told her, 'every time you are feeling stressed put it on and it will bring back memories of this lovely holiday.'

From time to time she worried about Peter and whether or not he was settled at the nursing home. Tim phoned a couple of times to reassure her that everything was fine and to ask if she was enjoying he holiday.

'It's perfect,' she told him. 'Both of us are enjoying every minute and the weather has been wonderful.'

She really was sorry when it came to an end, yet at the same time anxious. As they travelled home she wondered what she was going to find at the other end. Was Peter frustrated at being put in a nursing home; had his moods improved; would he be pleased to see her?

Tim had made sure that she would have a couple of days to shop and do anything else necessary before Peter came home, and she took advantage of the time to have her hair done and make one or two changes in the layout of the flat.

The day Peter was due home she cooked his favourite meal of chicken in a lemon sauce and made a sherry trifle, that was another of his favourite dishes. He arrived late afternoon, accompanied by Tim. He was talking animatedly to Tim as they came up in the lift but, when he saw Betty waiting for him at the door of the flat, his face darkened.

'Who's that woman and what is she doing here in my home,' he demanded.

'It's Betty, your wife,' Tim said. 'She's here welcoming you home. I understand she's cooked you a special meal.'

Peter drew in a deep breath and then gave a deep sigh. 'That sounds good,' he said. He walked in, straight over to his armchair, sat down and closed his eyes.

'Thank you for bringing him home,' Betty said squeezing Tim's arm.

Tim shook his head and looked worried. 'Are you sure you are going to be all right? I'm not sure that he knows where he is.'

'Of course I am,' Betty said confidently. 'Now, don't worry. If I need you then I'll phone you.'

Thirty-Nine

Betty found that looking after Peter was almost like caring for a young, but inactive child. He seemed to have no idea about doing anything or talking about anything. He was content to simply sit in his armchair and either stare into space or doze.

He ate or drank whatever she put in front of him without comment. If she asked him afterwards if he had enjoyed it, he smiled and nodded. Sometimes Betty wished he would complain just to show some interest.

She took to going out every day, choosing the early afternoon when she knew he would be sleeping after his main meal of the day. She never went very far, or stayed out more than half an hour, but she looked forward to the break from being confined to the flat.

When she encouraged Peter to come down and sit in the garden he showed no interest in the flowers or what was going on. Occasionally, there were other people out there and if they spoke he would completely ignore them, leaving Betty to try and speak for both of them in order to cover up his silence.

Most of the time he was compliant, although he didn't like visitors; not even Tim. Sally ignored his rudeness but after she had gone he grumbled about her and told Betty to stop opening the door to her. The only other time he seemed to be aroused was when Betty wanted him to do something and he didn't want to comply. He was loath to take a shower or to shave. Because he was now so thin and gaunt he looked even worse when he was in need of a shave. In the end, Betty compromised and trimmed his facial hair so that it had some resemblance to a beard.

When she held up a hand-mirror so that he could see the results he nodded, as if satisfied. 'You are very good to me,' he told her. 'You feed me and you look after me, what more could I ask.'

As the summer waned and was replaced by the shorter days of autumn, Betty missed their walks more than ever. Soon, she reflected, it would be winter and the chances of getting out would become less and less possible. Stoically, she resigned herself to a new lifestyle. She tried to interest Peter in television programmes that she enjoyed, or listening to plays or talks on the radio, hoping that perhaps it would stimulate him to talk about them afterwards. Usually he simply closed his eyes and went to sleep.

For her own entertainment, Betty started knitting again; something she hadn't done for many years. To her surprise she found she was enjoying it and it helped to pass the time.

She still went out on her scooter most afternoons and enjoyed the feeling it gave her, whether it was merely a drive round the village or a short expedition.

'Don't you think it would be better if you ordered online? I thought you had been impressed with this arrangement?' Tim asked.

'I enjoy going out,' Betty told him. 'You have no idea what it's like to be shut up in four walls day after day.'

'Yes I do,' he told her with a grin. 'I am shut up in my office from early morning until evening.'

'Maybe you are, but there are other people around you, different faces, challenging conversation, stimulating projects.'

As the days became shorter and the weather inclement, Betty realized that what Tim had suggested made sense; it was time to return to the deliveries even if this did mean she had less reason to leave the flat.

Whenever she felt disgruntled about the way her life was going she tried to remember that really, she was very fortunate. The flat was comfortable and easy to manage, Peter wasn't very demanding, and she went short of nothing. Soon it would be Christmas and then she would see more of the rest of the family, so she had something to look forward to.

It was early in December when overnight everything changed.

She had just made their afternoon cup of tea, brought it in from the kitchen on a tray, which she put down on a low table before gently shaking Peter's arm to waken him.

Before she sat down in her own armchair she handed him his cup. 'Be careful it's hot,' she remarked as she handed it to him.

He made no reply but immediately took a drink. The next thing she knew was that he had given an angry exclamation and thrown the hot liquid at her, catching Betty full in the face and almost blinding her.

'There's no sugar in the damn stuff!' he shouted.

Betty mopped at her face, her eyes were stinging and so was the skin on her face.

'No good standing there crying, get me a fresh one,' he ordered.

Betty stared at him in dismay, he has been so quiet and docile over the past few months that she couldn't understand his outburst. She had obviously made a mistake and given him her cup instead of the one intended for him, which did have sugar in it. Silently, she passed him the other cup. He tasted it and then sat back in his armchair to drink it without a word.

Betty went back into the kitchen and dabbed her face with cold water to ease the pain. Then she poured herself another cup and wondered if it was safe to take it into the sitting room to drink it. As she sat down in her armchair, she watched him nervously but he was drinking his tea as if there was nothing amiss.

She decided not to tell Tim, but she did wonder if she should speak to the doctor and see if he thought that Peter's medication should be increased.

A couple of days later, Peter flew into a rage when she tried to tidy up his beard, which looked straggly and unkempt.

'Get away from me,' he shouted, and pushed her so hard that she fell backwards, narrowly missing the corner of the table. As it was, she jarred her shoulder as she tried to save herself from falling and this caused a searing pain down her arm and side.

Frightened, she knew she must take some sort of action, but by the time she had pulled herself together Peter was back in his chair, his eyes closed in sleep and looking so peaceful that it was hard to believe he had been so aggressive only a few minutes earlier.

They had a quiet few days; Betty wondered why he had been so upset. Was it something in his diet that had triggered his anger, or was it that he wasn't feeling well. He was so moody and depressed over the next week that Betty wondered if the darker days had anything to do with it. His outbursts seemed to coincide with rain or bad weather.

It was a bitterly cold, bright, sunny day when he committed his next attack. This time, he lashed out at her with his fist when she woke him because she was about to serve him his main meal of the day. He picked up his plate of food and smashed it against the wall. His eyes glittering fanatically, he then turned on her with his fist curled up.

One blow caught her on the side of her face, before she managed to make her escape out of the flat and into the corridor. She heard him bolt the door behind her, muttering curses all the time he did it. She stood in the corridor, shaking and unsure of what to do. She knew she must contact Tim but how was she going to do that now. She thought about going out on to the street and flagging down a passer-by as she had done previously when Peter had locked her out. She waited a few minutes and then knocked softly on the door to see whether he'd calmed down.

'Can you let me in, Peter, so that I can get your pudding ready?' she said, in as steady a voice as she could muster.

She heard the lock being undone and the door open, and felt a huge wave of relief. For a moment she hesitated, wondering if it was safe to go in.

'What are you doing out there in the middle of our meal?' he asked.

Betty merely smiled.

'You want to take your keys with you when you go out,' he told her as he made his way to the table, and pulled her plate towards him and tucked into it.

Betty went into the kitchen and took the apple crumble out of the oven and dished out a portion for Peter. Her hand was shaking as she poured cream on it before taking it to him.

He pushed aside the empty dinner plate, picked up his spoon and tucked into the pudding. She watched him in silence. What would he do next, she wondered.

She waited until he was back in his armchair and had dozed off, then she rang Tim.

'Can you come round? I need your help but I can't explain on the phone,' she said.

'Is something wrong, Mother? You sound strange, almost as if you are frightened?'

'Come round, Tim, please.'

'I'm on my way.'

'He really must have professional care, his behaviour is not only erratic but dangerous,' Tim told her, after he had heard an account of what had happened. 'Heaven knows what he might do next time.'

'But he's been so placid for the past few months,'

'Well, by your account of what has happened recently, his dementia has taken another turn. Leave it with me, I'll arrange for him to go back into a nursing home. Just be on the alert until someone comes to collect him.'

Betty didn't go to bed, she waited for Peter to go to sleep so that she could lie down on the settee and get some rest herself. It was almost three in the morning before he rose from his armchair and made his way to the bedroom. Even then, she waited, afraid to sleep in case he wondered why she wasn't in bed and came looking for her.

It was several days before Tim found a nursing home that was prepared to take a dementia patient when they heard that he had become violent. It had to be one with staff specially trained to deal with such problems.

Betty kept thinking she was letting Peter down by sending him away, but her thoughts went back to the episode when he had locked her out of the flat and she dreaded something like that happening again. The following day, when he had no idea who she was and again attacked her, his eyes so fierce that she was really scared of him, she knew in her heart that she wasn't capable of dealing with him and that it really was necessary for him to have professional care.

Forty

It was four days before they would allow Betty to visit Peter. When she was taken into his room he was sitting in a chair by his bed. He opened his eyes and looked at her blankly, then closed them again without even speaking.

'How are you, Peter?' Betty asked. She went over to him and kissed him on the forehead when he didn't answer.

'Leave me alone,' he muttered, as he pushed her away angrily.

'I'll bring you both a cup of tea, do you take milk and sugar?' The girl who had brought her from reception asked.

'Thank you, that would be very nice. Only milk for me but Peter takes both,' Betty said.

She sat patiently waiting, afraid to touch him and finding it useless to talk to him. She wasn't sure whether he heard her or not as he made no reply. She hoped that when the tea arrived he might show some interest in what she said. As it happened, he picked up his tea, drained the cup and put it back on the saucer without a word.

Betty scrutinized Peter as she sipped her own tea and thought how he had changed in a few days. He looked so frail and his hair was completely white. The beard that he'd been growing was gone, and she assumed that someone must have shaved him.

She finished her tea and then, once again, tried to hold a conversation with him, but he only stared at her angrily and told her to get out because he didn't want her there.

Saddened, Betty accepted the inevitable and didn't visit again for almost a week. This time, she took along some of his favourite chocolates but, instead of her gift pleasing him, it only seemed to anger him. Opening the box, he stared at the contents then threw it at her, telling her that he knew she was trying to poison him.

He made so much noise that one of the nurses came running in to see what happening. Gently, she guided Betty out of the room, leaving Peter still ranting and raving at the top of his voice, disturbing other patients and their visitors, many of whom looked out of their rooms to see what was happening.

Betty was shaking so much that they sat her down in reception and brought her another cup of tea and suggested she rested until she felt calmer.

'Could you ring my son and ask him to come and collect me?' she asked.

When Tim arrived, the matron took him to one side and said that she thought it might be better if his mother didn't visit anymore as she seemed to distress the patient, and afterwards he was so violent that they had to sedate him.

The news distressed Betty. She felt it was both her right and her duty to visit Peter. She took to standing outside the nursing home, looking up at the window of his room, hoping that perhaps he might look out and see her and ask her to come in.

Nothing like that ever happened and after about a month Tim asked the matron if his mother could visit if he came with her.

'She's very distressed by this enforced separation,' he explained.

'I do understand, but my concern is for the patient and my staff; he becomes aggressively agitated by her visits.'

They discussed the matter at great length and finally the matron agreed that Betty could visit if Tim accompanied her.

'You must agree that if it causes any disturbance then you accept my ruling that she won't be allowed to do it again.'

Betty was overjoyed by the news. This time she didn't take him anything, afraid of what his reaction might be, and she also agreed to let Tim go in on his own first, so that he could assess Peter's mood. Matron too was taking no chances. She stood with Betty outside Peter's door to make certain that all was well.

They heard Tim greet Peter who responded and then the two of them participated in a general conversation.

Matron smiled at Betty. 'Sounds normal,' she said softly. Then she quietly opened the door and propelled Betty inside.

Betty stood by the door for several moments until Tim noticed she was there.

'You have another visitor, Peter,' Tim said in a welcoming tone of voice.

Peter frowned and looked towards the door. When he saw Betty, his eyes narrowed and his hands balled into fists.

'Get her out of here, I don't want that woman in my room!' he snarled.

'Come on Peter, it's your wife, you mustn't be churlish. She has a right to visit you.'

Peter didn't answer, he was out of his chair and across the room, one arm raised to hit Betty before Tim could stop him.

Matron heard Betty's cry as Peter's fist caught her on the shoulder, sending Betty reeling backwards but, before she could enter the room, Tim had grabbed hold of Peter's arms, holding it in a vice-like grip.

'Leave us, Mother,' he ordered.

Betty hesitated, tears streaming down her face from the pain and the sight of Peter struggling in Tim's arms, then fled.

Other members of staff had heard the commotion and came to help. Peter was sedated before Tim loosened his hold on him.

Tim and Betty were taken into Matron's study and given cups of tea to help them to recover their composure. This time there was no question of any compromise. Betty was told she must not visit Peter again.

From then on, they were sent a weekly report telling them how Peter was progressing. His health was obviously deteriorating, and in early March of the following year they were sent for because he was so seriously ill with pneumonia that he was in hospital and it was it was unlikely that he would live more than a few days.

Betty was in floods of tears but she agreed to go to the hospital with Tim.

Neither of them were sure if Peter recognized them as they stood, one each side of his bed, in intensive care.

When Tim spoke to him, Peter managed a faint smile, then he turned his head to look at Betty. His hand that was lying on top of the covers seemed to reach towards her. Betty took it, holding it gently and smiling down at him.

'You've been so kind to me,' he said in a dry whisper. 'I hope I've never hurt you.'

Betty felt too choked to speak, all she could do was gently squeeze his hand and smile at him, shaking her head as if to assure him that he had never harmed her.

He nodded contentedly, then the hand holding Betty's became limp and Tim gently disentangled their hands and led Betty away from the bedside.

★   ★   ★

Peter's funeral was a very quiet one attended by Betty, Tim, Brenda, Mary, Graham, Shirley, and Sally.

Although she had been living alone for quite some time, Betty found the flat felt cold and empty when she returned after the funeral.

As she looked round, things that had belonged to Peter seemed to be everywhere. She spent the evening and the whole of the next day gathering them together and putting them into boxes where she wouldn't see them.

A week later, Betty told Tim that she had decided to go into a nursing home and asked him which one he though was most suitable.

Tim looked aghast. 'What do you want to do that for, Mother? You are still able to look after yourself and I'm always on hand if you need any help.'

'I know, but I am tired of the world,' she told him. 'I find coping with the hustle and bustle of everyday life unbearable. I no longer enjoy shopping, I find that even with my scooter it has become more and more difficult to get around. Most of the time I am so lonely, and some days I feel it isn't worth going on living.'

'You have your freedom and you have a lovely flat,' Tim persisted. 'You can have friends round to visit whenever you wish. You still see Hilda and Sally, don't you?'

'I never see Hilda, she's moved away to live with her daughter in Scotland. Like me, Sally finds it increasingly difficult to get around. We both feel it would be wonderful to be somewhere where we had our own room, but other people had all the worries about buying food and cooking it; somewhere where we wouldn't have to change the bed or wash the bathroom floor every week. No more coping with bills, or dealing with equipment that had broken down and has to be repaired or replaced. It would be like our little holiday all over again, but without the worry of it ending and returning to normality.

'All this would be taken care of by someone else if we were in a nursing home and we would still be able to have visitors, enjoy sitting out in the garden on sunny days, and probably have all sorts of entertainment laid on for us from time to time.'

Tim shook his head. 'Can you afford to do that, Mother? I'm willing to assist you, of course . . .'

Betty laid a hand on Tim's arm. 'If you sell the flat for me there will be more than enough money to keep me in a nursing home. Please don't try and dissuade me, Tim. I have given it a lot of thought, I can assure you, and my mind is made up and it is what I want to do.'

Forty-One

Betty, sitting in a comfortable armchair, looked round the sunny room with a feeling of pleasure and contentment. All her favourite possessions were on view: family photographs and those other possessions she treasured the most.

The window looked out onto the garden where hanging baskets and well-stocked borders were all in full bloom and she breathed a sigh of sheer happiness.

She had done the right thing by coming into the nursing home, she reflected. She had peace of mind, no worries, no responsibilities and no domestic chores. It was perfect.

Twice a week she met up with other residents in the communal lounge for coffee mornings and twice a month there were activities or entertainment of some kind in the same room in the afternoons or evenings.

Sally had moved in shortly after she had and her room was only across the hallway which was very reassuring.

Sometimes Betty felt she was more in touch with the world around her than she had ever been. In some ways it was a new type of world but she found it comforting to know that there were people she could call on if she needed any assistance as well as people less capable than she was; people to whom she could sometimes give a helping hand.

Tim seem to be amazed at how contented and happy she was but then, she reflected, good and considerate though he was, Tim really had no idea what it was like to be old. No one really did, not until they got there.

She leaned back in her armchair and closed her eyes. One of the joys of being in the nursing home was that she could have a doze whenever she felt like it without feeling guilty and she found that a cat nap was so wonderfully refreshing.